The GOLDEN PEACOCK

LAUREN B. GROSSMAN

The Golden Peacock

Printed in the United States of America

*****

Disclaimer

This is a work of fiction, a product of the author's imagination. Any resemblance or similarity to any actual events or persons, living or dead, is purely coincidental. Although the author and publisher have made every effort to ensure there are no errors, inaccuracies, omissions, or inconsistencies herein, any slights or people, places, or organizations are unintentional.

*****

Cover illustration by Evan Jaroslow

Formatting by Debora Lewis arenapublishing.org

ISBN-13: 978-1511807395

ISBN-10: 1511807393

DEDICATION

I dedicate this novel to my mother and father, Lillian and Lawrence Jaroslow. In all my endeavors, they have always been my cheerleaders. My greatest sorrow is that my father, though he read it chapter by chapter, did not live to see it published. I miss you, Dad.

JANA LUTKEN — FRECHEN, GERMANY, OCTOBER 1938

We jumped at the violent sound of glass shattering. An axe crashed through the window, ricocheted off the kitchen wall, and landed within inches of my back. It was close. Too close. Papa tightened his protective grip around us.

I began to cry and Papa hushed me straightaway. "Shush, Jana. Keep quiet. Not a noise." I had never seen my father so alarmed. The look in his eyes was frightening.

"Nobody move... nobody!" Papa warned us.

Papa, my brother Max, my Aunt Gertie, and my two cousins huddled with me in our neighbor's darkened kitchen alcove. My papa's strong arms encircled us. He held us so tight I could not breathe.

The angry voices of a mob got louder as they neared the house. There were shouts of *"Juden! Juden!"* I trembled with fear. Yelling, screaming, pounding at doors—it sounded as if it was happening throughout the whole neighborhood.

Herr Schenkel, our kind neighbor who owned this home in which we had sought safety, grabbed a rifle and rushed to the front door. Enraged, he could no longer restrain himself.

"Franz, no!" Papa cried out.

With no regard for his own safety, Herr Schenkel stepped defiantly onto his front porch.

There was an exchange of threats, but my heart's pounding deafened me, and I could not hear what they said.

Shots fired into the air forced the small mob to flee. They spewed, "Jew lover! Jew lover!" The group continued down the street, only stopping to inflict their abuse on yet another home.

Herr Schenkel came into the kitchen visibly shaken, still holding his rifle tightly. He wiped the sweat from his brow. "They are gone now. You are safe, my friends."

Papa let go his hold on us, and we all exhaled. "We may be safe for the moment, but I'm afraid we have put you in a terrible position, Franz. For that, I am sorry and will forever be in your debt."

My father and Franz Schenkel had been neighbors and friends as far back as my memories allowed. They had met seventeen years earlier when they'd purchased their homes within one week of each other. It had been three years since the Great War ended. Both houses were abandoned and neglected. Just by coincidence and fortune, Herr Schenkel's family and our own had moved into our respective houses in the same week and had helped refurbish each other's.

Our home was small but warm and inviting. One large room acted as our living room, dining room and kitchen. It was where we spent most of our time eating, talking, playing games and telling stories. Mother and Frau Schenkel made it pretty.

We had colorful curtains with a grassy forest pattern on them and a nice big chair that Papa always sat in. It had lots of padding and was fun to jump up and down on when Max and I were alone in that room.

My parents had a bedroom with a small chest where they kept their clothes and personal things. Max and I shared a room that was barren except for two small beds and one bureau. My clothes occupied the first three drawers and Max's the bottom three. We had a secret hiding place in the wall behind the beds. Max and I shared the small opening. We put some of our favorite keepsakes in there. Nothing was valuable, but we liked having a place to keep things that only we knew about.

Our bedroom wasn't fancy, but it was ours, and we loved lying in our beds talking and sharing secrets just before we said goodnight. Max would make me laugh often. He was very witty and spent a lot of time changing the words to songs and poems just to make me laugh. And I did laugh almost every night and sometimes for a long enough time that Mama would yell, "Quiet in there! *Schlafen!* You two go to sleep now!" We would giggle for a short time more and gradually our eyes would close.

The Schenkel family's house was bigger and grander than ours. They had more rooms that seemed fancy compared to ours. They even had a separate kitchen where Frau Schenkel spent most of her time preparing meals for their family. Max and I loved spending time in there with all of those wonderful smells. If we were lucky, Frau Schenkel, who was like a second mother to us, would sneak Max and me a pastry just out of the oven. She would hand it to us with a wink and tell us to keep it between us. Mama didn't like us to eat before our supper, but it was an irresistible treat.

My brother Max and Dieter, the eldest of the three Schenkel boys, were the same age and became inseparable friends. They shared the same birth month, and we combined parties for the two of them. Throughout the years, we shared many meals and happy occasions. When they were young, the boys played war games for hours on end, as boys do. Then it was for fun. This night was real, and it frightened both of them terribly.

Mama and Frau Schenkel became the best of friends and often relied on one another to watch us children. They shared recipes, advice, and womanly secrets. Each of our homes became a comfortable haven for children in the neighborhood. No one ever needed to knock; the door always remained open, as did the pantry.

Our world collapsed in February 1935. Mama got sick. When she passed away from pneumonia a few weeks later, the Schenkel family helped us out, especially Frau Schenkel, who made dinners for us and helped with the cleaning. She missed Mama almost as much as we did.

A few months later my uncle died, and Papa's sister Aunt Gertie moved into our home with her two girls, both a couple of years older than me. Aunt Gertie took over the household duties. She was small in stature yet was as strong as an ox and had the rosiest of cheeks.

Max joked privately, "Aunt Gertie looks like a perfect square. She's as wide as she is tall."

Adelheid and Mathilde, my two cousins, became like sisters to me. It was good having other girls in the house. We played with our dolls, made up stories and whispered many secrets.

Great sadness had filled our home after Mama died. Papa became depressed and didn't speak much, but Aunt Gertie and the girls brought life back into our home. The house became crowded and full of commotion. She brought laughter, love and a feeling of normalcy with her. *Danke Gott.* Thank the Lord for Aunt Gertie.

Herr Schenkel paced back and forth. "We must find you a safe place to hide. At least until this lunacy is over. Until people come back to their senses."

Papa shook his head, still in disbelief. "Franz, I'm not sure that will happen anytime soon. The papers have been warning us for months that this day would come. Last week at the town pool, while my children were swimming, boys no older than Max posted a sign that read NO JEWS ALLOWED. Max said people were pointing and laughing as he hurried Jana away. The Nazi Party wants Jews out of the country. They blame us for everything wrong with the world. That group out there was a... a hunting party." Papa's voice rose, and anger reddened his face. "I recognized some of their voices. There were people I have known all my life. People I have worked—" His voice cracked. He eased himself onto a kitchen chair.

Aunt Gertie asked, "What shall we do, Henrik? Where shall we go?"

"Go? Leave Frechen? This is our home. We were born in this town, when it was just a tiny village, Gert. A small group of people who hate Jews are running us out? No. No. This is unbelievable. Unimaginable." He pounded the table with his fist. "Unacceptable!"

Frau Schenkel, who was sheltering her children in the back room, quietly entered the room. Her husband continued. "I do not think they will return this evening. Henrik, you must start planning. They were a small group tonight, but hatred breeds hatred. It will grow. There is much talk in the town center. That lunatic in Berlin is stirring up a frenzy of hate. It is growing throughout this country and other countries, too. People are getting hurt."

Herr Schenkel pulled my father aside. "Henrik, three Jewish families were tarred and feathered in Essen. In the town square! People laughed at them, and the soldiers shot the families. One by one, shot in the head, and still the people laughed. No, my friend, this is expanding into a firestorm of hate. Please, please consider leaving Frechen. Go. Be safe."

"Go? To where?"

"Amsterdam. I have a cousin there who writes me that the Nazis have not entered Holland. It is safe in Amsterdam. My cousin will employ you. I will write you a letter of introduction. Leave Germany!"

"But—"

"Think of your *Kinder*, Henrik." Frau Schenkel gently placed her hand on Papa's shoulder. "This is only a town. This is only a house. Your family... they are your valuables. Keep them safe."

"I will do all I can to protect your house until you return," Herr Schenkel vowed.

I held my breath as Papa focused slowly on each of our faces. He nodded and sighed. "Go collect your things. Pack two bags each. We will leave after midnight. Gertie and I will pack food and family items. We must fit the six of us and our belongings into the car."

He walked over to Herr Schenkel, and they locked in an embraced. Neither said a word. There was nothing left to say.

JANA — AMSTERDAM, HOLLAND, 1939

Herr Schenkel's cousin, Tomas Wertzelman, hired Papa to make men's caps. For almost eleven months, we were content. Then, without notice, he fired my father.

It was the Sabbath. After we recited the Sabbath prayers, Papa lovingly folded his prayer shawl, and then quietly said he had an announcement. He described to us what had happened. His boss had called him into his office and apologetically said, "Please try to understand, Henrik. I can no longer pay you because you are a Jew. People talk. Our customers talk, and they don't want to buy caps from someone who is sympathetic to Jews. They threatened that employing a Jew would get me into trouble. Please understand, Henrik. I could be shut down altogether."

Papa said, "Herr Wertzelman would not look me in the eyes. He handed me my salary and added one week's extra pay."

"He walked me to the door, placed his hand on my shoulder and said he felt terrible. He said, 'You are a good worker and a good man, Henrik. What is happening out there is... is... well, there are no words to describe it. It sickens me.' We shook hands, and I left."

Papa looked for work. Wherever he went, doors were shut before him. Papa seemed to age quickly. His shoulders slumped, and his walk was slower than usual. He sighed with every movement. Three weeks later and with no warning, Aunt Gertie, who had found work cleaning the home of a wealthy merchant's wife, was told her services were no longer necessary.

There was no more money coming in and soon there would be no food.

Papa appealed to a Jewish aid organization associated with the Central British Fund for German Jews. He reported that even they had their own troubles. Painted swastikas appeared almost daily on their doors, just to be washed off and then reappear. Windows were broken. Drunken men had broken into their offices and damaged everything. In need of their own support, they said they could offer us nothing.

However, before their offices closed for good, a kind director sent for my papa. Forbidden now to attend school, I went along. "Herr Lutken, since you cannot provide for them, there may be a way to help your *Kinder*. Burgerweeshuis is an orphanage taking in Jewish refugee children. They will not go hungry. I can arrange for that. However, I must do it by tomorrow."

"No! How can I leave my children?"

"How can you watch them starve to death? I am sorry. I know how hard this is. Nevertheless, this is the reality. There are many families now doing this. I implore you, let me make the arrangements."

I did not want to believe any of this. "Orphan? Papa, I don't want to be an orphan."

"My sweet Jana, you don't understand what is happening... why this is happening." He sighed. "How could you? You're only twelve. You would not be an orphan. See. Look at me. I am still alive. I'm right here."

"I heard her. She said orphanage, she—."

"It's a place that takes in children. Some are orphans while others are there to be taken care of."

Papa turned to the woman and sighed deeply. "Please make the arrangements."

Papa and Aunt Gertie had no choice. We were becoming desperate for food. They had sold most of our belongings, and Papa had long since sold the car. There was no money to bribe our way out of Holland.

Papa did not know of any place we could go where the Nazis had not created terror. He said Holland stood in the way of the Nazis invading France, but it was just a matter of time before the streets would fill with marching German soldiers.

The thought of separating from us—handing us over to someone else's authority—broke Papa's heart. The night before we were to leave, I listened to him crying in his bedroom—his cry turned into a wail. I did not know that such a sound could come from a human being. I wanted to climb into his bed and have him wrap his strong arms around me. I didn't, because I knew he would not want me to see him that way.

Aunt Gertie slept with her two children that night. I imagined her holding them fiercely close, knowing what the daylight would bring.

The next day came too soon.

"Papa, Papa, you will come and visit us, won't you?" I pleaded through my tears.

"Jana, my sweet child, I will come many times each week. This is a promise I make to you. This orphanage loves children. They will take good care of you and Max. They will feed you. You will have hot water to bathe in and fresh clothes to wear. I can no longer provide for you. I am sorry it has come to this. I have failed you both."

I gushed tears. "Don't say that, Papa."

"What about you?" Max asked, standing tall and straight. He held back his tears, for boys his age were not supposed to cry. "What about Aunt Gertie?"

"You do not worry about us. We will be fine. I will look after my sister. You do the same, Max. You watch over Jana. You will do that, won't you? You will do that for her. For me?"

"Yes, Papa, I will. I promise."

"Say that again!"

"I promise, Papa."

I felt secure knowing if Max made a promise to Papa, he would stick by that promise.

The six of us walked to the Burgerweeshuis in silence. It was the longest walk of my life. I held tight to Papa's hand, and he held Max's. Aunt Gertie, flanked by my two cousins, walked behind us. She needed privacy with her children and Papa needed the same.

The silence was cruel. There were no birds chirping, no vendors selling their wares, no streetcars running. The only sound was our footsteps, and each step took me farther away from the person I loved most in the world.

I could no longer bear the eerie silence, and in my nervousness, I began to hum. It was a Yiddish song Mama and Papa had sung to Max and me called "The Golden Peacock." Max had changed the words to make it funny and about me. It became our song, and we used to laugh at his lyrics. He came to call me his "golden peacock." Soon, Max began to hum and then Papa, too. It must have overwhelmed him, for suddenly Papa's legs buckled, and he fell to his knees crying. He embraced us both very tightly as we huddled together.

Aunt Gertie sniffled. "Henrik, we must keep going. They are expecting us."

We wiped away our tears. Max helped Papa to his feet. Papa took a deep breath, and we continued our walk.

I felt Papa's grip tighten when the massive brick building that was to become our home loomed into view.

Tall black metal gates surrounded the building and made it look like a prison. I feared that once I entered I would never see my papa again. Papa's finger trembled as he rang the bell.

A nun walked unhurried to the main gate and unlocked the door. She and Papa stepped aside and spoke in hushed tones. She smiled at the four of us and said, "Come children, we have been expecting you. You will be safe here."

She smiled at Aunt Gertie and Papa. "God bless you and keep you safe." She turned around and started to walk toward a long corridor. I stared at her figure draped in black as she distanced herself from us. She did not turn to see whether we were following her. I panicked.

I turned to Papa and jumped into his arms crying, "Papa! Oh Papa, please don't leave me!"

I clung to him with a strength I had never before felt. Papa lifted me up and held me. Through his tears, he said, "I will be back for you, my sweet Jana. This I promise. Never forget who and what you are. I love you, Jana, my *shayna madel*. My pretty girl. I love you. I love you both. Remember that always." He brushed my hair away from my face and gently set me down.

He grabbed Max and pulled him into a tight hug. "Never forget, Max. Never!"

Aunt Gertie had her private moment with her daughters. The girls were walking at a quick pace to catch up with the nun. Aunt Gertie faced away from us, her shoulders drooping, her head trembling, and with a shaky voice, said, "Come Henrik. We must go now."

Papa took Aunt Gertie's hand, and they walked away. Max stood tall and led me to catch up with the others.

I turned one last time and cried out, "Papa! Papa!" He did not turn around. His shoulders slumped, and he kept walking.

Max held my hand tighter as I kept turning around and watched my papa walk farther away. I wanted him to wave goodbye and have one last look at his face. He did not look back.

RAINEE ALLEN — BOSTON, MASSACHUSETTS, MAY 1997

Crap! This isn't working. I can't think. I can't work. I can't write. The nagging anxiety had returned.

Her agent Gary was going to call any day, and she had nothing to give him. She questioned whether maybe she was just a one-hit wonder. She thought, *I have to come up with a story, or they'll ask for their advance back. Think, Rainee think. Something will come to you.*

She crumpled the paper from her printer and tossed it into a wastebasket already overflowing with discarded attempts. She leaned back in her desk chair and closed her eyes, willing an idea to burst forth. It didn't.

Frustrated, she sighed and looked out her window. Pecking at the red, plastic birdhouse suctioned to the glass was a chickadee. The chirping of the bird became a distraction and an excuse to procrastinate. When she stood and walked to the window, the bird sensed her nearness and flew away.

Activity in the street below caught her attention. From the third floor of her Marlborough Street condominium, she watched six young children playing tag on the cobblestone street of Boston. Their mothers sat together on a nearby stoop, chatting, sipping coffee, and keeping a watchful eye.

A man with an ice cream cart approached, and Rainee watched the children's excitement grow. Even through double-pane windows, their delighted squeals of "Please, Mommy, please!"

were easy to hear. Mothers reached into their pockets for money. Rainee envied the innocence of childhood. She envied the mothers.

The sunlight streamed through the window and warmed her face. Moments passed as she became lost in thought, massaging her belly with the maternal instinct she had forced herself to bury long ago.

The children's loud laughter shattered her reverie. She shook away the memories, letting them fall onto her carpet like dust. She scolded herself. "Just shadows of a previous life, Rainee. Knock it off and get back to work."

She shook her head at the chaos of papers that cluttered the desk. She entertained guests so infrequently that cleaning the house was never a priority. Finishing this next novel, however, was.

Rainee reasoned, "Maybe if I clean this room and clear away the dust and the cobwebs, it'll clear the cobwebs in my head. I do my best thinking when I'm cleaning. And, hey, where better to start than this dusty desk?" She opened the closet and took out some rags and cleaning supplies.

Her once-patient literary agent's voice had begun to sound annoyed with her excuses. Gary called every few weeks requesting chapters of the novel. There was nothing to give him except delay tactics.

Rainee had been fortunate to have Gary Edwards read her debut novel three years ago. Her query letter had caught his interest. His response was one of five she received. The other four wanted her to send money for the privilege of reading the manuscript. Gary requested no money and only the first fifty pages.

Two weeks after the pages were mailed, he called. "I like your writing style. It's fresh. You pulled me into the story immediately. I'd like to read more."

"Really? That's great!"

"Well, let me read more. Then we'll see how great it is. I can't make any promises yet."

Rainee's first impression of Gary was that he was an egotist, but he was an expert. The next day she mailed him the entire manuscript.

Despite knowing the improbability of signing with an agent, she was hopeful and felt like celebrating with her two closest friends.

The bar filled with people meeting after work seeking warmth from the cold stormy March that Boston had been experiencing. Rainee and her friends found a booth away from the noise. The waitress placed a bowl of peanuts on the table, ready to take their orders.

"Miss, a bottle of champagne, please." Rainee's contagious excitement raised her friends' curiosity.

She turned to them. "I want to share some promising and potentially—and I stress the word potentially—great news with both of you. First of all, do you know how hard it is to get a literary agent nowadays?"

Shelley and Jimmy shook their heads.

"Well, there is someone who's interested in my manuscript. *My* novel!" She pointed to herself and giggled.

Her friends congratulated her with applause, hugs and compliments. "Oh, m'God, Rain, that's fabulous!"

"You go, girl."

"Always knew you had it in you."

"I'm so very proud of you!"

The waitress returned with a bottle of champagne and fluted glasses.

Typical of Rainee's self-effacing personality, she added, "Of course, he could read the rest of the manuscript and hate it."

Her closest friend, the ever-optimistic Shelley, said, "On the other hand, he might love it, sign you up with a publishing house, and get your novel into every major bookstore. Not to mention, you'll win the Pulitzer Prize, of course and—"

"Oh, of course," Jimmy said.

"And get a movie offer for it." Shelley raised her glass. "Here's to my friend, Rainee Allen and the incredible success of her book. We want to be in the audience when you accept that Pulitzer."

"Thanks, Shel, but I think that's a huge jump. First, he has to like it. One step at a time."

Ever pragmatic, Jimmy asked, "What's the next step, Rainee?"

Rainee smiled. "A refill?"

"No, I mean... well, yeah sure. Oh, you know what I mean... with this Edwards fellow? What happens next?" He refilled Rainee's glass.

Rainee was starting to feel the effects of the champagne. "Dunno. Guess I have to wait and see." She raised her glass and grinned. "Here's to waiting and seeing."

Clinking their glasses together, they cheered, "To waiting and seeing! Here, here! Bravo!"

Throughout the next three years, her book had indeed won several prestigious awards, made the *New York Times* Bestseller list and, as Shelley had prophesized, became a movie. With the royalties, she purchased her Boston condominium. Gary became a happy agent, and the publishing house signed her to write another novel, this time with a substantial advance.

However, developing a new idea for a book frustrated her. Rainee was experiencing writer's block.

She was discouraged and felt like a fraud. Again she wondered whether she was a genuine writer or a one-hit wonder. Rainee fell back into her desk chair, looked at the jumble of papers, and rolled her eyes. "Maybe if I start with one drawer at a time, I'll be able to clear up this mess in say... oh, a month?"

To celebrate her success, Rainee's father had bought her a roll top desk in a Newbury Street antique store. He restored it, taking care to stain it the color of her paneled study. During the restoration, he discovered a secret drawer and took special delight showing it to Rainee. It was a sliver of a hiding place, built to hold secret documents. It was there that Rainee kept her passport and the acceptance letter from the publishing house.

She loved the desk and its many drawers. Each drawer had its own purpose: a tiny drawer held her postage stamps and paper clips, another drawer held pens and pencils, and one held her private stationery and correspondence.

More in keeping with her personality, the bottom drawer was a clutter of papers. She groaned at the amount of work that it was going to take to organize it.

She pulled the drawer fully out and sat down on the floor. There were college term papers yellowing with age. Her attention turned from cleaning to reading. Rainee forgot that twenty-two years ago she had received excellent grades for her writing. At the time, she was a business major. It was not her intent to become a writer.

After graduation, she floundered a little until she found a job with a marketing company where she stayed for nineteen years. When her book became a success, she handed in her notice.

Culling through her many papers, Rainee came across a passport. It was not hers. It did not even look like the passports of today. Printed on the grey cover was *IDENTIFICATION CARD—For the dead and the living we must bear witness* and the words *United States Holocaust Museum*.

She flashed back to a business convention in Washington D.C. six years earlier. A co-worker had suggested they visit the Holocaust Museum. Picked arbitrarily from a large bin, the ticket clerk had handed each of them a passport/identification card of a Holocaust survivor.

She thought, *Now why did I keep this all these years*?

When she began to read it, the reason became evident. Rainee had received the passport of a woman who shared her birthday. It was coincidental that this survivor's birthday was February 9, 1927 and Rainee's birthday was also February 9th, but thirty years later. Rainee recalled this odd coincidence had touched a feeling deep inside her. She did not know why, but it had affected her emotionally.

She pointed it out to a co-worker, wiped some tears from her eyes and said, "I know it sounds silly, but I tend to believe things like this happen for a reason."

Her friend agreed. "These types of coincidences are one of life's little gifts."

When she returned home, she had put it aside and, after a while, it had found its way into the bottom desk drawer.

Well, this is as good a time as any to reread this, she thought.

She pushed herself off the floor, stretched her legs and straightened her spine, feeling an ache where her doctor had diagnosed some arthritis. He had said that it was common for a woman her age to have it; which was not something a woman her age wanted to hear.

Rainee switched on the lamp next to the futon and settled into a comfortable position. She began to read the story of Jana Lutken, born in Frechen, Germany, on February 9, 1927. She could not know it then, but the story would soon send her on a life-changing adventure.

JANA — APRIL 1940

The nun who had taken us inside first brought us to the dining area and fed us. Max ate greedily. I was still weeping and did not have an appetite. She was kind and put her arm around me.

"My name is Sister Hendrina. This orphanage houses about seventy other Jewish children. There are many non-Jews housed in different buildings. You boys stay in separate quarters, as well. The children here range in age from babies to sixteen."

Max was busy stuffing his mouth. I am not sure he even heard her.

"After Max finishes eating, I will take you to the bathroom to shower." She said, "Then you will be given uniforms to wear."

I had seen the girls' uniforms. As we walked down the long corridors, doors were open to different rooms where people were busy working. Girls wore white caps, black dresses with white aprons, black stockings, and black shoes. They reminded me of Aunt Gertie's maid uniform, in reverse colors.

"After you dress you will find the other children outside in the yard. They will be working, some planting, and some hoeing. Only the very little ones will be at play," Sister Hendrina said. "Here, everyone has assigned tasks."

"Ja, Fräulein," Max and I said at the same time.

"You must address me as Sister."

"But—"

Max shook his head to quiet me. I was about to tell her we don't address people that way because we're Jewish.

She said, "You must obey the clergy and carry out your assigned duties."

I didn't mind that because I expected to work for my room and stay.

After that day, I only saw Max occasionally. He was in a separate building and had to do different jobs around the other house. When we did see each other from a distance, we would wave. It made me cry. I missed Papa and my brother. I missed my family.

Once a week, the nuns did allow all of the children to sit together during an evening meal. I looked forward to that meal all week long. I sat between my cousins and Max. The dining hall was usually quiet, but on this night, everyone would talk and even laugh. They called it Family Night.

I expected it was better for me than for other orphans. Some children spoke of the Nazis shooting their parents right before their eyes. They had witnessed their loved ones murdered. I couldn't imagine how awful that must have been. The Nazis shot two sisters, too. They were left to die, and a kind stranger brought them here. The nuns fixed their wounds and nursed them. However, one girl lost a leg, and the other an arm. I heard that a teenage boy had battery acid thrown in his face, and now he was blind and horribly scarred. I suppose I had it better than most.

At night, in the dormitories after the lights were out, I overheard whispered stories about cruelty from the clergy. This I could not believe because they seemed so kind to us. However, sometimes a girl would return to the dormitory after we had been in our beds for hours. She would be sniffling.

"What's wrong?" one of us would whisper.

No one ever answered. None of them ever talked about it. It was as if they were ashamed. I could not understand what might have happened in the late hours of the night. I just felt sad for them.

One Family Night as we devoured our meal, Max told me and cousins Adelheid and Mathilde, that he overheard the adults talking about the war, and horrible rumors were plentiful. Some were inconceivable. I was young, but I understood that the Nazis were killing Jews, not just in Germany, but everywhere.

Max whispered, "I'm worried about Papa and Aunt Gertie. Are they still alive? Are they still in Amsterdam? Four weeks has passed since Papa brought us here. Where was he? He swore that he would visit us, and Papa always kept his word."

Mathilde said, "There's no way of knowing; no one who can give us answers."

"I am not going to wait around for that. Listen—" Max lowered his voice. We leaned in to hear. "—I am going to go look for them."

"How? How can you leave here?" Adelheid asked.

"How can you leave *me*?" I asked raising my voice. "You promised Papa!"

"Shhh, Jana. You can come too. All three of you can come. I have thought this out and I have a plan. You must trust me."

My cousins whispered together for a moment. They turned to us and Mathilde said, "Max, we cannot leave with you. We cannot take the chance of being caught. We are older than both of you and almost the age when the nuns will not accept us. Mama lied to the nuns about our ages. They toss you out into the streets when you turn seventeen. I am eighteen and Adelheid is already seventeen. We can't take that chance."

"I know, Mattey, but what if we do find your mama?"

They both lowered their eyes and shook their heads.

"It's all right. Then it is you and me, Jana."

"Tell me how, Max." He whispered his plan and I nodded.

The next day during afternoon chores, I groaned loudly and convincingly. The nun in charge of the kitchen said, "Come here. What is the matter, child?"

I stood holding my belly. "I do not know. My tummy hurts so much." I groaned again, hoping to sound like I was in genuine pain.

"You may report to the infirmary."

That was it. That was all I needed to hear. "*Ja,* Sister. *Danke,* Sister."

I left the kitchen holding my belly. I groaned all the way there.

The infirmary was in a separate building. Parked outside the entrance was an ambulance. Each morning a doctor from the hospital arrived in it to see sick children. I cautiously looked right and left. There was no one. I opened the back door and climbed in.

"Psst." The sound came from under some blankets bundled in the corner. It was Max. I joined him under the musty covers.

"Good girl. I'm proud of you. Now, we must pray that no one is sick enough to need this vehicle and we must not make a sound."

Twenty minutes, maybe thirty must have passed and we were both sweating from the heat under the wool covers. "Max, can't I just lift this up a little. I can't breathe."

"*Nein,* Jana. Be patient. Now, hush."

I wanted to tell him how much he sounded like Papa just then. But we heard voices outside the ambulance. My body stiffened. The doctor was giving last minute orders to the nuns. Then he opened the door, settled into his seat, and turned the key in the ignition. The vehicle made some sputtering noises, and then the engine sounded like it died. The doctor swore a few times, which almost made me giggle. I cupped my mouth with my own hand. He tried again and the engine turned on. I could feel Max let out a very quiet sigh of relief. The doctor drove the ambulance out the gates and off the grounds. We were on our way.

The ambulance arrived at the hospital's back entrance. The doctor slammed the door and that was our cue. Max threw the blankets off and very slowly unlatched the back door. He looked around and motioned me to follow him. We slid out the back, closed the door as silently as possible, and ran for the nearest bushes.

Max whispered, "We have to wait until it gets dark." We waited in those bushes for hours.

I had fallen asleep with my head on Max's lap. He gently shook me. "Wake up, Jana. It's dark enough. Let's go."

Max held my hand as we walked in the direction of our apartment. The streets looked different to me. They were empty and there were flags with swastikas everywhere. Every now and then, we would hear a car coming and duck behind the nearest tree or building.

"Where is everyone?" I asked.

"I'm not certain. Perhaps it's a curfew."

"Max, I'm hungry."

"I am too. We'll eat when we see Papa."

"But, what if—"

"No *what ifs*, Jana. We will eat when we see Papa."

I didn't complain from then on. We walked in silence, retracing the steps we had taken many months ago. I had forgotten how far a walk it had been. At that time of night, we did not have to avoid many oncoming cars or soldiers.

I was tiring and slowing down. Max pulled me at a faster pace than my shorter legs allowed. I tripped and skinned my knees. They began to bleed. "Max, I'm bleeding."

"We will wrap it when we see Papa. We must keep moving."

We finally came to a street that looked familiar to me. My heart leapt at the thought that we were close to home. I quickened my step.

The sound of trucks rumbling grew near. We sprinted into an alley behind the apartment buildings. It was a good thing that Max knew the way, because I was lost. I rarely played in the back alleys. Things were not recognizable to me, especially at night. Thankfully, Max knew where he was.

He stopped abruptly. His chest heaved with a big sigh. "This is it."

It was the back of our apartment building. The only way to our floor was to use the fire escape. With no hesitation, Max jumped up and grabbed the metal ladder. Very slowly, so as not to make a sound, he lowered it. When the ladder squeaked from metal touching metal, he stopped and patiently waited. Then he lowered it a little again. I was the lookout. We were fortunate that no one was around.

We started the climb to the window that used to be our living room. My heart was aching at the thought of holding Papa. I imagined what his look of surprise would be. We would climb through that window, go to his bedroom, tap him on his shoulders and throw ourselves into his arms.

Max motioned for me to stop. He had heard a noise. We crouched low, tried to be invisible, and waited. No more sounds. He looked through the glass, but it was too dark inside to see anything. Grabbing the window handles, he began lifting it slowly. I watched his face grimace with each squeak as he inched it higher. The opening was just enough to allow our bodies to crawl through. We moved slowly, not knowing what or whom to expect.

The living room was empty. Not even one piece of furniture. We opened the door to Papa's bedroom. Empty.

I sat down on the floor and cried silently. Max held me in his arms, as Papa would have done. I'm sure he was crying too because his chest was heaving up and down. Eventually, we both fell asleep exhausted from crying.

Max woke up before me. He gently nudged me, "Wake up, Jana."

He removed his shoes and moved through the apartment looking for any sign of Papa and Aunt Gertie. They had not even left a letter for us. There was not even a scrap of food. Not even a crumb left for a cockroach. The apartment had been picked clean.

"I really need to use the toilet, Max" I told him. "Badly!"

"Okay, use it quietly, and don't flush!" Max responded.

The little room was cold and empty. It was not at all as we had left it. There was a brown ring around the toilet hole. The seat was partially broken, which made it uncomfortable. The chain was missing, so I could not flush, even if I wanted to. Worse yet, there was not even a slip of toilet paper to use.

I sat there thinking of Mama. She made every room in our home warm and welcoming, including the water closet. There was lace on the windows and always fresh-smelling flowers on a small table. It had never occurred to me before that the flowers were likely to hide smells. I smiled when I realized that.

We spent the day in the empty place we used to call home. Since it would be dangerous to make any noise, we just lay on the floorboards and whispered. The *what if* became *what now*? We knew we could not knock on a neighbor's door for fear that a familiar face would not meet us.

There was plenty of activity throughout the building and on the street. We peeked out the kitchen window as life in our neighborhood had resumed to normal. I suppose one could call it normal, if motorcades of Nazi trucks passing and soldiers marching uniformly were normal. What we didn't see was a Jewish face. Not even the children playing in the streets looked familiar.

What had happened to Papa and Aunt Gertie? Did they leave on their own or were they taken away? What happened to the Klein family, the Hinkleman family, the Steinfeld family, neighbors all. And what of their children?

We were both hungry. "Max, can't we please knock on someone's door and just ask for food?"

Max said, "Absolutely not! You know we can't take the chance, Jana. There is no one we can count on."

We looked out the window again. "See those children playing with the ball over there—the ones wearing the brown uniforms? See them? Some are younger than you. They are called Hitler's Youth. They would report us and not think twice about it."

"Max, we can't stay here, tiptoeing around forever. I am really hungry."

"I know. Tonight, I will go out and rummage for food."

"You mean scraps from someone's garbage cans?"

"Yes, Jana, that's exactly what I mean. I will be grateful if I can find anything." Max pointed his finger at me and added, "You should be grateful too."

"Yes, Max." I sniffled. "I will."

At least in the orphanage there was food. "Max, should we go back? To the orphanage, I mean."

He was quiet for a long time. "You know they take a bed count. They already know we are missing. They might not let us back in."

"Then again they might!" I was trying to be optimistic.

"Not without a punishment, Jana. Are you prepared for that?"

"I don't know. What could be worse than not finding Papa?" I started sobbing again. "That hurt more than anything they could do to us."

"Don't be so sure. Look, let me try to find food tonight. We'll sleep on it and rethink it tomorrow."

I nodded.

That night, when there was no activity outside, Max slowly opened the living room window and left to look for food. He warned me that if he didn't return, I should get back to the orphanage as quickly as possible. I didn't want to think about that.

It felt like hours had passed when I heard two shots ring out. The sound echoed in the night air. I was scared. Was Max all right? I sat in the dark trembling, repeating his name, Max, Max, Max. It was as if I was willing him to appear. He had been gone a long time.

There were sounds of soldiers arriving at our street. I went to look out the window afraid of what I might see. It was happening three apartment buildings down. Soldiers knocked down a front door. You could hear their boots marching up stairs and knocking down another door. A woman screamed. The night air amplified sounds—the scuffling of shoes, the desperate pleas of a woman. Then the soldiers emerged dragging a man into the street. They dropped him in the gutter. A soldier raised his gun and aimed it at his head. The woman screamed again. But not loud enough to muffle out the sound of the bullet leaving its chamber.

A noise rising from somewhere deep inside was about to exit my throat. Suddenly, a pair of hands from behind covered my mouth and muffled my screams. It was Max. He pulled me away from the window, and down on the floor. His hands never left my mouth. I shook uncontrollably. He held me tightly as I cried into his shirt.

He tried his best to console me. "I'm so sorry you saw that, Jana. I wish I had returned sooner. I'm sorry."

Slowly, I began to calm, and my shaking stopped. Max raised his pointer finger in the air, and like a magician would, said, "Aha!" He removed a piece of stale bread from underneath his tear-soaked shirt. We split the small piece in half. He went to the living room window where he had quietly placed a bottle of wine and handed it to me to drink first. There was but two thimble-sized sips left. "Drink it slowly," he warned.

We slept until the sunlight's glare entered the room.

This time I awoke before Max and just watched him sleep. I thought, *Papa, you would have been so proud of him. He tried his best to take care of me, just as he promised you. But what about you? Where are you? What have they done to you? You have to be alive. You just have to.*

"You just have to." I accidentally repeated the words aloud and woke Max.

"Huh?" He asked, wiping the sleep from his eyes.

"Sorry, Max. I was just talking to Papa."

"That's all right. I was just dreaming about him. You know what he told me in my dream?"

I shook my head.

"He said we should return to the orphanage, beg them to take us back, and then take whatever punishment they dole out."

"I agree, Max. If you think that's what Papa would want."

"Jana, we will have to do it in daylight. If we go back at night, they may not come to the front gate."

"Okay."

"We will have to be careful and act like all the other children on the street. We can walk a little and then play a little, then walk some more, and then play some more. You understand?"

"Uh-huh."

Max looked out the front window. I was afraid to. He said, "There's no sign of last night's shooting. Not even blood in the gutter. If we are lucky, maybe it rained. Then we could get some rainwater and clean our faces a little. Look more presentable. Not like two children on the run."

"When should we leave?"

"Let's leave before there's activity. That way no one will see us using the fire escape."

We left the apartment as we found it… empty. Or maybe, it was a little emptier than before, because before there was hope that Papa was there. Now that hope was gone.

On the road back to the orphanage, we found an empty tin can that had rainwater in it. We washed the dirt off our faces and hands. We were passable. Max warned, "If anyone stops us, let me do the talking."

Keeping to the plan, we made our way back slowly, stopping to play along the way. We cut through a park, and even found a ball. We faked our laughter as we threw the ball back and forth.

At the end of the park, four German soldiers were sharing a cigarette. I froze. Max lowered his voice and said, "Keep moving and act natural."

One soldier yelled, "*Werfen mir den Ball.*"

I asked Max, "What do I do?"

"Do what he said. Toss him the ball. Act like you're having fun."

I threw him the ball, and he started kicking it with his foot. Then he kicked it over to his comrade, then the other, and before long, they had a game going. Max pointed to himself and yelled, "*Schieß zu mir.*" They kicked it back to him and he joined them in the game. I suppose they were not much older than he was. I could not believe what I was witnessing—just some boys playing ball. I sat down on the grass and waited.

The game continued until a different soldier came by and yelled at them all to stop. The soldiers scrambled to attention and saluted him. Max picked up the ball, waved at them, and we left.

"What were you thinking?" I asked.

"Just trying to fit in." He laughed and added reassuringly, "We may make it back okay after all."

That is how we made our way to the Burgerweeshuis. It took us a while, but we were there before dinner.

Max rang the bell. Sister Hendrina came out and she had a scowl on her face. "Where have you children been?"

Max let me explain that we left to find our father. He knew I would cry and maybe we would receive some sympathy from the nuns. We received no sympathy whatsoever. She sent me to the head sister's office, and Max was sent to the head brother's. Although they took us back, we were both severely punished. I later found out that Max was ruthlessly beaten. They hit me with a switch across my knuckles. It bled a little, but it was not as bad as Max's beating. The cruelest punishment we faced was that they took away our Family Night.

From that day on, I only saw Max from a distance. We waved to each other, but that was as close as they would allow us to get. I became very lonely.

I was lonely but not alone. I became friends with a girl who was my age. Even though Hannah was a German Jew, she had short, blond, straight hair and crystal blue eyes. Not like me. Not like most Jews. My eyes were dark brown and matched my hair, which was always frizzy and out of control. I looked Jewish but Hannah could pass as Aryan. She came from the town of Essen, not far from Frechen. Together we dreamed how we would visit each other when we returned to our homes.

"My father was a teacher." Her blue eyes sparkled with pride and then clouded over with sadness. "One rainy day, the Nazis arrived at our house and dragged Papa out into the muddy streets. They called him *Judenschwein*."

"Jewish pig?" I gasped and laid my hand on hers. "But why?"

Hannah gulped back her tears. "They kicked him and beat him. I ran out of our house and screamed at them, 'Leave my father alone!'"

"Oh, Hannah—"

"The Nazis picked me up and tossed me aside like a sack of potatoes. I hit my head and almost passed out. They pointed their guns at me. That is when I saw my mother come running from our home screaming at them. She had a broomstick in her hand. She tried to defend our family... with a broomstick!" Hannah was silent for several minutes. "The Nazis shot her. Then they shot my father in the head. That's when I fainted."

Hannah told me she awakened in a neighbor's bed. The kind woman arranged for her to be smuggled out of Germany to this orphanage. Some nights I would hear her cry. I didn't know how Hannah could finally fall asleep with those pictures in her head.

All the children here keep pictures in their heads. Each child has suffered the loss of parents, family members, or friends. I still cling to the hope that Papa is still alive somewhere, that he will come and take Max and me away from here. However, each day takes him farther and farther from us. Images of my past life have started to blur into a mixture of muted colors. No longer sharp, memories of my past are becoming hazy shadows. The past and present have been muddied by an uncertain future.

RAINEE — MAY 1997

"What? Are you serious? I would love to go with you! When are the dates?" Rainee dug into her purse and grabbed a calendar. In her excitement, she broke her pencil tip. "Hold on! Let me find my pen. It'll make it more permanent that way." She pulled out the pen she used when autographing her novel. When her book became a movie, Shelley had presented her with a Mont Blanc pen.

Rainee wrote down the dates of their departure and return.

"And this is all on your boss? Two months in London for training with all expenses paid? I'm speechless! I'm thunderstruck! I'm dazed! I'm nonplussed! I'm—"

Shelley was laughing. "Apparently you are not that speechless."

"Why would he pay for my flight?" Rainee was jumping out of her chair with excitement. The couple at the next table glared at her. She hadn't realized how loud her voice had become, and she apologized to them. "Sorry, I'll tone it down."

"I told him I was afraid of flying and needed a companion to hold my hand. It was the only way I could go."

"Oh, you are such a smart one."

"Well, I did give up one first-class ticket for two coach tickets. But for my best friend... and to see that look on your face... well, it's worth it. Now, are you sure you can clear this with Gary?" Shelley was always pragmatic.

"Oh right... well, uh... I know. How does this sound? I will tell him it's research for the novel. I feel a little guilty that I've kept him in the dark so far." Rainee leaned in closer. "But you know, Shel, I've come up with a possible storyline. It should take place in London, anyway. There's someone I want to visit there if she's still alive and if she still lives in London and if I can find her."

"Sounds like a lot of ifs."

"I know. She doesn't even know I exist. I have this feeling of connection with her. I can't quite explain it. I do think she would make a great story."

"This sounds intriguing. Tell me more."

Rainee ordered a round of White Russians and told Shelley the story of Jana Lutken—what little she knew of her.

"It's so cool that you share the same birthday. This sounds like fate," Shelley said enthusiastically.

"Yes, well, even if she's not alive, I consider her to be my muse. Because of her, I no longer have writer's block. She's inspired me to come up with something. First, we share a birthday. Second, I kept her museum ID card for all those years. Now third, you've asked me to travel to London. See? That is fate!"

"How do you know she's still in London?"

"I don't. I'm going to contact Yad Vashem in Israel. The institution keeps very thorough records of Holocaust survivors. I can also do some research in the British Library. Then, if I still can't locate her, I'll write a nice fictional story instead of a biography. I can change the names to protect the innocent."

"Sounds like a plan. I like it."

"You got it, sister." They clinked glasses and spent the remainder of their meal talking about the logistics of their trip.

JANA — OCTOBER 1940

Weeks have passed since our escape, and I have not seen Max. Rumors about the clergy continue to grow. I am very worried about him. I sometimes see other boys when we're working outside in the yard. Priests in long black robes, wearing crosses on heavy chains, watch over them. The boys never seem to smile or talk to each other. At least we girls make friends and chat. Someone tells a joke, and we laugh. The world does not weigh heavy on our minds, and we feel safe within the borders of these walls. The boys look exhausted from worry. I want to ask them why, but contact with them is forbidden.

At least, I still get to see my cousins, Adelheid and Mathilde. Because they have a different last name, the nuns never caught on that we are cousins. So I see them at meals and in the lavatory on shower days. When the nuns are not looking, we hug.

"Oh, Jana," they'd sob. "We miss our Mama so much." When they cried, it made me cry too.

I reminded them in a whisper, "The nuns don't like to see us cry."

One beautiful fall day, we were busy preparing the soil for next year's crops. The rumbling sound of approaching vehicles brought our chores to a standstill. The gates of the orphanage swung open as four trucks and a jeep bearing flags with a swastika entered.

Soldiers with guns jumped from the back of the truck and stood at attention. Soon a very expensive automobile arrived behind them. A chauffeur stepped out and opened the passenger door. A strikingly beautiful woman emerged from the car. Her blonde hair, tucked neatly under a fashionable hat, made her look like a movie star. She wore a white fur coat and used a white cane. Everything about her appeared pure and good.

One soldier from the jeep must have been a powerful man because he had many stars on his uniform, and the other soldiers saluted him. He greeted the woman and together they walked into the orphanage.

We could not control ourselves and began whispering. "Who is that beautiful woman?"

"Who is the Nazi?"

"Why would they meet here in our sanctuary?"

"Hush, hush, children!" The nuns hovered about, silencing our questions.

We returned to our chores, stealing glances at the front door.

I remember that night as if it was yesterday. It was hot in the girls' dormitory. In the past, October had been a chilly month leading us gently into the winter. This particular year it was unseasonably warm. Windows in our dormitories were nailed shut for our own protection. That night, most of us lay sweating on our cots as we speculated about what we had witnessed earlier.

I had finally fallen asleep when the loud sound of jangling keys unlocking our room woke me. It had to have been the middle of the night because the full moon was shining through our windows softly lighting our room. An odd feeling crawled through me; something important was about to happen.

The head sister snapped on the overhead lights, and clapped her hands to awaken the other sleeping girls. She had our full attention. Alongside her was the blond woman.

"Children, this is Frau Wijsmuller-Meijer. She has brought us some wonderful news. There has been an arrangement made with the Germans to transport you to Great Britain. This special plan made with the Wehrmacht allows you to leave Amsterdam. All seventy Jewish boys and girls will ride a *Kindertransport* to a safe haven, where you will stay in various parts of England. Families have agreed to take you in and care for you. You will be safe from the Nazis there."

Sounds of disbelief rose until the nun clapped her hands to silence the room.

"You must leave immediately," the head nun continued. "Take whatever you brought. Quietly, line up, two by two. And please, as you march past Frau Wijsmuller-Meijer, I would like each of you to curtsy. It is only proper to thank her for this selfless deed and for the opportunity she is giving you."

Frau Wijsmuller-Meijer spoke to us, her voice soft and gentle. "There is no need to curtsy, *Meine Kinder*."

The head nun was insistent. "Children, please do as I requested."

She turned to Frau Wijsmuller-Meijer and spoke in softer tones, "Geertruida, you have gone to great lengths to arrange their safety. I cannot begin to imagine how you convinced the *Generaloberst* to allow this. I should have known that someone of your prominence in this community could convince the Germans to permit these children to leave."

"Sister, they have agreed to a limited number of *Kindertransports*. The Nazis have been clear about that." The blonde woman sighed. "I fear they will soon change their minds and stop deporting the children. We must get as many out and as quickly as possible. We must hurry to the train station now. There is no time to waste."

Frau Wijsmuller-Meijer waited until the last child had left the room and then followed behind us, like a shepherd herding her flock.

That is what I felt like. I followed the girl in front of me, like sheep. What else was I to do? As we gathered outside the tall gates of the orphanage, I looked around for the boys and did not see them. What of Max?

Frau Wijsmuller-Meijer said, "Children, wait here."

As we waited, the cold air that had not entered our dormitory started to seep through my clothes. I shivered, reached in my satchel, and took out my one coat. It was a good coat, made of thick wool. It felt like we were standing there a long time.

At last, there was some commotion. It was the boys being ushered from the orphanage, and they formed into a group behind us. Max was with them! Relieved, I waved and he waved back. I was so happy to know that he was going with me.

But what of Papa? I was leaving the country. He would not know where to find me. Would I ever see him again? The thought left me with a cold shiver.

We were a large group, so we walked the distance to the train station. I do not know how many miles it was or how long it took. I was happy to be outside the gates of the orphanage, walking toward my freedom. At the station, a train, surrounded by Nazi guards with rifles, was waiting. The first seven boxcars were padlocked, and there were sounds of children talking inside. The cars toward the end of the train were open, ready to be loaded. Once again, they made sure the boys were separate from the girls. Perhaps thirty girls filed into one car; the boys entered another. I found my way to a corner and sat down. The doors closed swiftly. We were in total darkness.

Everyone was afraid to talk. The silence and the darkness were eerie. I thought of Hannah. Was she here? Consumed by my own thoughts and fears, I had not once considered my friend. I stood and whispered, "Hannah? Hannah?"

"Hush!" one of the older girls said.

The train screeched as the metal wheels began to move. It rumbled, slowly at first, and soon picked up speed. After a little while, the rocking back and forth lulled me into sleep. I awakened several different times when the train halted as Nazis herded aboard more children. They entered with the same bewilderment the rest of us felt. Quietly, we made room for them, and the boxcar became crowded.

Hours must have passed as light started to show through the slats of the boxcar. We all stirred and wiped sleep from our eyes. It became evident that the train was slowing again as it approached the next station.

"It's a port!" squealed one of the girls. "I can see the signs." She was able to see through the rotting wood of the boxcar.

The train came to a halt. We heard shouts from the Germans.

"Schnell, Schnell! Aus dem Zug!"

The car doors opened, flooding us with sunshine. Atop the station building a large sign spelled out *Hoek van Holland Strand*—Hook of Holland Station. I thought, *What a silly name for a town.*

Soldiers led us to waiting tables that held large vats of porridge. We stood in single file and were handed a cup of porridge with a slice of stale bread. It was then I realized that this was my breakfast coming at nearly the same time as at the orphanage. *This will not be so bad,* I thought.

The soldiers still kept the boys distant from us. I looked for Max among them. He was there devouring his meal. I smiled. Since he was a little boy, he always ate too fast. Papa chided him to chew his food and not gulp it down. It made me giggle.

Frau Wijsmuller-Meijer appeared with an announcement. I had not realized that she had accompanied us to this point and felt relieved to see her. She stood on a crate so we could all see and hear. Her face was in shadows as the sun backlit her. Her blonde hair blazed like a halo. I strained to see her kind face. Thankfully, as she began to speak, a cloud formed in the sky, so I could look upon the face of the woman who was our liberator. Like a mama taking care of her children, her mere presence comforted me.

"Children, please listen closely. From here, you will take a boat to England. Volunteers will greet you. When you hear your name called, you will go to a designated spot. Foster families will be waiting for you there. They come from many different places throughout Great Britain. They will take you in and shelter you. Do not take this for granted. They do this at great risk to themselves. Your very presence creates danger to those families, especially if the Nazi army does invade England."

People interpreted her words into different languages. The news was met with mixed emotions. Some children were in disbelief; some had smiles on their faces. She understood that this was a lot for us to comprehend and patiently waited for the murmuring to stop. "Now listen carefully; you must learn to fit in. Some of you will be encouraged to attend church, to adopt a new last name, to eat foods that have been forbidden by your Torah."

There were sounds of objection.

She spoke louder. "Children, this is a matter of survival. I have no doubt that God would not consider this a transgression, but would allow it. I also encourage you to learn to read and speak English. Again, I emphasize that you must try to fit in."

The Nazi officer signaled to Frau Wijsmuller-Meijer. She stepped off the crate to speak with him. I watched her frown as they exchanged whispered words and could tell how unhappy she was with the conversation. She emphatically clenched her fist, shook her head in disagreement and pointed her finger in emphasis and objection. The Nazi straightened his posture and towered above her. She reluctantly pocketed her hand. After a few minutes, the tense conversation ended. Frau Wijsmuller-Meijer slowly turned to face us. She squeezed her lips tight and resumed her place on the crate.

"Children, the *Generaloberst* has brought to my attention that you are not all leaving on the same boat and at the same time. I assure you," and she turned to glare in the officer's direction, "that this was not the intended plan. However, we must all adapt, just as I was encouraging you to do before I was interrupted."

She paused as if weighing the right words in her head.

"The girls will be the first to leave on the ship in the harbor. The boys will follow on a separate ship later this afternoon. If you have a relative amongst you, take a few minutes to say your goodbyes. God be with each of your precious souls. I pray you will find each other again in Great Britain."

Some of the children stood to protest. Immediately, the Nazi guards raised their rifles, silencing any demonstration.

Frau Wijsmuller-Meijer raised her hands to get our attention and to quiet us. "Please children, please. Do not provoke the soldiers." We calmed down and she continued, "I will be leaving you here so that you may continue your journey. I pray to God you all find safety in your new lives. Remember to be grateful. Unlike many children your age, you have been given the gift of life. Do not waste this extraordinary gift. You will be in my thoughts and my prayers. God bless you all."

With those final words, Frau Wijsmuller-Meijer turned and walked to a waiting automobile. In silence, we watched her drive away.

I stood immediately and ran to Max, thinking this may be the last time we would see each other. I was losing faith that we would reunite in England. Already the Nazis proved they did not keep their promises. I did not understand how anyone could deny the requests of a woman like Frau Wijsmuller-Meijer. In changing her plans, they had proved deceitful, and I was beginning to recognize the danger.

Max was running in my direction too. We caught up with each other and hugged. He held me tightly, like Papa would. "I promise I will look for you in England," he vowed. "I promised Papa I would take care of you. After we were let back in, they didn't allow me to be near you. I'm sorry; I really tried."

Max wiped away the tears that trickled down his cheeks. He held me at arm's length and looked me straight in the eyes. "Jana, you must be brave. You must try to fit in as the lady said. Wherever you end up, you must try. Do not be stubborn, my proud golden peacock. You will always carry being Jewish inside of you, so do whatever is necessary."

"But—"

"Be smart. There is great danger in practicing our Jewish laws now. God understands. Break them if you must. You will always be Jewish in God's eyes."

"Max, I'm scared." I trembled. "I miss Papa. I miss Mama. I miss you. Now you are leaving me too. Why is this happening?"

Max pulled me into him and held me tighter. "I do not understand why. I do know not to trust the Nazis' words. Be very careful whom you trust. These are dangerous times." He could see how frightened I was. He added, "Do not worry about me. I am strong. You be strong, too. I will find you even if I have to look all over England. I will find you."

A soldier blew a shrill whistle and the Nazis started breaking up the farewells of families. They were physically tearing people away from each other's grasp. When people protested, the Nazis stopped being polite. They used the butt of their rifles to wedge people apart.

Shockingly, two shots rang out and someone screamed. Then there were more screams. I looked and saw a boy lying on the ground. Blood was pouring out of his skull forming a crimson puddle. His sister could not stop her screaming and was inconsolable. She threw herself on his body.

The Nazi who shot him pulled her off and pushed her onto the ground. He lifted his rifle and aimed it at her.

A different soldier came quickly and stopped him from shooting her. "*Nein! Nein!*"

The first soldier walked away disgruntled, spit on the ground and said, "*Judenschwein!*"

Max said, "Go, Jana! Go now! I will find you! I will!" He pushed me away.

I ran to where the girls were. I saw Hannah and we grabbed for each other. We huddled together with fear and a new understanding. If the Nazis could get away with murder in public, what would stop them from murdering all of us? Max was right; there was great danger, and I had to stop being naïve about the world. I had to grow up fast and face the reality of this new world that was being thrust upon us.

I jumped when the boat's piercing whistle sounded. We girls were rounded up and walked up the metal plank in silence and tears. My two cousins were ahead of me and boarded holding hands. None of us looked back at the boys, frightened we would show weakness or, worse yet, dissent. I feared I would never see my brother again. I could feel the collective hearts of all of us as they silently broke—not in half—but into a million pieces.

Another shot thundered in the air. I jumped again. We all turned to look. Some of the boys started to protest, yelling names at the Nazis and arming themselves with rocks, ready to fight. What were they thinking? Did they really think rocks would stop the Nazis? I strained to see Max. Thankfully, he was not part of the group of protesters. He was too smart for that. He knew the danger.

That first shot had been a warning. Still it did not stop the growing number of boys ready to fight.

The *Generaloberst* came forward and spoke with the soldiers. Without hesitation, and apparently without any remorse, he and the soldiers shot each protester.

The boys' bodies crumpled to the ground. Blood flowed onto the docks and spilled into the water below.

Some girls screamed, and some fainted. I froze. My body felt like lead. Starting at my feet and slowly working up to my head, I began to quiver from fear. I knew then the horror of that moment would live in my mind forever.

I stared at the *Generaloberst*. He had a large and bulbous nose, a high forehead, a balding head, overgrown eyebrows nearly linked together as one, and black eyes, cold and lifeless. His ugly wide smile showed missing teeth. I had no doubt his hideous face would forever haunt my dreams and be a permanent memory.

He stomped out his cigarette and started laughing. Laughing! Then he sneered. "*Untermenschen!*" he said and spit on the ground. The other soldiers joined him in laughter. This amused them.

I thanked God that Max stayed on the ground. He was smart. I knew that at that very moment, he wanted to get up and charge at the soldiers. He restrained himself, which must have taken a lot of self-control. He had made a promise to me. I knew he would do whatever was necessary to keep that promise.

Something compelled me to stare at Max's face, and then the *Generaloberst's* face, then Max, and then back at the Nazi. My head bobbed back and forth, like watching a tennis match. I think I was afraid that the moment I looked away, the Nazi would shoot my brother.

"*Schnell! Schnell!*" We were hustled onto the boat by the sailors. They had also witnessed the horror and understood the danger. We quickly moved up the plank and onto a ship named *De Praag*. We joined another hundred or so girls already on the boat. We stood by the rails and waved goodbye. I cried inconsolably as I waved goodbye to Max, not knowing what his fate would be at the hands of these murderers.

His head remained bowed. He would not look up.

RAINEE — 1997

The lights in the jumbo jet dimmed. Passengers attempted the impossible—finding a comfortable sleeping position. The steady drone of the airplane's engines soon helped put many to sleep.

Shelley shifted in her seat, obviously unnerved.

Rainee asked, "You okay, Shel?"

"No. I lied to you before. I am afraid of flying."

"It's okay, Shel. These planes are all computerized. We'll be fine." She noticed Shelley's knuckles had turned white from gripping the armrest. Rainee placed a calming hand on her friend's arm.

Shelley took a sip of her scotch and water. "It's going to be a long night, isn't it?"

"Well, it will be if you don't fall asleep."

Shelley playfully said in a child's voice, "Tell me a story, please."

Rainee laughed at her friend's silliness. "You want me to tell you a story? Sorry, I don't do bedtime stories."

"I know... and now you know that I wasn't lying to my boss. I am terrified of flying. Scared to death actually. Thank God you're here. So now, it's your turn."

"My turn? For what?"

"I just revealed the truth to you. Tell me something about you that I don't know. Anything. Maybe something that terrifies you. Talk to me. Lull me to sleep."

Rainee laughed. "You mean bore you to sleep. You know everything about me. I'm an open book."

"Everyone has a secret. What do you writers call it? Skeletons in the closets?"

Rainee tapped her fingers on the tray table. She squirmed nervously in her seat.

"What's the matter, Rain?" Shelley could tell her friend had become a little disconcerted.

"Nothing." She gulped down her Scotch and nodded. "Okay, I will tell you something... something that terrifies me. I haven't talked about this in... well, I don't know how many years." She drained her cup.

Shelley could tell that her friend was genuinely anxious. "Take your time."

"I've... I've... I've honestly wanted to tell you for years, Shelley. But frankly, I couldn't. I'm ashamed. It's not a subject I'm comfortable blurting out, y'know?"

"Hey, you're my best friend. I won't judge you."

"All right, but there is a caveat. You have to promise that you will never repeat it to anyone." She faced Shelley. "That's including me. I don't want to discuss it or analyze it."

Shelley raised her eyebrows. "Seriously?"

"Yes, seriously. It's not up for discussion."

"Now you've got me nervous, but I'm curious too." She sighed heavily. "Okay, I promise."

"Here, pour me some more." Rainee held out her plastic cup, and Shelly poured the last drops from the miniature bottle.

After a moment of collecting her thoughts, Rainee said, "Shel, do you remember soon after we met, I told you about a friend of mine? A guy named Ricky. He was one of my best friends from junior high school right through college. People said that men and women couldn't have platonic relationships. Well, ours was platonic. Really. He was like a brother to me."

"Yeah, I remember. You told me after college he moved to California, and you lost touch with him."

"Right. There's more to our story, however. A lot more." Imitating Bette Davis in the movie *All About Eve*, she said, "Fasten your seat belts. You're in for a bumpy night."

"Nice imitation, but, please no puns about bumps while we're on a plane." Shelley opened another miniature bottle. "Why do I feel we're going to need a few more of these?" She stopped the stewardess and ordered more Scotch.

Rainee adjusted her pillow and began her story. "It was 1977. We were seniors in college. Ricky and I went to a frat party at Boston University. We hung out at B.U. a lot, because they had better parties than our school. We weren't exactly potheads, but both of us occasionally smoked. It was the 'seventies. There was a lot of it going around. We walked into a frat house, and there was a cloud of smoke hanging in the air. The place reeked of grass."

Shelley nodded.

"The party was crowded and rocking. Everyone was stoned or drunk. Pretty typical for those days."

"I remember those days," Shelley said. "The good old days."

"Yeah, some of it was good. Ricky and I grabbed a spot that opened up on the couch. A girl there was smoking from a hookah, and she offered us a hit. She told us it was 'really good stuff.'"

"Synonym for really strong stuff, right?" It was more of a statement than a question.

"Yeah. It was strong all right. A couple of hits and I had no memory of the rest of the night. Apparently, the grass had been laced with PCP."

"PCP?" Shelley gasped. "Angel Dust?"

"Exactly. It was a hallucinogen. We didn't know someone had laced it with PCP. I always stayed away from hallucinogenic drugs. Not my cup of tea."

Rainee fidgeted in her seat and was silent for a few minutes. Her hands folded and unfolded the small square cocktail napkin. She stared at the imprinted airline logo.

"That's your big secret? You got high?" Shelley asked.

"No, I'm not done. There's more to this bedtime story. I've never told anyone else, and I'm trying to put the words together. Give me a moment."

"Sorry, hon. Take your time. It's a long flight, and I'm not going anywhere."

Rainee leaned her head back and inhaled deeply, letting her breath out slowly. "The next morning I awoke under the dining room table. Ricky's body was next to mine; one arm draped over me. He was out cold. I shook him to make sure he was still alive. He awoke slowly and then asked me that quintessential question: 'What happened?' I didn't know. Our heads were throbbing. We were groggy and dazed. What I didn't tell him was that my thighs hurt like hell, and so did my vagina. Shelley... I was still a virgin."

"You mean, you think—."

"Maybe three weeks later I noticed that I didn't get my period. And my period came like clockwork. Like clockwork!"

"Oh shit."

"Yeah, oh shit. I went to the school's clinic and took a test." She paused. "I was pregnant! I was pregnant with Ricky's baby. Christ, my first time, and I got pregnant. And pregnant from my best friend. Just my luck, right?" Rainee took another sip.

"What did you do then?" Shelley asked.

"Well, I knew I had to tell him. You know, I was just twenty, and I hadn't even lived yet. Having a baby was not in any of my plans. I had dreams to travel, to start a career, to... well anyway...."

"Wow, Rainee. It must have been rough."

"I was determined to get an abortion and then get on with my life. To me, it was the logical thing to do. I met Ricky in the Public Gardens, and we went for a walk. It was fall. The flowers were still out. People were enjoying the swan boats. It was a beautiful day, even for some lousy news. I knew I had to tell him. I felt that he had the right to know."

"What did he say?"

"At first, he was speechless. When I told him I wanted to get an abortion and needed to borrow $200.00, he lost it. He started to rant, saying things like, 'How could you? You can't abort a baby. That child is half-mine. You can't kill,'—and he did use the word kill— 'our baby.'"

"Oh my God."

"When I told him it was just a tiny clump of cells, he went berserk. He asked how I could even consider killing it. Then he went on and on about the Holocaust and all the innocent Jews killed in the war. Ricky was Jewish. Apparently, his family had lost many relatives in the war. His grandparents even met in a concentration camp. Once they had invited me to their family's Seder dinner. Inevitably, they started talking about their lost loved ones. Everyone began to sob. Including me! It was a very emotional experience. I had never given much thought to the Holocaust because it didn't affect me."

She sighed and continued. "I was stunned by Ricky's reaction. I couldn't equate the two things. I didn't get how the Holocaust related to me having a baby grow inside my body. But he did! In all the years I knew him, I had never seen him so passionate and angry about anything."

"What did you say?"

"First, I apologized for the words I used and then I tried to explain that this situation was not the same. I told him that I didn't want to have a child. I said, 'We got stoned out of our minds and screwed. We made a baby. It was not a child conceived from love. It was just a mistake.' Well, let me tell you, when I said that, he looked like he was going to blast off into the stratosphere. He was positively apoplectic. He ranted and raved. He went on and on for... oh, I don't know how long. My head was pounding. It felt like it would explode. Finally, I caved. I gave in."

"He wore you down?"

Rainee's lower lip began to tremble. Tears slipped down her cheeks. "Yes. I told him I would have the baby and then give it up for adoption. I was not going to be a mother at twenty. Well actually, I would have turned twenty-one by the time the baby would arrive. July, after graduation."

"Wow, what did he say?"

"He said he would take the baby. He calmed down a little when I caved. He said he had a job offer from a computer company in California that would start just after graduation, and he would take care of his child. He also said that we would have an entire country between us, so I would be free to pursue a career. In all honesty, that hurt. Though, I must say, I did feel a little relieved."

"What did your parents say?"

"Oh, I dreaded telling them. But, it turned out that they were supportive. They said they would have had no problem either way, if I aborted or gave up the baby for adoption. It was my decision. They're pretty liberal thinkers."

"So, you had a baby, Rainee. All these years I've known you, and you never told me. How is that even possible?" Her alcohol consumption only slightly muted Shelley's annoyance.

"Can't you understand how painful a subject this is, Shel? I wanted to put it all behind me. But it inches into my brain at times. I'm not sure whether it's guilt or regret."

The plane hit turbulence. Shelley reflexively grabbed Rainee's arm, loosening her grip only when the vibrations stopped. "What did you have? Boy or girl?"

"A healthy seven pound, six-ounce baby boy. Ricky named him Joshua. We were in the hospital. Joshua was in my arms. I kissed his forehead. Then Ricky took him from me, kissed me goodbye and left. Left with Joshua. I cried and cried. Oh, I was a mess for a while. The nurses said it was hormonal, but I knew that wasn't why. Ricky moved to California, and that was the last time I saw him. I heard through mutual friends that he married a Jewish girl. They had two more children and lived happily ever after. Joshua would be nineteen now."

"Do you regret your decision?"

"Yes and no. I know I made the right decision at the time. I was too young and inexperienced to be a mother. About that, I have no feelings of guilt. But now that I'm forty... yes, I do regret giving up Joshua. Who knows whether I'll ever be a mother?"

Shelley attempted to lighten the mood. "Wow! This could be a book."

"You asked me to tell you a story. How are you going to fall asleep now? I know I'll be up for the rest of the night." Rainee let out a slow breath. "Y'know, Shel, the truth is that it feels somewhat liberating, now that you know. I've carried that secret for years."

"Does Joshua know about you?"

"I don't know. If he does and wants to meet me some day, he certainly could find me. You wanted to know what terrifies me: it's coming face to face with the child I gave up. Okay, end of discussion."

"But, what did—"

"End of discussion. Anyway, we need to get some rest or we'll have trouble adjusting to the time zone in Great Britain."

Shelley fell asleep quickly from all the Scotch. Rainee took a Valium. Despite the pill and the alcohol, she was wide-awake for most of the flight. Her mind was full of memories. Somewhere around three o'clock in the morning, she fell into a restless sleep.

The smell of coffee woke Rainee. Her head was fuzzy from having taken the Valium along with the alcohol.

Soon the garbled words of the captain came over the intercom. Rainee caught every third word, yet understood the gist of his communication. They would soon be serving breakfast and were on schedule to land in an hour and a half.

Lines quickly formed at the bathrooms. Rainee gently nudged Shelley awake.

After going through Customs and collecting their bags, they hailed one of the many black taxicabs that were queued up waiting for passengers. Shelley loved the taxi, checking out every little detail. It was distinctly different from the cabs in the United States: very roomy, with seats that could fold down and face backward, allowing for extra people.

As they passed the sights Shelley had only read about, her excitement grew. "Look at this! Look at that! Look over there!"

Rainee smiled at her friend's delight. She said to the cab driver, "Would you mind driving past Buckingham Palace and give this lady a real thrill?"

"No worries, love." He winked and took a circuitous route to their final destination.

Shelley's company owned a condominium where they housed visiting employees and special guests. It was in an upscale area known as Mayfair. The buildings were similar to Rainee's brownstone on Marlborough Street.

The taxi driver carried their many suitcases up the stairs to the front door. Rainee paid him while Shelley fumbled through her purse for the keys.

Inside the foyer, Shelley was amazed at the elevator that would bring them to the third floor. Rainee instructed, "They're called lifts, here. Oh, and an apartment is called a flat."

The lift was tiny and had a sign that warned of "two-person only" occupancy. Shelley laughed. "What do you think? Three feet by three feet? Glad I'm not claustrophobic." Because of the lack of space and the multiple suitcases, it took them a couple of trips.

Even in daylight, the third floor hallway was lit poorly. There were several bulbs in need of replacing. The flowered wallpaper was peeling in some areas, and bits of something unrecognizable littered the floor. "And they call this area upscale?" Shelley said. However, nothing could quell their excitement at being there.

They followed the hallway to their flat. Shelley turned to Rainee and with a huge grin, unlocked the door. They were pleased to find a roomy, three-bedroom condominium with an eat-in kitchen and a spacious living room. The refrigerator was empty. However, to their delight, they found the bar fully stocked.

Considering the amount of clothes they brought, they were a bit disappointed to find no bedroom closets. Each room had large wardrobes, and Shelley suggested that they share the third bedroom to store extra clothes and, since it had a desk, Rainee could use it as an office.

The third bedroom had a single window, which brought in sunlight and overlooked a colorful garden. Rainee set her laptop on the wooden desk. The room would serve well as her temporary workplace. She then went around the flat lifting all the shades and opening windows to let out the stale smell. Happy to be there with an objective, she breathed in London's air.

Following inspection of the apartment, the women wrote a list of what they would need to purchase: food to stock up the refrigerator, laundry detergent, toilet paper, etc. They decided to celebrate their arrival at a restaurant recommended by Shelley's boss. The next day they would spend exploring London. After that, Shelley would begin her training and Rainee was anxious to commence her research.

Because she was writing for publication, Yad Vashem assigned Rainee a researcher named Ilana Zahavy. She had worked at Yad Vashem for four years and had success in locating Holocaust survivors.

Ilana's last email to Rainee revealed that when the *Kindertransport* arrived in England, Jana was fostered by a family named Wickham who had a farm in Berkhamsted. They changed her name to Janet to sound Protestant. Berkhamsted was her last known location. Ilana assured Rainee that she was continuing her research and was optimistic that she would find more up-to-date information.

Rainee hoped that if she started her search in Berkhamsted, she might find the Wickham family. With some luck, they might have kept in touch throughout the years.

The train took a little less than one hour. At the Berkhamsted station, she asked for a telephone directory. The ticket agent pointed to several graffiti-covered, fire-red phone kiosks. With the one remaining phone book, she looked up the name Wickham and found two listings. She wrote down the numbers and addresses for both.

Rainee hailed a taxi. "Your town library, please."

The taxicab dropped her off in front of a two-story white house. The library appeared to be a refurbished residence. A white picket fence lacked a lock to keep people out and had a sign welcoming people in. There were flower boxes under each window filled with healthy-looking gardenias, penstemon, and begonias. The porch wrapped around the house and had many small groupings of comfortable-looking white rattan chairs. There was even a hammock, which swung gently with the breeze. Rainee smiled. *What an inviting setting to sit and read!* When a little bell jingled as she entered, she was charmed even more. With the exception of an elderly woman behind the front desk, the library appeared to be empty.

She approached the librarian. "Good morning."

Behind the woman, a large picture window with rare English sunshine streaming in caused Rainee to squint at the woman. She held her hand up to shield her eyes from the light.

The diminutive, gray-haired woman wore her hair pulled tight in a bun. She looked at Rainee above her half-glasses. "Good day. May I assist you?"

"I'm hoping you can. I'm trying to locate a woman who lived here during World War II. I have reason to believe she may still be alive."

"I'll do my best. What information do you have about her?"

"She lived with a family named Wickham. They were farmers. As I understand, she left right after graduating high school. Would your archives hold that information?"

"Perhaps. Wickham, you say. There are some Wickham families still living in town. However, I'm not sure you will find who you are searching for in our archives." She leaned forward. "The library, which held land deeds and such during the war, was bombed by the Luftwaffe. We lost many important papers. Oh, that bombing left such a ghastly mess." She shook her head as if it had been a personal affront. "Whatever survived was moved to the National Archives in Richmond. They put much of it onto microfiche and returned some to us."

Disappointed, Rainee groaned, "Oh no... it seems I may have come all this way for nothing." A second thought crossed Rainee's mind. "Were you living here then?"

With pride, the librarian answered, "Oh yes, I have lived here all my life. I was a volunteer aide to the head librarian, Mrs. Collingsworth."

"You mentioned a bombing. May I ask what happened?"

"Well, I was not in the building when it happened—obviously. I was fortunate. The alarms had gone off, and I went to one of the bomb shelters. I tried to convince Mrs. Collingsworth to come with me. Nevertheless, she would not leave her precious books... her precious building. She was a brave and loyal woman."

A foolish woman, Rainee thought.

"In any case, let me see if I can be of help."

"Thank you, Ms...?"

"Mrs. Numan." She added a curt smile and raised a curled finger to indicate that Rainee should follow her.

"It's nice to meet you. My name is Rainee Allen."

Not missing a beat and with no sound of surprise in her voice, Mrs. Numan asked, "The author?"

"Well, yes."

"There's a long list of readers waiting their turn for your novel. I haven't read it myself. I hope to get around to it one day soon." Mrs. Numan reached into her desk drawer and took out a large brass ring. It held an abundant assortment of keys and jangled loudly as she walked.

Rainee smiled as she followed her through a maze of doors, each leading to more rooms filled with shelves of books. "Charming... you have a truly enchanting library."

Mrs. Numan stopped to find the exact key she needed. Rainee was not surprised that she was able to locate the right one swiftly since it was the largest. It was a very old-fashioned cast iron key. It must have weighed three times what the other keys weighed. It fit easily into the old lock. The door, which led to a cellar, squeaked open. Mrs. Numan turned to Rainee. "Wait here, please."

She descended into the darkened cellar, holding the banister for guidance. When she reached the bottom, Rainee heard her click on the cellar lights, illuminating the steps and the room below. "Okay, it's safe, just hold onto the railing, dear. The stairs are a bit rickety."

Rainee did as told.

Filling the room were clearly labeled vertical and horizontal file cabinets. There was a desk in the center of the room with a plastic-covered microfiche reader. The musky smell and the dust that had settled all around indicated to Rainee that people did not often visit the cellar.

Mrs. Numan instructed Rainee how to begin her research and pointed out which of the filing cabinets might contain useful information. Then she left her alone.

Rainee removed the plastic cover on the microfiche reader and went to the filing cabinet that held the film. She removed those related to the period when Jana was in Berkhamsted and began the tedious task of scanning the local newspaper for the Wickham name.

Like most of Europe during the war, resources were scarce, and Berkhamsted had been no different. The village newspaper was less like a typical newspaper and more like a bulletin. Its circulation to the townspeople was infrequent. An event had to be very newsworthy in order for someone to expend the effort and money to produce this small publication. Rainee noted that it was not a propagandist bulletin. Rather, it would update folks about the war, death tolls, crop pricing, local stores going out of business and, on occasion, a shocking rumor about a pending divorce.

After two hours, Rainee yawned and rubbed her eyes, which were becoming tired and bleary. *This is leading me nowhere,* she thought.

Finally, one microfiche mentioned the word *Kindertransport*.

Rainee sat upright. Goose bumps crept along her arms. The bulletin reported, *Throughout Great Britain, refugee children from different countries are being accepted and integrated into families.* It continued on for several paragraphs describing the pride of the British people in their assistance of these children escaping from the horrors of war.

The reporting was sophomoric and puerile, and though there was no way of knowing, Rainee suspected it had been a high school project. She kept reading as more and more microfiche films began to expose events of the war. As she read, she noted that the writing became more stylish and erudite. It seemed obvious that if begun as a high school project, the teacher must have taken over the reporting as the subject grew more serious. Rainee became engrossed and energized. The bulletin expanded to several pages. The reporter increasingly took a political stand, dangerous for those days. *What bravado that must have taken*, she thought. With renewed exhilaration, she could feel her heart racing.

The October 1940 *Berkhamsted Broadsheet* reported that three families had accepted five young refugees into their homes. It named the Jameson, Wickham, and Ellington families. The community was encouraged to welcome the children and accept them as new citizens. Rainee considered it very naïve of the reporter to reveal the names of the families who had taken the children into their shelter. Had the paper fallen into the wrong hands, or if one of the citizens of Berkhamsted proved to be a traitorous Nazi sympathizer, those families would have been in great danger.

There it was: the Wickham family. Rainee was elated. In the privacy of the cellar, she did a little victory dance. She printed out the *Bulletin*, and headed upstairs to see whether Mrs. Numan would know how to follow this lead.

As it happened, the librarian was very helpful. She was even delighted that Rainee had been able to locate the data she'd sought. Reading the paper, Mrs. Numan kept nodding in acknowledgement. Absorbed in the article, she muttered, "Of course! Yes! Brilliant!"

Rainee wasn't sure whether she was delighted with the finding or the fact that someone was using her cellar sanctuary.

"Ah, now I remember this. Oh, so very long ago. Quite. You are a very lucky lady. The very same Wickham family is indeed still living here. I can give you their address. Of course, their farm's land was long ago transformed into a marketplace. You know, dear, I remember this. In fact, I remember the young girl they took in. Jane, Janice, Janet... something like that. She was always shy. Always sad."

"Yes! Jana was her name. It's pronounced with a Y, like Yana. She was German and came here from an orphanage in Amsterdam. What else do you remember, Mrs. Numan?" Rainee clapped her hands. "Oh, I can't tell you how wonderful this is!"

"Well, we remember her as Janet... I think. I seem to remember that when she arrived, none of the townspeople met her for a few weeks. I suppose the family wanted her to adjust to her new surroundings. When she finally emerged from their farm, it was to enroll in school. Naturally, her English was very poor. Oh, she learned a few words from the Wickhams. None of us could really understand her, so we left her alone. Poor child. She was a stranger. And a Jew too. That set her apart from everybody."

"I can imagine."

"All the European propaganda at the time blamed the Jews for the war. Hitler was trying to make his once-powerful country great again. But she was just a child, an orphan at that. We all took pity on her, Jew or non-Jew. She was a child. It wasn't her fault. All the while, Nazis were on the march toward England." Mrs. Numan continued reminiscing about the time she had lived through. A time she had witnessed.

Rainee reflected. What awful times had she experienced in her life? The war had ended twelve years before she was born. Soldiers had returned and started families; some had gone back to school on the G.I. Bill and most had begun to rebuild their lives. Europe was cleaning up the mess left by war, putting itself together brick by bombed brick.

"I'll write down the Wickham's address for you. You'll find them lovely people, though quite aged and a bit forgetful. Nevertheless, farmers tend to be made of sturdy stuff. Here you go, dear." She handed Rainee the notepaper. "Please do keep in mind that the war carries awful memories for people, whilst many others have tried to put it behind them. The men who went to war still have memories as vivid as if it were yesterday, not fifty years ago. I'll call for a taxi, dear." The librarian smiled. "I wish you luck with your research. I do hope you find Janet... that is, Jana."

"You've been very helpful. Thank you so much, Mrs. Numan."

She noticed how careful the librarian was to pronounce the German girl's name correctly. *Girl?* Rainee smiled at the thought. Jana Lutken, if she were still alive, would be in her seventies. She stepped outside into the cool, damp country air to wait for her ride.

The taxi arrived within five minutes. She handed the cab driver the Wickhams' address. Even though Berkhamsted was small,

Rainee figured he must be like the cabbies in Boston; they resented short drives and the lower fares. When she noticed he looked glum, she said, "I'll be calling you to pick me up as well."

"Well now, that's bloody exciting." He said with homegrown cheek.

The ride lasted less than five minutes. If she had known where to go, Rainee realized she could have walked. The driver stopped in front of a housing complex of small apartments crowded onto a lot. A bent and rusted industrial steel fence surrounded the property, as if to keep people inside. The gate was unlocked and wide open. The building's exterior was in need of a coat of paint.

Where the library had planted colorful flowers lining the walkway inviting people to visit, here overgrown and dying bushes overhung the path to the front door. Rainee looked about, wondering how depressing and dreary a place this would be for anyone to live.

She rang the doorbell for apartment 5B and waited several minutes. A diminutive, gray-haired woman, hunched over a walker, greeted her. "May I help you?"

Rainee took a deep breath. "I'm looking for a Mr. and Mrs. Wickham. Do I have the correct address?

"May I inquire what this is about?"

"Please, excuse my manners. My name is Rainee Allen. Mrs. Numan, from the library, gave me your address. I hope that was all right."

For a moment, her quest seemed like a crazy dream, and she thought, *Here I am, some strange American woman knocking on your door, coming from out of nowhere. Please let me invade your distant memories*. She lowered her voice, trying to hide her own jitters. "I'm a writer. I'm trying to locate Jana, or as you knew her, Janet Lutken. I was hoping you might still be in touch with her."

The woman gasped, then hesitated a moment. "Forgive my manners. I am Gloria Wickham. Please, do come in." She turned and moved very slowly, leaning on her walker. Toward a closed door, she called, "Harv, dear, there's a lady here who wants to speak with us."

A few minutes later Harvey Wickham joined Rainee and Mrs. Wickham in the sitting room. He was a big man. His hair was full and white, and he did not look as aged as his wife. His face was wrinkled, rugged and weathered. Rainee assumed it was from spending years working outdoors. Although he walked with a slight limp, he did not use a cane.

"Hi, I'm Rainee Allen." She extended her hand.

The man failed to acknowledge it. He walked across the room and claimed the only armchair.

"My husband, Harvey Wickham." Mrs. Wickham completed their introductions. She gestured toward a worn settee. "Won't you please sit down, Miss?" Mrs. Wickham moved slowly and, with a quiet sigh, eased down onto the tattered furniture.

"Thank you." Rainee sat beside the woman, suddenly unsure how to continue. She had come so far and had so many questions to ask. However, these people appeared frail and so old to her. She hoped their memories were intact. For Mr. Wickham's benefit, Rainee explained again about her search.

Throughout her discourse, the couple remained silent.

Mrs. Wickham finally broke the silence. "M'dear, I'm afraid you've made a long trip for naught. We lost touch with Janet many years ago. She moved to London after her graduation from high school. She came home to visit us once, and then stopped coming. I was never sure why. She was a lovely girl. Very helpful around the farm."

Mr. Wickham grunted, "Uh-huh."

It appeared to Rainee that he had listened with great interest, leaning forward in his chair.

Rainee looked back to his wife. Had the woman's eyes started to brim with tears? She wasn't sure.

"We loved that girl like she was our own." Mrs. Wickham stood, pushing herself up with the walker. "Where are my manners? We don't get visitors often. Miss Allen, would you like a cup of tea?

"That would be lovely. Thank you."

Rainee wanted the conversation to continue, but waited politely. Mrs. Wickham returned, balancing a worn silver tray, laden with cups, sugar, milk, cookies, cake, and scones.

The woman glanced down at the crowded tray. "Oh my, I've probably overdone it a bit, haven't I? As I said, we don't often get visitors. This is like a party for Harv and me." She glanced at her husband. "Isn't it, Harv?"

Her husband helped steady his wife as she placed the tray on the coffee table. "Uh-huh."

Rainee smiled at the woman's kindness, yet what Mrs. Wickham had revealed saddened her, and she thought, *This couple managed to live a long life, yet they seem so lonely. How does a family spend a lifetime in the same town and yet no one comes to visit?* "Mrs. Wickham, would you mind telling me about Jana? I'm sorry—your Janet?"

"Well now, that was long ago, Miss Allen. My memory has started to fade. You know, m'dear, I'm ninety-five years old." She smiled with great pride and continued chatting as she poured tea. "Sugar? Milk?"

"None for me." Rainee observed that Mrs. Wickham was missing two of her front teeth and the rest were yellowing with age. Nonetheless, she possessed a smile that was warm and sincere.

"Well, she came to us from what they called a *Kindertransport*. Do you know what that is? Harv and I had read there were orphans headed to England and needed families to take them in. We didn't have any children of our own...." Her tone had grown wistful. She shook her head, clearing away whatever memories might have pained her. "Nevertheless, we had a farm and needed help running it."

Rainee sipped her tea. "Thank you. This is very tasty." She was conscious of Mr. Wickham, silent and noncommittal in his corner of the room. She caught him staring at her, and she shivered. *He is odd,* she thought.

Mrs. Wickham continued as if memories were flooding back and she needed to share them. "We thought it would serve two purposes. We had hoped to get a boy, but we took Janet. Well, let me tell you—"

Now Mr. Wickham was glaring at his wife.

What's happening here? "Yes?" Rainee said. "Please do go on."

"When I saw her, she was a pitiful sight. She was dirty and smelly too. Just like a street urchin." Mrs. Wickham's voice caught in a sob. "We took her in, we did, and we scrubbed her real good. She cleaned up nicely. Very pretty too. Wasn't she, Harv?"

"Uh-huh. She spoke only German. We taught her English."

Rainee was startled at the first sentence Mr. Wickham had spoken since she had arrived.

Mrs. Wickham continued. "That's right, though she already understood a bit. Just certain words. Took her a while to learn, and she never did lose her accent. When we enrolled her in school, the students made fun of her. Kids can be terribly cruel. She was a child, for goodness sakes. But no matter what they said to her, she would not cry. Isn't that right, Harv?"

"Uh-huh."

Rainee studied him. Something troubled her about him. She was more relaxed asking questions of Mrs. Wickham, who seemed very willing to respond. "Could you tell me what she was like? What kind of work did she do here?"

"Oh my, she was very helpful on the farm and—" The woman glanced in her husband's direction. It seemed she was about to say something else, but stopped.

Rainee noticed her reticence but was unable to decipher what was happening.

"Eventually, we began to feel like family. Janet became the daughter I never had. Oh, she was often melancholy. She missed her father and brother. She never learned whether they were still alive. Janet told me that her brother—what was his name—oh, yes… Max. He had promised to find her in England." Mrs. Wickham's voice had grown pensive once more.

Rainee wondered whether she was reliving the long-buried pain of not being able to make her "daughter" happy.

"Some days, I would find her looking out the window, watching and waiting for him. Poor child. That went on for years, even after the war."

"Naïve kid." Mr. Wickham was picking some morsels of scone from his teeth. He looked up and spoke. "There was a rumor that

German submarines torpedoed the ship carrying the boys. We didn't have the heart to tell her that he was probably dead."

Rainee gasped. That rumor was missing from the articles she had read.

Mr. Wickham put the toothpick aside and continued. "She held onto this hope like rosary beads. You know, close to the heart. Rumors were that a second transport was two hours late leaving port. They separated the boys from the girls at the last minute. The first ship's captain had cargo, and he had a bloody deadline. He had to leave. If the sub had struck with all the kids on board, Janet would have died along with her brother." He crossed his arms and settled back in the armchair.

Mrs. Wickham spoke as if confiding something dear to her heart. "We were churchgoers. We took her to church with us. Thought it would be a good way for her to fit into the community. Janet went and never complained, but she never took Jesus into her heart. You can't force that."

Rainee smiled. "No, you're right. You can't force the heart."

"Now, where was I?" Mrs. Wickham paused for a moment before continuing. "Well, Janet went to London after graduating high school. That was where she married. She invited us to visit, but we didn't go. We never were ones for traveling."

Rainee tried to hide a smile. It was perhaps forty miles to London and they were concerned about "traveling." "Did you stay in touch?"

Mrs. Wickham shook her head and wiped away a tear on her cheek. "I'm sorry... what was it you asked m'dear?"

"Did you stay in touch with her after she moved?"

"Not really. I posted some letters to her, and she would write me back. The one time she visited with me; we met for lunch at a pub by our train station. She seemed to be in a hurry to return to London."

Rainee was anxious to discover what had happened. "I'm hoping to find her while I'm here. Do you have her last address? Did you know her husband's family?" She leaned forward on the settee. "She'd be in her seventies now. Mrs. Wickham, I have this... this feeling that she may be alive. It may seem silly to you. Somehow I feel a connection to her."

"That's not silly at all, m'dear." Mrs. Wickham patted her hand. "I have some old address books back in my desk. Harv thinks I'm daft for saving them. Now, you see Harv? They do come in handy eventually."

"Uh-huh."

She returned with an overstuffed book held together with rubber bands, small bits of paper poking from its frayed edges.

"Let me see. Yes... here it is! She married a man named David Bowman. Sounds Jewish, doesn't it? Let me write down his family's address. It was in London too. Can't guarantee it's still the same. They might be all gone by now. Ah! Here's Janet's last address. It was a small flat in London."

Wanting to be a good guest, Rainee finished her tea though it had grown cold. She had been busy listening and making mental notes. She had not meant to neglect the lovely tray Mrs. Wickham had prepared in her honor. She leaned forward and picked up a raspberry cookie.

"May I use your telephone?" she asked. "I'd like to call a taxi to take me back into town."

More an order than a request, Mrs. Wickham said, "Harv, would you mind doing that for her?"

Mrs. Wickham accompanied Rainee to the door of the apartment building. "If Janet is alive, praise the Lord, please tell her we loved her and we miss her."

"I will, Mrs. Wickham, I will," Rainee promised. "Thank you so much for the tea and for sharing Janet's story with me."

As she waited for the taxi, she considered that not all the orphans were as fortunate. She had read that many ended up working as slave labor for families. Countless foster families abused children verbally and sexually. Some of the children even took their own lives. She thought despite Mr. Wickham's frosty personality, Jana indeed had been lucky to end up with this family.

JANA — ENGLAND, OCOTOBER, 1940

Our boat docked in Harwich, England. When we arrived, I was dazed from hearing so many different languages. There were children from Austria, Czechoslovakia, and Poland. Children below in the ship's hold, not knowing what to expect, were afraid to come up on deck.

I looked in the crowd of children for my cousins. I could not see them and knew intuitively that I would never see them again. I felt panic crawl through me.

Before we could leave the ship, doctors examined us. Customs officials took our documents and wrote things on them; some used rubber stamps with different colored inks.

Hannah whispered to me, "They're validating our documents. I don't know why. I know who I am."

I giggled, but I was nervous and held Hannah's hand tightly.

The families who met our ship were called guarantors or foster families. They were crowded together waiting behind a fence. One of the officials would call out a name, and a family would come forward and pluck one of us away like cabbage from the garden.

After a long wait, an official called out, "Lutken, Jana."

I heard him say my last name, but he mispronounced my first name. I wasn't sure what to do. Did he mean me or someone else?

He repeated, "Lutken, Jana."

Hannah, who was standing by my side, nudged me. We hugged.

I walked slowly to the man and pointed to myself. I tried to correct his pronunciation. "Jana. Ya... ya... Jana Lutken." I was still unsure whether he meant me.

"Okay, sure... whatever you say, darlin'."

Then he gripped my arm and called out, "Mr. and Mrs. Harvey Wickham."

There was some stirring among the crowd, but no one came forward.

He repeated, louder, "Mr. and Mrs. Harvey Wickham. Last call."

For a moment, I was afraid no one was going to come forward. Then I noticed a couple pushing their way through the crowd. Were they the Wickhams?

The man spoke with one of the officials. Even though I couldn't understand him, I could tell by the sound of his voice he was annoyed. The words, so many words, rattled in my ears. I understood one thing: "boy." Maybe they were waiting for Max!

While the man continued to bark at the officials, the woman who had accompanied him came close to me. Was this Mrs. Wickham? She stooped down and looked into my eyes. She had a kind face.

I did not speak English, yet her eyes and her warm smile broke through our language barrier, and I was able to comprehend. It felt like she was telling me not to be afraid and that everything would work out.

Mr. Wickham returned with papers in hand and grumbled quietly. His wife patted his arm, reassuring him. Later I would learn that Mr. Wickham had specifically requested a boy to work on their farm. However, Mrs. Wickham had told him that because I could help her, she would be able to help him more.

"Humph!" The burly man walked away briskly, grumbling, and we followed. The woman took my hand in hers, and we walked together. "I always wanted a daughter," she whispered.

I smiled, pretending to understand her, and I think maybe I did.

Sitting between the Wickhams in their truck was uncomfortable; they continued their argument as he drove through the pretty countryside. After a while, he sighed and stopped talking, which seemed to signal acceptance. His wife tried to hide her smile; she peeked down at me and winked.

"Your papers say your name is Jana." She pronounced my name with a *J*, not with a *Y*. She said the words slow and even, as if maybe I would understand their language if she was patient.

I shook my head. *"Ich heisse Jana. Ya... ya... ya... Jana."* I was trying so hard to teach them, though I understood that I was the one who had much to learn.

Mr. Wickham snorted. Even though I didn't know more than a dozen words in English, whatever he said sounded like a bad word. It was the way he snarled it. "Bugger! It sounds like a German name."

"You're right, dear." His wife turned to me. "Let's make it easy for you. Hmm... I think we shall call you Janet. Yes, Janet! That's a fine and proper English name. And it's spelled almost like Jana. There now, that's settled. You are now Janet Lutken." She patted my hand.

I vaguely understood what they were saying. I wanted to correct them, but my head was spinning from all that had occurred since that morning's breakfast. Had it been just that morning? I wasn't only losing the sense of time. I was losing the sense of my own identity.

It was a long ride. Most of the roads were rough and unpaved, and a bump tossed me into the air. Mrs. Wickham grabbed me and held me tight.

Finally, we arrived in a town called Berkhamsted. We continued the drive out to the countryside and to their farm. A metal gate with the words Wickhill Farms blocked our way. Still grumbling, Mr. Wickham climbed down from the truck, slammed the door, and unlatched the gate. He swung the gate wide open, got back in the truck, drove through, stopped, and again stepped out to re-latch it. It seemed like a lot of work. I had a feeling that would become my job in the near future.

As we topped a knoll, Wickhill Farms came into view. I gazed at the bucolic scene as we drove toward the house. The dirt road was lined with trees and opened up to expansive fields of green, rolling hills. The farmhouse was in the center of the field with a grove of fruit trees as its back yard. The image of a mother standing protectively in front of her brood came into my mind. I thought of Hannah's story of her mama running out of their home to protect her and realized that, other than a hug, we never had a chance to say goodbye.

The truck stopped at the house that was to become my new home. Mr. Wickham climbed down from the truck, slammed the door, and headed toward the barn, still grumbling.

I followed Mrs. Wickham into the house. We went straightaway up the stairs to what would be my own room. I had never had a room to myself, one I could call my own. The room was small, with a bed, a dresser, and a chair in the corner next to a window. Towels were stacked neatly on the foot of the bed.

With a pleased look on her face, Mrs. Wickham said, "Ah!" Then she left the room in a hurry and returned after a few minutes, carrying a hairbrush and a small mirror. She placed them on the dresser. "This was my sister's." She pointed to herself.

I understood her. *"Eine Schwester?"* So she had a sister, like I had a brother.

She tried to hide her sadness and shook her head. Later I would learn that her older sister, Ina, had died, and the treasures she had given me had once belonged to Ina. She blinked, and for that minute, I shared her sadness. I longed for my brother too.

"For you." She pointed at the dresser where boys' clothes lay folded neatly on top. "Oh my! Well, now, we will go straight into town tomorrow and exchange the boy's attire for pretty girl's clothing. Shall we take a bath now?" Making pictures with her hands, she was communicating with me quite well.

I understood and nodded, *"Das Bad."* I was filthy, smelly, and needed a bath. "Bath" in English sounded almost like German!

Mrs. Wickham showed me the bathroom on the first floor, and then gestured toward the kitchen. After my bath, I supposed I was to go there. She must have known I was starving. She prepared my bath and took my clothes away, holding them at arm's length. I thought they would burn my clothes, and I understood why, but they were my last connection to home.

I hesitatingly objected. *"Waschen?"*

A puzzled look crossed her face. "*Waschen*? Oh, wash them? Why, these clothes are positively filthy and somewhat tattered, my dear."

"Bitte?" I put my hands together as a plea.

Mrs. Wickham laughed and said the only German word she knew. "Oh, all right. *Ja*."

She closed the door, giving me a privacy that I had not experienced in a very long time.

I lowered myself into the claw-footed cast iron tub and let the warm water envelope me. The grime of many days floated away. I scrubbed myself raw, attempting to scour away events and memories etched in my head. No amount of scrubbing could erase the face of that wicked soldier, *Der Generaloberst*.

I lost track of time as I lounged in the tub. I fell asleep and dreamt of Papa, Mama, and Max. I dreamt of the happier days in Frechen, sitting around our kitchen table, lighting the Sabbath candles, Mama saying the prayers. Then Max was teasing me with his silly version of *The Golden Peacock*. Everyone laughing until there came a loud and sudden knock on our door and a German soldier ordered us out.

"Time to come out, Janet."

As I slowly awoke from my dream, I heard Mrs. Wickham's voice coming from the farthermost back of my head. "Time to come out, Janet dear."

It was her knocking and not the Nazi. I must have been in there for a long while. She must have wanted to know if I was all right.

"*Ja. Ja.*" I said still a bit hazy from my sleep, but relieved she awakened me before I would have to see the *Generaloberst's* eyes again.

I stepped out of the tub with reluctance, wanting to stay waterlogged for much longer. My fingers were noticeably wrinkled. I toweled dry and dressed.

My mouth was watering as I followed the smell of food into a large kitchen. She was at the stove, stirring a big pot.

"Hungry?" She pulled out a chair at the wooden kitchen table. "Have a seat, Janet."

I obeyed. *"Ja, Frau Wickham."*

"Oh no, Janet dear. We can't have you calling me that. Let's see. Suppose you call me... Auntie?" She pointed to herself and repeated the word, *Auntie.*

Aunt Gertie quickly came to mind, and sadness overwhelmed me. Not wanting Mrs. Wickham to think me unhappy, I pointed to her. "Auntie," I said, and then pointed to myself. "Janet." I wanted her to think me grateful.

She poured stew into a bowl and placed it before me. "This is to be our dinner this evening." She sat down at the table with me and watched as I devoured the stew. I realized I was eating just like Max, gobbling down my food. I was surprised at how hungry I really was.

RAINEE — LONDON, ENGLAND 1997

So far, everything that Rainee had discovered supported the details Yad Vashem had provided. During her ride back to London, she read her notes and reviewed what she had learned to date.

The researcher, Ilana Zahavy, dug deeper and had followed Jana Lutken's life until she became a widow at age sixty-two. At that point, information about her stopped. It was almost as if she had disappeared.

As the Wickhams reported, she had married David Bowman when she was in her early twenties. They had no children. He was an accountant, and they had lived a comfortable life in London. Her foster mother Gloria Wickham had taught her sewing; she found employment as a seamstress in the prestigious theatre, the Palladium. Her husband was diagnosed with lung cancer, and she retired to be his caregiver. For many years, she nursed him, and his cancer went into remission for quite some time. He continued his career for another nine years until the cancer metastasized to his brain. He died at the age of sixty-nine.

It was early evening when Rainee arrived at the flat in Mayfair. Shelley had left a note propped up against the coffeepot: *Sorry to leave you alone—again. Having dinner with friends from work. ~ S.*

"Shelley, always the party girl," she said to the empty apartment. "That's okay with me. I'm exhausted. A shower and some soup would be just about right."

Before heading to bed, she stopped to check her email. It was an automatic habit.

"You've got mail," the familiar announcement sang out. The single email was from Yad Vashem. She clicked on the message and gasped. Ilana had discovered more information!

I admit to having lost track of Jana Lutken Bowman and had almost abandoned hope. After checking thirty-four nursing homes in Great Britain, we have confirmation at last: Jana is alive and living there! She is listed under the name Janet Bowman. Good luck! – Ilana Zahavy. She added the address.

Thrilled with the news, Rainee hit Reply and typed, *Would you believe I'm here in London right now? Thank you for everything you've done. ~ R. Allen.*

At last, she had an address! Tomorrow she would come face to face with Jana Lutken Bowman.

Located between Euston Station and the British Library was 130 Chalton Street. A tall, white, wrought iron fence surrounded the red brick building. A security camera hung at eye-level, and a sign on the gate directed visitors to ring an intercom buzzer.

Someone with a cheerful voice said, "Hello. May I help you?"

Rainee spoke to the intercom. "Yes, please. I was hoping I might be able to visit one of your residents."

"Do you have clearance?"

"Well… no. She doesn't know me, and I don't have an appointment." Rainee realized how foolish this sounded and was instantly sorry she had not arranged a visitation. "I'm writing a story about Holocaust survivors and I've come to England in search of Jana Lutken."

Smiling at the security camera, she hoped her image in the fisheye lens would not give away how foolish she felt.

"Sorry. There is no Jana Lutken here."

"Oh, yes, that's right. Her married name is Bowman. You have her listed as Janet. Would it be possible to speak with a supervisor?" Pleading her case, she continued. "I've come such a long way. You can't imagine the lengths I've gone to find her. Please?"

"Wait one moment."

The silence at the end of the intercom lasted for almost five minutes. Thinking she had been forgotten, Rainee was about to ring again, when the voice said, "Are you there?"

"Yes."

"I'm going to buzz you in. Hold down the latch for a few seconds; it sticks a bit."

The buzzer sounded. Rainee held the latch and opened the gate. She passed through a brick arched entryway and found a small, lovely courtyard obscured from the street. Benches with umbrellas speckled the manicured lawn while rows of mature chestnut trees and colorful flowers lined the curved walkway. She found the grounds pleasant. It created the feel of walking into a residence rather than an institution.

The front door had a weathered brass knocker, several locks, and another security system.

A smiling receptionist opened the door. "Sorry for all the fuss, but we do have rules to safeguard our residents."

"Of course you do. I totally understand. I'm so sorry for not calling in advance."

"I'm Sally." She smiled and extended her hand. "You can call me Red," she pointed to her dyed, cherry-colored hair.

Rainee returned the greeting. "I'm Rainee Allen. It's nice to meet you, Red."

"Our manager is John Pritchard. He suggested you have a seat. He's on the telephone with the NHS and will come out soon as he's available." She rolled her eyes to indicate that it could be a while. She led Rainee through the foyer to the reception hall with chairs and comfortable-looking couches. Feeling the excitement of finally meeting Jana, Rainee could not sit down.

Vases filled with fresh bouquets of English primrose sat on the side tables. Black and white pictures of aged faces decorated most of the wall space. Rainee assumed they were the residents and wondered which face was Jana's. It was well lit, clean, and not the antiseptic notion of a nursing home she had anticipated. She found herself smiling that Jana was in what appeared to be a quality facility.

After several minutes, John Pritchard entered the room. His height made the room shrink, and he dwarfed her five-feet, four-inch frame. He had wavy dark brown hair that complemented the flecks of brown in the irises of his hazel eyes. A convivial smile erased any apprehension that she would be dealing with a dull, by-the-book, bureaucratic administrator.

"Ms. Allen? I'm John Pritchard. A pleasure to meet you." He took her hand in both of his, a simple warm gesture that Rainee found appealing. "Let's go to my office to talk." He held the door, allowing her to walk in front of him.

A gentleman... and an English gentleman at that, Rainee thought.

The office was small and orderly. A Victorian roll top desk, similar to hers, was against one wall, and a table with four chairs was in the center of the room. Before she could point out their similar tastes in desks, he said, "Please, have a seat. Now, how may I be of assistance?"

Rainee told her story of receiving the passport at the Holocaust Museum. "I feel like Jana has become my muse. I've previously written a novel, and I'm under the gun to write another. I hope to write about Jana."

John had been listening intently. "Allen! Oh, brilliant! Yes, of course. Rainee Allen. I read your book. It was marvelous. They made it into a film, didn't they? However, I must admit I didn't see the movie. Terribly sorry. You see, I don't go in for that sort of thing."

"That's quite all right." Laughing, she added, "I'm sure many people didn't see the movie."

"Actually, what I meant to say is that movies don't usually do a book justice, so I rarely see a movie after reading the book. Oh, I'm meeting a famous author. What a delightful surprise."

Rainee thanked him. "I'm glad you enjoyed my story. You see, I'm here to—"

"You know, I think it could be in my bookcase. Would you mind autographing it for me?" He jumped up to look through his shelves, which were bulging with books. John shuffled through his books, knocking some down and making futile attempts to catch them.

His clumsy response touched Rainee, and she smiled.

"Forgive me. It must be at home with my collection of fiction. These are mostly clinical. I'll make sure to bring it. That is if you'll be returning."

Rainee smiled. "I'd be honored to autograph it for you, Mr. Pritchard."

"Please, call me John."

"Thank you, John. Call me Rainee. Now, about Jana... or Janet—"

"Yes, of course, Mrs. Bowman. Normally we don't allow visitors that aren't on a patient's roster. However, she has no family, so there is no one listed. Frankly, I believe she could use a visitor and— Oh! Will this lead to another movie?"

"Um... I'm not sure where this will lead. Would you like to see her Holocaust Museum ID card?" Rainee reached into her purse, and as she anticipated, he nodded.

He looked at the cover. "It seems we have a renowned resident in our home."

"Please, take your time. I think you'll find it a captivating read."

Instead of staring at him while he read, she stood to look at his pictures and certificates, which covered the walls. *What's an Oxford law school graduate doing in social services?*

After a few minutes, he handed it back to Rainee. "Interesting. Very thought provoking indeed. I can understand why you would want to interview her. You say you share a birthday. You look good for someone in her seventies." He laughed at his own joke.

"Very funny. There is a thirty-year difference, thank you very much." She liked his humor.

John's expressive face turned serious. "You may have wondered why there is so much security here. Why a residential building would have several locks on their doors."

Rainee nodded.

"The fact is that most of our residents have dementia. Forty-five percent have advanced dementia, which is probably Alzheimer's disease. Because they're prone to wander away, we keep them locked in for their own good." He paused. "And... I'm sorry to have to tell you this... Mrs. Bowman has early onset dementia, likely Alzheimer's."

Stunned, Rainee was unable to speak. It felt as if something had knocked the wind out of her.

"We're still learning about this disease. She has good days. Patients with Alzheimer's do. I don't know how much you know about this bloody awful disease, but—"

"Not much."

John continued. "The Alzheimer's Association estimates that forty-seven percent of people who reach age eighty-five have the disease. About nineteen percent between seventy-five and eighty-four and three percent for those ages sixty-five to seventy-four. Mrs. Bowman's came early."

Seeing that Rainee was still stunned, John said, "Sorry... I'm droning on like a medical brochure. It's terribly unfortunate that I have this conversation with so many families."

Rainee shook her head in disbelief. "Please continue. Tell me more about Alzheimer's."

"Well, here's an example of what happens in their brain. They can remember things from their distant past, but not what they ate for breakfast. They live in the past, and the past becomes their present reality. Patients can have long instances of being lucid. Sadly, for most of them, their memories are being erased… slowly. Spouses come to visit and are not recognized on one day. On a different day, they are greeted with loving arms. You can't predict what the day will bring." He paused. "You know, I believe it's hardest on the family. They spend a lifetime creating memories together only to have those memories expunged by their loved one."

Rainee gasped at the impact of what that might mean for Jana. "You say that their past is their present? Do you mean to say that she's reliving the Holocaust? That she survived the horrors of those years… created a somewhat normal life… just to relive it all over again?"

"Well, we haven't seen any signs of Mrs. Bowman reliving the Holocaust. We can only hope she doesn't remember it. To my knowledge, she hasn't even mentioned it."

"May I meet her?"

He looked at his watch. "I'm sure she has returned to her room for an afternoon nap. Patients like regimens. Come back tomorrow around ten o'clock. She'll probably be in the great room watching the telly. That's a good time to meet her. Just... well, try not to expect too much."

This new and surprising information saddened Rainee. "Okay, I'll be here. Thank you for that information. Since you're located so close to the library, I think I'll head over there and read up on Alzheimer's."

John smiled. "Are you all right? Can I offer you some water? You look a little pale." He sounded sincere.

Rainee stood to leave. "No, no. I'm okay. I don't know what I was expecting. I appreciate your concern, though."

"I know this is a lot to take in." John walked her to the exit. "I look forward to seeing you tomorrow. Oh, and I shall bring in your novel for that autograph."

She managed a weak smile.

JANA — BERKHAMSTED, ENGLAND 1941

The reason Wickhill Farms was not named Wickham Farms was that the acreage the family owned had rolling, green hills as far as you could see. It was lovely. Jersey cows and English Oak dotted the landscape.

Though it was a dairy farm, it also had fruit trees, and lots and lots of pigs. Dirty animals, pigs. One of my chores before heading off to school and on the weekends was to get up with the sunrise and feed them.

The Wickhams hadn't known that I was not supposed to eat pig meat. They were not familiar with Jewish laws. Though they never spoke about it in front of me, I suspect I was the first Jew they had ever met. Like most English folk, they were Protestant. I think they were the first Protestants I had ever met.

We went to church every Sunday morning. Mr. Harvey would take a long bath and scrub the pig smell off—well, as best he could—and try to cover the smell with fragrant waters. Auntie and I would dress ourselves in our best outfits. I didn't mind going to church. I liked the singing. It seemed to take my mind off missing Papa and Max, at least for a short while.

Most of our meals had bacon or some sausage mixed in. Never having tasted it before, I didn't even know I was eating pig. It was when my English started to improve that I began to understand I was breaking my ancestral laws. However, I remembered Frau

Weissmuller-Meijer warning us to fit in and that God would not want us to starve. After a day of school and working the farm, I was so famished that I would eat anything placed in front of me.

Mr. Harvey would eat his breakfast silently, and then go to the barn to begin his chores. There were many mornings I didn't even see him before I set off for school.

Auntie was a good cook. She was a hard worker, too. She would be up at dawn, feeding the chickens, making breakfast for Mr. Harvey and me, and putting it in the oven to keep it warm while I dressed. Her hands were always busy with her cooking, sewing, or cleaning. In time, she taught me to do all those things too. Somehow, Auntie always managed to keep the house very clean. I was awed at how it was possible to do that, living on a muddy pig farm.

On Saturdays, when I was home from school, I witnessed their daily routine. On a farm, the weekend does not interrupt routine. There was no rest. "A farmer must farm his farm." That was Mr. Harvey's favorite saying. Every afternoon, he would come in to a hearty lunch waiting for him. We would sit down and eat together, in silence. He wasn't a big talker. Then, back to work until dinner.

During the week, I would come home from school, and a snack was always waiting for me. Auntie insisted I did my homework straightaway. When I needed help, I'd ask her. We would sit at the dining room table—my makeshift desk—and work. Gosh, did I need help, especially in the beginning.

My English was slow in coming. I tried very hard and eventually, with her help, I did learn. My accent was impossible to lose, however. Some children made fun of me because of my accent. I tried not to let it bother me. Still, it did hurt. A couple of students would do the Nazi salute when I passed. I suppose it was because I am German. Auntie said, "Never mind those mean kids. They're just trash." It hurt, anyway.

Months went by and Max did not come for me. I sat by my window at night, looking at the night sky, wondering if he was looking at the same stars. Or was he up there amongst them? I was afraid that the reason he didn't come for me was that he might not be alive. What other reason could there be? Yet I felt that I would have somehow known in my heart if he were dead. Like when Mama died, my heart ached so, just as if a part of me died with her.

Max promised me, and he promised Papa he would take care of me. He would not break that promise. I refused to believe he could be dead. Instead, I convinced myself that his boat had taken him to another country by mistake. Mr. Harvey said that mine was a child's dream. Sometimes, I wondered if I would be able to recognize Max's face as a grown man.

The faces of my family—Mama, Papa, Max, Aunt Gertie, my cousins—were beginning to fade like the tide ebbing from the shore, leaving only disappearing footprints of my history. Each day, each face, and memories of my past life were evaporating slowly. I heard my father's voice saying, *Always remember who you are*. But who was I?

One day I cried in Auntie's arms. "I'm beginning to forget. How do I stop this from happening?"

"You can't stop it, Janet dear. This is life. Always know that you carry the spirit of your family in your heart. You will always be Jana Lutken."

She lifted my chin, smiling with tears in her kind eyes. "I do feel, dear, that you have become like a daughter to me. The daughter I never had. You have brought sunshine to this dreary old pig farm. Imagine. Sunshine in England—a rarity to be sure. And that is what you are—a rarity."

She held me tight as I continued sobbing. "Janet, you know that since you will not take Jesus into your life, we cannot adopt you. It would be an honor to me if you considered me like your second mother. I know I'm not her and can never take her place. Knowing the girl you are now, I have no doubt that she was a wonderful mother. And I'll understand if you cannot ever come to call me mother."

I did not want to hurt her feelings. She had been so kind to take me in. Of course, over time my feelings for her did grow.

Even during this war they were calling a Holocaust, there was goodness and compassion, and there was kindness and love. I knew how fortunate I was to find it at Wickhill Farms.

RAINEE — LONDON, ENGLAND 1997

Gary Edwards had given Rainee a letter of introduction so she could access the archives in the British Library. After going through the process of registering for a library card, she entered the inner sanctum. The room was enormous with tables arranged in rows with military-precision, and computers atop most of them. Shelves and shelves of reference books lined the periphery of the room. Sitting in front of computers were people engrossed in their study and writing notes on legal pads.

Rainee spoke with a librarian, who directed her to a computer and showed her how to access information using the library's search engine.

She began by typing in Jana's name and hometown. All that came up was the same information written on her Holocaust Museum card.

Frustrated, she approached the librarian, who suggested, "Since Jana was not a notable person, the only way to locate information on her history may be in the official British Archives. However, they moved the Archives outside the city. Perhaps, if you knew where she had lived, that town's library would have information."

Rainee thanked him and didn't bother to mention that she had already researched there.

The ID card named "Mama Wysmueller" as the Dutch woman who arranged for the train that took Jana from Amsterdam to England. Rainee typed in the name but came up with nothing.

She typed in the word "Kindertransport," and a plethora of information filled the monitor. In her reading she came across the name Geertruida Wijsmuller-Meijer, a woman recognized by Yad Vashem and named one of the Righteous Among the Nations—people who had risked their lives to save Jews. This Christian banker's wife helped arrange the *Kindertransports* that saved ten thousand orphans. She had to be the Mama Wysmueller that Jana referred to in her ID card. Now, she was a notable person.

Rainee scribbled extensive notes about Jana's rescuer.

Next, she went to the bookshelves to look up Alzheimer's disease. Although there was lots of information, she found nothing on Holocaust survivors with Alzheimer's.

Discouraged but better informed, Rainee left the library and walked wearily to Euston Station.

The day had been informative and eventful. She was ready for a relaxing bath and would meet Shelley for dinner. At her friend's suggestion, they'd stocked the refrigerator with dinners that had gone untouched. Since Shelley's business was picking up the tab, Rainee sensed they would be eating out a lot.

Rainee arrived at the nursing home the following day promptly at ten o'clock. John entered the reception hall and greeted her with his sincere smile and warm handshake. "It's a pleasure seeing you again, Rainee."

She smiled as well. "The pleasure's mine."

"Mrs. Bowman is in the sitting room, watching television. Routine, even something as mundane as watching the telly, is important for those with various forms of dementia."

"Yes, I remember what you told me." After learning so much about the woman she would soon meet, Rainee's pulse quickened. Would her visit lead to something more—or to absolutely nothing at all? There were times she had almost forgotten her primary goal, which was to find material for her next book.

"I suggest that when you first go in, just sit quietly with the others and observe a bit before you attempt to interact with her." John sighed. "She is one of our more withdrawn residents. Lately, she has been vacillating back and forth in the awareness of her surroundings."

He led her into a room where sunlight broke through the grated windows, creating a lattice pattern on the worn rug. The television blared while several residents sat in a semi-circle, their expressions uniformly blank as they faced the small screen. Placed about the room were chairs and tables. One card table positioned under the window had a jigsaw puzzle half-finished. Beneath the scent of some disinfectant, there lingered the faint acrid smell of urine, bringing Rainee grim reminders of her grandmother's last days in a hospital room.

"Mrs. Bowman is the lady sitting alone, at the edge of the group." He whispered, indicating a gray-haired woman slumped in a wheelchair. "I'll be back in a bit."

Some looked up and stared at Rainee when she entered. Apparently satisfied that she was not there to visit with any of them, they turned back as a group to face the television. Jana did not glance in her direction at all.

Rainee sat down at one of the tables, notepad at the ready, and studied this person she felt she already knew. Janet Bowman, née Jana Lutken, was in her late seventies but appeared much older. Her mouth seemed fixed in a permanent scowl, the face deeply wrinkled. Riding low on her nose, thick-lensed tortoise shell glasses dominated her face. She slumped in the wheelchair, as though she had shrunk into a withered husk. Life, age, and her mental deterioration—whatever the diagnosis—had not been kind to her.

With the exception of the nonstop noise from the television, the room was silent. No one spoke to one another, nor did they laugh. Rainee considered this strange since they were watching an old black-and-white movie—a Danny Kaye comedy from the '50s. Studying the room, she noticed a chalkboard announcing the weekly schedule of events. Today, at two o'clock, a piano player would come to entertain. Tomorrow promised an ice cream social. *What would constitute "sociability" for this group*?

By ten thirty, small groups of visitors began to arrive. Slowly, the residents and their family members departed. Jana, alone in her wheelchair, was the only one left watching the movie. Rainee noticed that Jana showed no interest as the visitors arrived.

She recalled what John had said yesterday; *She never has visitors*.

Rainee moved from the card table to a chair closer to Jana. She smiled at the older woman. "Hello. Do you mind if I sit here?"

Since Jana said nothing, Rainee sat beside her and continued to watch the movie. Rainee could not resist the urge to laugh at the predictable lines and familiar clownish acting of the 1950s. She noticed that as she laughed, Jana's deep scowl would flicker into a hint of a smile. Once, she emitted a small sad ghost of a chuckle.

Rainee reached into her tote bag and produced the box of chocolates that she had purchased. John had reassured her that Jana suffered from no health issues that would make her gift inappropriate. She unwrapped the box and extended her hand toward the other woman. "Do you like chocolate?"

Jana turned slowly toward Rainee. "Chocolate? I like chocolate." Expressionless, she peered down into the opened box, back up at Rainee, and then down once more at the box. She hesitated, then reached over and selected one piece. "Thank you, miss."

"You're very welcome."

Would she be able to start a conversation with this woman, she wondered. Together they finished watching the movie while Rainee occasionally laughed at the actor's antics. She watched for Jana's response, but her interest seemed more and more focused on the box of candy.

Rainee lifted the gold foil wrapped box and offered the chocolates to her. "Please. Have another piece."

Jana selected one glossy-mounded chocolate cream, popped it into her mouth, chewed once, and swallowed. She reached out again, this time gathering up several pieces that she slipped into a pocket.

Rainee glanced away, allowing her opportunity to hide the candy. In her research, she had read that people with Alzheimer's would often hoard food. She turned back to Jana. "My name is Rainee Allen. It's nice to meet a fellow chocolate lover."

Jana bowed her head, then retreated into silence. Finally, surprising Rainee, she said, "I am Janet Bowman."

"It's lovely to meet you, Mrs. Bowman. I love Danny Kaye. He was so funny. His movies always make me laugh. Have you seen his other movies?"

"Whose movies?" Jana asked anxiously, the frown lines deepening.

"Danny Kaye's."

"Who is he?" Bewilderment flickered in her eyes.

"He's the funny actor we just watched in the movie." She gestured toward the television.

"Oh... yes...."

Rainee sighed, saddened by another aspect of Jana's mental deterioration. She had already forgotten the movie and probably the stranger sitting beside her.

John entered the room. "Ah, Mrs. Bowman, I see you've met Ms. Allen." He tapped the gold-colored box of chocolates. "It seems you two have something in common—a sweet tooth. Hmm... and right before lunch too." He grinned and wagged a finger at them as though they were two naughty schoolgirls.

"My fault entirely," Rainee said. "I'm sorry if I've upset your routine. But as far as we're concerned, there's always room for chocolate. Right, Mrs. Bowman?"

"Chocolate? What chocolate?" Jana said, then suddenly burst into high-pitched laughter, startling Rainee. Understanding it was simply a joke, Rainee joined her laughter.

Rainee was delighted and surprised, because she had seen Jana's face light up, and at that moment, she had glimpsed a hint of a younger woman. Laughter was a sign there was someone inside. Always a believer in the power of positive thinking, she was confident she could reach her.

"Many of our residents are already in the dining room. Mrs. Bowman, may I take you there now?" Then John asked as an afterthought, "Do you mind if Ms. Allen accompanies us?"

"As long as she brings the chocolate," she said.

"What chocolate?" Rainee joked, and John and Jana laughed with her. She wedged the box into the side pocket that hung from the wheelchair. "Actually, I believe these belong to Mrs. Bowman."

Jana's eyes twinkled again for a moment and beamed her thanks.

They walked down a long corridor, its walls decorated with letters from primary school children who had visited the nursing home. Rainee paused to read one or two written in the carefully cramped printing of the five or six year olds, amused at their simple, kind messages.

The clean and tidy dining room had tables covered with white linen and centerpieces of vases with fresh flowers. In contrast with the sitting room, the aroma of roasting chicken filled the air. It was obvious to Rainee that the staff had worked to create a warm, comfortable environment.

Setting the brakes carefully, John placed Jana's wheelchair at a table where a man and another woman already were awaiting their midday meal. Then he introduced Rainee to the others. "Mrs. Cartwright, Mr. Saunders, this is Rainee Allen."

She smiled at them although neither glanced in her direction. "This has been fun for me, Mrs. Bowman. May I come back and visit you again?" She reached for Jana's hand.

Jana started to jerk her hand away and then nodded. "Yes. I'd like that." She motioned for Rainee to lean closer. "I like almonds too," she whispered.

Covering Jana's hand with her own, Rainee grinned and nodded. She felt better already. Perhaps she had reached through to her.

As they left the lunchroom, John nodded his approval. "Good show. You've done well. She normally doesn't say much to anyone." He walked with her to the exit.

"May I come back the same time tomorrow?" Rainee asked.

"Certainly," he said. "Sorry I was so busy this morning. Tomorrow we should have time for a chat."

JANA — WICKHILL FARMS 1942

As I began my journey into womanhood, Auntie taught me what I needed to know about feminine hygiene. My body was changing, changes that I could feel and notice. Changes others must have recognized too.

When my monthlies started, Auntie showed me how to secure fabric to absorb the bleeding. We sat down together, and she was very patient and kind as she talked with me. She explained to me how babies were made and how they emerged from a woman's body.

"It will hurt a lot," she said, "but having a child is well worth it and something very important that women must do." Her eyes welled with tears. She must have been sad about not having had her own baby. I listened to her words, half in disgust and half in disbelief. She explained what I needed to know about becoming a woman. My breasts were forming where there had once been little bumps. There was no putting that off. I was grateful for her patience.

One day, on a trip into town, she bought me my first brassiere. She had used four of her precious rations stamps for me. "Don't let Mr. Harvey know," she reminded me as we left the store.

Growing up was not easy. Other girls whispered and giggled about boys, but no boys showed any interest in me. Maybe it was because I was Jewish. I pretended not to care, but I did.

On the rare occasion, a boy would stare as I walked past him. That's when I started to take an interest in my own looks. My hair was full, shiny, and naturally curly; I never needed to get a home perm like so many of the other girls. My eyelashes were long and dark. I thought I must have been turning rather pretty.

A small, precious collection of makeup now sat atop my bureau. Although Auntie did not wear makeup, she knew some tricks, which included using burnt cork for mascara and beetroot juice for lipstick. Auntie even purchased a larger mirror for me, since we could not yet afford a full-length one. How I longed to see how my body was changing. Was it nice? Did I have a good figure? Each night I brushed my hair one hundred strokes, because the magazines wrote that this was what the movie stars did.

I noticed hair appearing in private places that had once been smooth and soft bare skin. Embarrassed yet needing to know, I asked, "Auntie, is this normal?"

She just patted my arm and nodded.

Much to the displeasure of Mr. Harvey—a man I never could bring myself to call Uncle—I spent too much time in the bath, scrubbing away the pungent smells of the farm. For my fifteenth birthday, Auntie bought me scented water, so I would smell nice. She enjoyed sewing dresses for me. She was fond of reminding me that "I was the daughter she never had."

Mr. Harvey must not have liked what he saw. At meals, he would leave as soon as he finished, as if he were uncomfortable in just being around me. When he could not avoid being alone with me, he refused to meet my eyes and always looked away. His reaction to me was truly confusing and, to some extent, upsetting. He spoke to me less and barked orders more.

At the start of winter, the ground froze. That year the farm needed more attention than usual and there was constant work to do. I helped round up the pigs as soon as the sun began to set. We had to cover the chicken coop every night to keep the fowl from freezing to death.

That year Auntie's youngest sister became ill and sent for her. They called it pleurisy, which Auntie said could become pneumonia or tuberculosis. She hurried so she could be by her sister's side. We did not know how long she would be gone. She placed me in charge of the household duties on the farm. My main job was to keep Mr. Harvey fed.

Each morning, I awoke even earlier than usual and prepared his breakfast and lunch. Then I would leave for school. After school, I would cook our evening meal. It was the supper meals when we would eat together, as we had when Auntie was there. He never talked with me as Auntie would. He didn't ask what had happened in school that day or how my studies were going. Except for his occasional grunts, we ate in silence.

Weeks passed and Auntie wrote, *My sister has taken a turn for the worse. I need to stay longer as she needs me more than ever.*

I could tell that her absence agitated Mr. Harvey. Eventually, his agitation changed to anger.

"When will she be back?" he constantly griped. "How much longer do I have to put up with this? Things will bloody well fall apart here!" He paced and grumbled in his bedroom each night. Once it sounded like he even threw a chair across the room.

RAINEE — LONDON 1997

The day after meeting Jana, a cold, dreary rain showered London. Emerging from Euston Station into this characteristic weather, Rainee watched pedestrians snapping open their umbrellas. London's rain brought the kind of cold that reached deep into her bones. As much as she had always loved this country and had enjoyed the year she spent as an exchange student, she had never loved its weather.

She shrugged as raindrops rolled off her shoulders, refusing to let the chilly rain bother her. Securely wrapped against the damp and tucked in her tote bag was a half-pound of chocolate-covered almonds. She turned the corner to Chalton Street, quickening her step as she neared the nursing home.

When she entered the sitting room, she was dismayed to find no one there. The notice on the chalkboard stated that today was Game Day in Xavier Hall, and the receptionist directed her to another part of the building. From down the corridor she heard voices rising in excitement. Double doors to the hall stood open, and Rainee leaned against the wall to observe.

The nursing home occupants were sitting at round tables playing Bingo. She noted that John was in charge of today's game. "B-3!" he called out. There was some protests of disappointment. Then he called, "I-19."

"Bingo!" a voice shouted from the back of the room, followed by a collective groan from the other players.

John clapped his hands, encouraging the others to applaud. "Mrs. Wacker! A winner! You've won a £10 gift certificate to Foyles Books, donated by the Kelly family. Congratulations!"

He gestured to Rainee standing by the door. "I see we have another Bingo player. Are there any objections to letting a visiting writer from across the pond join us and play?" As usual, no one spoke up. He indicated the table where Jana was sitting.

"Thank you. I'm honored," Rainee said, addressing the room at large. She sat down. "Good morning, Mrs. Bowman."

Jana stared at her quizzically.

"We met yesterday."

"We did?" Jana looked puzzled.

She doesn't remember me. "Indeed, we did," she said as one of the aides handed her a Bingo card and chips.

The game continued. Instead of playing, Rainee watched Jana. As John called out numbers, she would place the chips on her card, regardless of accuracy. Was she simply apathetic or had she actually forgotten her numbers? Her card was nearly full, yet she played on, oblivious to the rules of the game.

Again, someone shouted "Bingo!" Rainee sighed with relief. Game Day ended. The players wandered out of the room, and an aide wheeled Jana to the sitting room to watch television.

At John's invitation, Rainee followed him to his office. "She didn't play very enthusiastically," she said, then chuckled. "Does she even know the rules?"

John shook his head. "I'm not surprised. I've noticed that she doesn't take much pleasure in any of our activities. I don't know. Perhaps that's typical behavior of a Holocaust survivor."

"Yet according to what I know of her story, she lived with an English family on a farm," Rainee said. "Her lot was much better than that of many. She lived freely and not in a concentration camp or in hiding."

"That's true. Here's what I believe is the difference: survival meant hiding in a way. Not standing out. Being wary of strangers." John leaned back in his chair, steepling his fingers in thought. "She was cast out of her own country and probably felt like an outcast in her new one. Janet might have been the only Jew in an English Protestant village. Even here, she's our only Jewish resident, so we try to level the field for her."

"Level the field?"

"Well, like Christmas time, for example. We put up a tree and decorate. We also take out a menorah for her and light the candles. However, she really doesn't show any interest."

"She was very young when she came to England. A decorated tree probably makes as much sense to her as anything else," Rainee said.

John leaned forward and pulled a manila folder from his desk file drawer.

Rainee had caught a glimpse of his neatly ordered and meticulously organized hanging folders. He would not have a bottom toss-away drawer like hers. Order reigned everywhere in his office. His shelves were labeled, files were color-coded, and even his books were shelved alphabetically by author. The pinned notes on a cork bulletin board were evenly spaced. She wondered what he would make of her messy office and what it revealed about her character.

"I've been reviewing Mrs. Bowman's file. Nothing extraordinary, actually." He flipped through the first few pages.

"She did have a brother. Max, an older brother, I believe. Their parents sent them to an orphanage. But, you knew that already."

He turned another page, one finger marking his place. "They were separated on their voyage to England. Girls left on a different ship. The boys were to follow. That was not the original plan. A benefactress, Geertruida Wijsmuller-Meijer, had arranged for the families to stay together on their journey to England. A Nazi commandant ordered a change in plans at the last minute."

Rainee gasped. She had an awful premonition of what would follow.

"There was little that could be done. The commandant promised Mrs. Wijsmuller-Meijer that the families would reunite in England. The first ship with Janet aboard arrived uneventfully and docked at Harwich, England. A Nazi submarine torpedoed the ship with the boys. All passengers and crew perished."

Horrified, she said, "Sounds like a mission to me. I wonder why the Germans would blow up a ship full of children."

"Probably it was not the children they wanted to destroy, but the cargo. It doesn't report what cargo they were shipping. Arms. Oil. Could've been anything." John continued to read from the chart. "Whilst living on Wickhill Farms, Janet Bowman waited for her brother to come take—"

"Jana," Rainee said, correcting him for the first time.

"Excuse me?"

"Her name was originally 'J-a-n-a,' pronounced with a *Y*." Rainee took a pencil and paper, then wrote it. "The Wickhams changed it to Janet to help her fit in."

"That makes sense. These papers list her middle name with the letter *L. Must be for Lutken.*" He indicated the name on the form.

"What a sad story." Rainee edged closer.

"She left the farm after she graduated secondary school and moved to London. Apparently, she was a very good seamstress and managed to earn a living sewing. She married David Bowman, who was several years older."

He returned to the file. "She waited for Max, apparently convinced he would come for her. When she was in her thirties, she finally learned about the torpedoed ship and fell into a deep depression. Janet—sorry, Jana—spent three months in a sanitarium. Her husband visited her daily." John flipped over another page. "On her medical form it was determined that she could not have children 'due to trauma.' It doesn't say what kind of trauma. They never adopted. And... well, you know the rest." He closed the file.

"Who filled out that report? It seems quite detailed."

"It was before I became director. Let me see. The signature is almost illegible. I can barely make out the last name. Yes, yes, Bowman, to be sure. Her husband had already died, so I assume it was a member of his family." He squinted at the signature. "Samuel... maybe."

"The poor, poor woman." Rainee felt tears burn and blinked them away.

John smiled at her. He took out a box of tissues from his desk drawer. "She's gotten under your skin, I see."

She nodded slightly. "When did her dementia begin?"

"As best as we can tell about two years ago. The Health System's forms are only as good as who's filling them out. I suppose it isn't like that in the States." He winked at Rainee conspiratorially.

She shrugged and smiled.

"Mrs. Bowman has some very lucid moments and at other times, her memories are cloudy. Much like today's weather, actually. If it's Alzheimer's, it is progressive. No one can predict when it will overtake her."

Rainee shook her head. "That's so very sad."

John slipped the file back into the desk. He smiled. "I hope that was helpful."

"Well, it explains an awful lot," Rainee said without cheer.

"Say, if you aren't busy tonight, I'd love to take you to dinner. Perhaps we can talk more about Mrs. Bowman."

Rainee hesitated for only a second. "I would like that very much. Here's my address." From her purse, she pulled out a business card and wrote on the back.

There was an awkward silence as he escorted her to the front door, then stood there waiting as she descended the long stone steps.

"Shall I pick you up at seven?"

Rainee looked back, nodded, and waved goodbye. She noticed John was still smiling.

JANA — BERKHAMSTED, ENGLAND 1942

That winter, while Auntie was still with her sister, dreadful snowstorms blanketed Wickhill Farms. I had never seen snow piled so high. Winds howled outside, and Mr. Harvey had much work to do to protect the farm and to make sure that the pigs and fowl survived.

It was New Year's Eve and the world was ushering in a blustering 1942. That night Mr. Wickham was out in that cold for over two hours. As I sat at the kitchen table, finishing my homework, the door burst open with a blast of icy wind.

The wind propelled him into the kitchen like a billowing sail. He was covered in white with snow. Ice had formed on his mustache, and his entire body was shaking from the cold.

Feeling sorry for him, I said, "Go sit by the fireplace."

He swung around and raged at me. "Blasted storm! Half of me pigs is dying! The hens won't be laying no eggs anytime soon, I guarantee that! That's *if* they survive!" He hurried over to the fireplace and removed his coat. His hat, scarf, and gloves were sopping wet.

"You're soaked right through!" I exclaimed, but he seemed not to notice. "Should I bring you some dry clothes?"

He nodded, though I wasn't sure he had heard me. Uncertain, I ran upstairs to his room and brought down a choice of clothes. I wasn't positive that I had brought the right things, but I placed a shirt and sweater on the rocking chair. For once, he did not object. I left the room, allowing him a few minutes to change. When I stepped back into the living room, I saw that he had stripped down to his faded red flannel long johns and was shivering by the fireplace.

I averted my eyes. "I'll go reheat the stew. It'll warm you."

He was finishing off the small bottle of whiskey he had taken with him outside earlier, gulping it as if it were water. He opened a second bottle and began drinking that. He glared menacingly at me.

What had I done this time? I hadn't brought the weather. I wasn't responsible for his pigs.

"What's the matter, gal?" he snarled, his body rocked unsteadily. "Never seen no man in his underwear? Rather see me naked?" He grabbed at his crotch and stared at me, his eyes blazing with anger and alcohol.

I had never seen this side of Mr. Harvey before. I was frightened. I panicked at his sudden onset of drunken rage. Most of all, the look in his eyes terrified me. I turned and ran to the toilet. Would I be safe in there? There were no locks on any doors in the house. I grabbed hold of the doorknob and placed my feet on either side of the doorjamb, bracing to protect myself.

Through the door, I could still hear him as he called out for his wife.

"Gloria! Gloria! Goddamn this bloody weather!" he bellowed. "Goddamn those bloody awful stinking pigs! Damn this fuckin' farm and damn that little Jewish bitch too!"

I shuddered, but he didn't come after me. After a while, my arms grew weary from holding the doorknob. When it grew silent in the other room, I opened the door slowly, hoping it would not squeak. I peeked out around the corner into the living room. Mr. Harvey was half-sprawled across the rocking chair, the whiskey bottle dangling from his hand. Had he passed out?

Cautiously, I took a blanket from the sofa and crossed the room to cover him. Ever so gently, I placed it over him. I was leaving him to sleep it off, when he shot his arm out, grabbing me.

He held my arm tightly, pulling me close. I gagged. He stank of whiskey and pigs. He pulled himself up, rocking back and forth. He almost lost his balance, then caught himself, never letting go of my arm. "Blimey, gal. You tryin' to warm me all over, ain't ya? I'll bet y'are. I seen you, puttin' on makeup and smilin' at the boys. You're no better than a whore. You women are all alike. All of you, all whores."

He pulled me closer, forcing me to endure his smell. The look in his eyes reminded me of the Nazi on the pier who shot the boys. Black, angry, hateful eyes. In my fright, I began to shake and could not stop.

He locked one of his big arms around me and started tearing my clothes off with the other. I fought against him. He was much stronger than me, his muscles strengthened by years of farm work. I squirmed, trying to get out of his arms, just as I saw pigs squirming before Mr. Harvey slaughtered them.

I wanted to run, but to where? Where could I go?

RAINEE — LONDON 1997

This was the fifth day in a row she had come to the nursing home, with the hope of somehow reaching through to Jana Lutken.

For three days, she had carried the same bag of chocolate-covered almonds in her tote bag. Maybe today she would have a chance to talk with Jana. Maybe today she would see one of those lucid moments that John had described.

When she reached the sitting room, Rainee found her seated near the sofa and for once not in front of the television. Perhaps that indicated a good start. "Mrs. Bowman, would you mind if I sat with you?"

Jana looked up at her, smiling warmly in recognition. "Chocolates?"

Rainee laughed. "Even better. Chocolate-covered almonds!" She whispered, "Our secret."

Jana clapped her hands like a child, and Rainee slipped the bag into the side pocket on the wheelchair.

"Mrs. Bowman, I've found out that we share something in common... besides the chocolate, of course."

"Oh? What's that?"

"We share a birthday. February 9th. However, I was born thirty years after you."

"Aquarius!"

Rainee smiled. "Yes, that's right." Pausing for a moment, she was uncertain how to continue. "Mrs. Bowman, do you remember being my age? I turned forty this year."

"Certainly. When I was forty, I was married to my David, the most wonderful man in the world." Jana paused for a moment, lost in memories from long ago. Timidly, she asked, "Would you like me to tell you about him?"

"Oh, yes. I would love it."

"It's been such a long time since I've talked to anyone about my life. I don't have visitors... you see, I have no family." She massaged her neck. "Most young people aren't interested. Why would you even want to know?"

"Well, you see, I'm interested in people. I think everyone has a story to tell. Everyone." Rainee faced Jana directly, curious about her seemingly unconscious neck massage. The gesture was as if she was twirling a necklace, a necklace that wasn't there. "For example, you lived through a very bleak era in history and survived. What could be more interesting?"

"I did?" A quizzical expression replaced Jana's lively interest of a moment ago.

Was she rushing in too quickly? Perhaps it would have been better to ease into this woman's history. Rainee's Holocaust research cautioned that many survivors never spoke about their experiences.

"I apologize, Mrs. Bowman."

"John said you were a writer." Her eyes twinkled again. She was with Rainee in the present and purposely changing the subject.

"Well, yes. I am a writer."

"A successful one?"

"A lucky one." They both laughed. "My novel was made into a movie. Perhaps I could rent a copy at the video store. We could watch it together."

"I would like that very much, my dear. Was it Reenie? Renée?"

"You have a good memory, Mrs. Bowman. It's Rainee."

"Like today? Rainy outside?"

"Yes!" She was delighted that Jana's memory was so acute today that she had almost remembered her unusual name. "It's spelled a little differently. However, it is pronounced that way."

After lunch, they sat side by side on the sofa, chatting about the weather, television shows, and current events. The rain had subsided. It remained cold and cloudy outside, casting weak shadows into the room. An aide hurried from room to room, putting on the lights, which did little to alleviate the gloom of the afternoon chill. One by one, the other residents' heads drooped as they fell asleep, slumping into their chairs.

She watched Jana's eyes begin to close too. "May I come back tomorrow?" she asked her softly. She hoped that tomorrow would bring improved memory. Rainee questioned herself if was cruel of her to ask someone to relive the sadness and fear of that awful period of history.

Jana nodded as her eyes were closing and her head melted onto her chest.

"This room is chilly, Mrs. Bowman." Rainee shivered, looking back at the sitting room's fireplace where the last few logs had burned down to embers. There was a basket of firewood, and she reached inside the screen to add more wood. "This may help."

Jana awakened for a moment, her eyes half-open, watching Rainee as she went about rebuilding the fire.

"I'm sure this will warm things up a bit." Rainee took one of the long iron tongs that rested beside the hearth and reached in to stir the embers. The tinder caught, flaring quickly, and then one of the logs started to burn. "Won't that be better, Mrs. Bow—?"

Jana's scream blocked out anything Rainee was going to say. Her scream went on and on, higher and higher, as if she had not even stopped to draw a breath. Her body stiffened, and she grasped the arms of the wheelchair.

John rushed into the room followed by one of the aides. "Mrs. Bowman? What is it? What happened?"

"I-I was just starting to rebuild the fire," Rainee said. "Then she began screaming."

JANA — 1942

I had broken free of his grasp and thought I was safe. Defending myself, I grabbed the fire poker and pointed it at him, quivering. He seemed startled at first. He stopped reaching for me and then howled with laughter, nearly choking. He took another swig of whiskey, emptied the bottle, and hurled it against the fireplace. I watched the bottle as it sailed through the air, then shattered into a million pieces. Protecting my face from the glass, I did not see him lunge at me. In one quick movement, he easily knocked the poker from my hand, grabbed me and held tight.

He fumbled at his crotch, then changed his mind. He bellowed, "I'll show you what you can do with a real poker, Jewish whore!"

I kept struggling as he forced me down onto the rug—he was much too strong. He pulled and tugged at my underwear until my panties ripped. Forcing my legs apart with his knees, he rammed the iron poker up inside me. He pushed and gouged the poker so deep inside me that I thought he had reached my heart. Pain seared through me, and I screamed.

He leaned over me laughing. His drool dripped onto my chin. "You'll never be able to bring another Jew into this world!"

I was sure he was killing me. A wave of nausea swept through my body. I wanted to vomit. With my last strength, I reached for the wooden footstool and slammed it into his head. He grunted from the pain, almost as if in surprise, and half-rolled off me. I thought I had killed him, but his stomach heaved up and down with each breath. He was alive, though I wished him dead. I considered taking the poker, still dripping with my blood, and stabbing him where he lay. But I could not be as evil as he had been.

The pain! Oh, the pain! It was more horrible than anything I could have ever imagined. Surely more horrible than what Auntie said childbirth would be like. It was a dreadful agony of cramping and burning as blood gushed out of me. I knew I had to stop the bleeding or I would bleed to death. I think I passed out for a few minutes. I tried to stand up but Mr. Harvey was still unconscious, sprawled over me. The stink of whiskey hung over him like England's fog.

I heaved him off me. Trembling, I struggled to stand up. Bent and doubled over with the pain, I tried to clean myself, replacing rag after rag as blood soaked through. Panicked, I didn't know if I was doing things right. Auntie would have known of course. I woefully realized that I could never tell her. How could I hurt the woman who loved me so much? Would she even believe her husband was capable of so heinous an act?

I nearly collapsed with the throbbing as I struggled to remove bloodstains from the rug. I kept thinking if I could just remove any trace of what happened, maybe I could remove my memory of it too. Perhaps he'd be too drunk to remember anything when he woke up.

Throughout the long night, I scrubbed away at the blood. While he was still unconscious, I bundled up the rags and burned them in the fireplace. I prayed I had erased all traces of his monstrous act.

The bleeding eventually did stop. It would be many days before the pain in my body finally faded. The pain piercing my heart would stay there forever. Something had died inside me.

I knew I could never look directly at Mr. Harvey's face. He had revealed his true feelings and his prejudice. He frightened me. Auntie always said that alcohol brought out the "real you." He had taken in a Jewish child, yet obviously hated Jews. It made no sense to me. I was confused and overwhelmed.

How could I continue to live here? Where would I go? If I left, how would Max find me? I was still too young to begin a life elsewhere. There were so many questions in my brain. I resolved that when I finished high school I would leave and never come back to this farm.

The night was long and snow continued to fall. All throughout the darkness and into the morning, I sat by him where he sprawled unconscious on the floor. As the house creaked, I worried that the weight of all the snow might cause the roof to collapse. Had it always creaked, and I was just not aware? Or had this long, frightful night heightened my senses so that every sound kept me alert for his movement?

I rehearsed a story about the growing bump on Mr. Harvey's head, hoping he had no memory of it. For the first time since I'd left Papa, I prayed to God. *Please God, let him not remember last night.*

The storm ended, and the sun broke through. Finally, icicles melted from the windows. I went into the kitchen and prepared his breakfast porridge as if it was any other day. Several hours had passed before I heard a moan. I stepped back into the living room where Mr. Harvey was moving around in a daze holding his head.

"What the hell happened?"

He did not remember. Thank you, dear Lord, thank you.

"Y-you came in half-frozen. You drank a lot of whiskey to warm yourself. I think it made you a bit drunk. You staggered around a lot. Then you fell and hit your head on the corner of the fireplace. Don't you remember?"

There was silence for what seemed a very long time. He sat very still and then belched loudly. He shook his head, still not facing me. "Nah. Don't remember a bloody thing."

I shuddered at his choice of words. From then on, he treated me differently. He was even more distant than before, and that was all right with me.

Did he remember? I would never know. If he did, he never would let on. Like the poker that seared and pierced into me, that night was seared into my brain. I could never forget. My life had changed yet again, this time forever.

RAINEE — 1997

John had made reservations at Claridge's, an elegant, world-renown restaurant and hotel. The maître d' formally greeted them, introduced himself as Lawrence, and escorted them to a corner table. He held the chair for Rainee, and then pivoted to return to his main duties.

The pivot made John smile. "How are you with pomp?"

"It depends on the circumstances." Rainee chuckled.

They laughed at the pun. Then John, wanting to share the hotel's history with her, said, "You might find the history of Claridge's impressive. Some tidbits of information you can take back to Boston. Did you know, for instance, that the Empress Eugènie of France made Claridge's her winter quarters?"

"No, I did not. Really?"

"Yes, indeed. In fact, during World War II, many of Europe's royalty escaped or were exiled to Claridge's."

"No kidding? Who?"

"Well now, let me think." He put his hands to his chin, and stroked an imaginary beard in a professorial look. "The kings of Greece, Norway, and Yugoslavia, and the queen of the Netherlands made Claridge's their temporary homes. There's a famous story—I hope I get this right—that a diplomat telephoned Claridge's and asked to speak to the king. The hotel clerk said, 'Certainly sir, but which one?'"

They both laughed.

"I was looking forward to seeing their changes. I read they recently updated the Art Deco decor with this new modern design. Fortunately, they managed to preserve their title as London's *Art Deco Jewel*." He leaned in closer and lowered his voice. "Call me old-fashioned, but I liked the old style better."

"Your knowledge is very impressive, John."

The sommelier offered a wine menu. They both decided on the house wine. Rainee had noted the wine expert's look of disappointment before he spun around on his heels. "I think he was looking for more of a challenge."

John sighed dramatically. "We are but simple folk."

"May I ask you a personal question, John? Feel free to tell me to mind my own business."

"Certainly."

"How does a person attend a prestigious college like Oxford, earn a law degree, end up working for social services, and still afford a five-star restaurant? Now is when you tell me to mind my own business."

John laughed, and Rainee noticed what a wonderful laugh it was. "Checking out my office walls, I see. It wasn't my idea to put up those certificates. Mum insisted."

The waiter brought their wines.

John sniffed, sipped, and nodded his approval.

"Here's the deal: I tell you all about myself—isn't that what a date's about?—and then you tell me all about yourself. Deal?"

Rainee agreed.

"I come from what some people call 'old money.' I refused, foolishly I might add, to take any money from my family. I wanted to make it on my own. Tell me, is rebellion synonymous with young and stupid?"

Rainee nodded and laughed.

"I earned scholarships and got a free ride through college and Law school. Obviously, I opted for a different route than Law. Mum and Dad were not at all pleased with the profession I chose. Father rather expected me to enter his law firm, as did Mum. He fully expected me to become a solicitor, or better yet, a barrister. Apparently, I was a disappointment to both of them." He feigned surprise, exaggerating a large O with his mouth. "Oh my! Good gracious, what could they say to their high-society circle of friends?"

They waited as a server filled their water glasses.

"I knew that the profession of law was not for me. As a child, I spent many holidays alone with Mum, because of Dad's workload. I intended to have a family someday with whom I would spend time and really know my children, have a hand in their rearing. My Mum never complained. She was a dutiful wife and very good at playing the role. Only I could tell that she was lonely. I could see it in her eyes and her expression when she'd receive that inevitable phone call that he'd be working late. I suspect that that's why I never had a sibling. He was never home to procreate."

They laughed, but there was a serious undertone in his assertion.

"So you were getting even with your parents by not becoming a lawyer?" Rainee grimaced, and immediately wished she could take that back. "I'm sorry, that was inappropriate. It's none of—"

"No, no, that's fine. You're probably right. Rebellious, remember? Isn't it the job of all youth to send a message to the previous generation? Righteous rebellion. After all, we know more about life than they do. I suppose each generation feels the same.

"I must say that I have not regretted my decision, not once. I love what I do. I hope I am good at it. And, no, I don't often dine at five-star restaurants. I save that for special occasions. I do, however and in full disclosure—that's the Law degree coming out—receive a monthly stipend from the family trust. That helps pay for my apartment. After all, how would it look to their friends and colleagues if their son were living in a hovel?" He chuckled.

Rainee realized that she was attracted to this Londoner. She liked his laugh, his smile, his intellect, and found his self-deprecating wit endearing.

The waiter returned to take their orders.

John asked, "May I take the liberty to order for you?"

"Please do."

"Okay, this Oxford scholar and this venerable author would like to begin with the Pâté de Foie Gras, followed by the Glazed Duck Confît, please." He looked over to Rainee for her approval, who tried to hide her giggle. She nodded her assent.

"Very good choice, sir." The waiter scurried to place their orders.

"Not haughty enough?" John asked. "I can up it a notch, if you prefer."

"No, that was haughty enough for me. Honestly, I did try not to laugh."

"I must, at all costs, protect the English reputation... or at least... my parents' reputation."

He raised his glass and Rainee raised hers. "I propose a toast—to you finding answers, and to me finding a new friend. Cheers."

"Lovely. Cheers." They clinked glasses.

"Turnabout is fair play, Rainee. Start with the day you were born."

Rainee laughed again. "Well, let's not go back that far. To begin with, I was not born into aristocracy. You'd call us working class. Dad was a car mechanic, now retired. He owned his own business. He was a hard worker, and he loves to do woodwork in our garage. He's very good with his hands. My mom worked in the school cafeteria, which I think was her way of keeping an eye on us. That enabled her to be there when we got home from school too. I have two brothers with whom I miraculously get along. I guess you could say that I had a fairly normal childhood." She added, "I too was a bit rebellious as a teenager."

"You? No, I simply can't believe it."

"Don't look so shocked. After all, I grew up at the tail-end of the hippie era—the sixties. Still, I enjoyed a normal childhood with adoring parents, both of whom still adore me, as I do them. Graduated college. Sadly, no scholarships. I earned a degree in marketing. Had a few jobs, then started with a company and lasted there until my novel became a movie."

She paused to take a sip of her wine. "Feeling confident to be called an author, I stopped being a renter and, with my royalties, bought a condominium on Marlborough Street in Boston. By the way, I love that street because it has cobblestones and gas lamps, albeit gas lamps converted to electric now. It has always reminded me of England."

John said, "I've been to Boston and I loved it. Quaint areas throughout the city. And you're right; it is a bit like merry old England. On my next visit, I shall look for Marlborough Street. Please, go on."

Is he making promises of the future? "Well, I love my life in Boston and my circle of friends. My closest friend, Shelley, is whom I came to London with. Or is that, with whom I came to London?" She shrugged. "Her company is training her and she asked if I would come along. How could I say no? I'm under a deadline to deliver another novel to my publisher or relinquish an already-spent advance. That's where Jana comes in, and you know the rest from there." She raised both palms as if an exclamation point.

John said, "Now, that was a much-abbreviated narrative of your life story. However, it does allow for more time to find out about you." His face became very solemn. "I do have one serious question. I mean, if it's not too personal."

"Okay."

"Rainee. Unusual name. Is that short for something? Does it mean something in some obscure language?" He smiled.

She liked the way his eyes crinkled when he smiled.

"You know, no one has ever asked me that before. I'm kidding, of course. What does it mean? How do you spell it? I swear, if I ever have a kid, I would never do that to them." She rolled her eyes. "I've spent a lifetime explaining it."

"My apologies."

"No, no, it's fine. Believe me, I'm used to it. Here's the story: My mother was pregnant with me and due any day. It was February and had been raining nonstop for several days. She was getting cabin fever. My Dad suggested they go see a movie that had opened several weeks before. It was *Raintree County*. Do you know the movie? Liz Taylor, Montgomery Clift. Anyhow, they arrived at the theater and it was still raining. The marquis displayed the movie title, with two letters missing. I'm sure you can guess which letters. *T* and *R*. So it spelled out *Rain ee County*. While they were watching the movie, my mother's water broke. They laughed in between contractions because it was raining, and my mother was too."

John's smile widened.

"It seems they thought it was appropriate to name me after a movie title that was missing a few letters. And this was all before the hippie era began, when kids were named Moonfrye, China, and Dharma. I suppose you could say they were ahead of their time."

They both were still chuckling when their first course arrived.

Rainee looked down at her hands and realized, as on the plane, she had been folding and unfolding her napkin while she spoke. She questioned where and when she had picked up that habit. She wondered whether John noticed. *Is it first date jitters? Is it because I intentionally left out a life-changing event in my life?*

Throughout the dinner, the conversation flowed. They enjoyed each other's company, and it was evident to both. Not wanting the meal to come to its inevitable end, they deliberately slowed the pace when their waiter served dessert.

Hailing a taxi, John asked. "Will you be visiting Jana tomorrow at the same time?"

She smiled. "I plan on it."

As they settled into the back of the taxi, he said, "You may want to look for her in her room. She won't be in the great room."

"Oh? Why not?"

"The visiting physician will be making his rounds. Mrs. Bowman refuses to see him. Instead, we transport her to another doctor's office. This doctor is new to us. He replaced a retiring physician three weeks ago. I noticed on his first visit that she became quite agitated when he entered."

"I wonder why."

"I asked her why, but she wouldn't talk. I mean, quite literally would not talk. She became almost catatonic. The look of fright in her eyes was perplexing. She went to her room and refused to let him examine her. The same response happened the following week."

"That's odd. I wonder what would make her so afraid of this doctor. I'll be there. You know, John, even though there's not been a lot of conversation yet, I'm growing fond of her. Perhaps it's because she reminds me a lot of my grandmother, may she rest in peace."

"Maybe you can get her to talk. By the way, I thought we could rent a video of your movie and invite the residents to watch. As a visiting lecturer, you could answer questions. I think they'd like that very much. Would you consider that?"

"I'd love to. As a visiting lecturer, I can even write off this trip." She chuckled.

The taxi arrived at her building and John walked her to the front stoop. "I enjoyed this evening very much."

Rainee had, too. "I hope we can do this again." She was aware of that awkward moment at the end of a first date, when the question of a kiss hangs in the air. He took her hand and kissed her cheek. He waited until she had entered the building, then left smiling.

JANA — 1942-1945

Auntie wired that she was returning. Her sister had passed away from complications of pneumonia. Mr. Harvey was so happy to see her finally return that he put on a tie and bought some flowers with which to greet her at the train station. He had tears in his eyes as he held her. Auntie was pleased to know how missed she had been.

We returned to the farm, and she was delighted to find things in order. She complimented me on how immaculate the kitchen was, the linens in order, and the house swept. I was relieved to see her because I knew if she was there, Mr. Harvey's anxiety would be gone.

He was ecstatic that she was home and became overly solicitous of her, making certain she was warm, not too tired, and not too hungry. He transformed into someone I had never seen before. Was he this attentive when they were courting? Was it his guilt over that horrible night? I would never know.

On the second night of her return, he took her into town for a special dinner. Since the snow had not melted completely, he shoveled paths around the house so she would not fall. Auntie seemed flattered by the new attention and joked that she should go away more often. I chuckled obligingly; he didn't find it funny.

For her everything seemed the same as usual. There were no apparent signs of change in the household. My life, on the other hand, was forever changed. Before Auntie came home, my fear had turned to anger. Excusing myself to do homework, I would not sit down to supper with him. The truth was that I had eaten before he came in from his chores. And I did not eat the same meal either because I would often spit or piss into the pot. My hatred was that strong. Respect for Auntie kept me from killing him, but that often happened in my dreams.

I loathed Mr. Wickham so much that my body reacted with nausea when I saw him even from a distance. However, because I loved Auntie I could never tell her about that awful night. How could I? I would be gone, and she would have to live with him, knowing his real nature. No, she would never hear it from me. She deserved better, but there could be no purpose in making her unhappy. She loved him.

Soon the same mundane routines resumed on the farm. My determination to leave grew stronger each day. I lived for the end of high school.

When that day finally arrived, there was no ceremony or pomp to mark the occasion. The school bell rang and the students left the building as if it were any other day. The expectation was that most would continue to live in Berkhamsted for the rest of their lives. Few would matriculate to college. Many would never leave the area. I had other plans.

To my surprise, Auntie was waiting for me outside the school. She had a big smile on her face, even though I knew her heart was breaking. She hugged me tightly and then handed me fresh-picked flowers. She told me how proud she was of me. We put my bicycle in the back of the truck. As we drove back to the farm, a tear trickled down her cheek. "Janet dear, when will you be leaving us?"

I was silent for a moment. How did she know? We had never talked of the future. "I think this week."

"Where will you go?"

"London. One of the other students knows someone in London who has a flat and is looking for another roommate."

"How will you live?"

"I'll try to get a job as a seamstress."

We grew quiet again. "Uncle and I bought you a graduation present. It's a leather suitcase. Somehow, I knew you'd be leaving us." Tears were still falling. "You must never tell him, but I have been secretly putting away some money for you." She reached into her purse with one hand still on the steering wheel and handed me a roll of bills. "My little cache for when you would need it. There's even some ration stamps. It's not a lot, but it should help you get started."

I felt awful knowing that she was miserable at the thought of me leaving, but I was elated. "Auntie, I can't thank you enough for all you have done for me. You made me a home; you gave me a life."

"It will never compare to what you have given me, Janet dear. I will always think of you as my daughter... *our* daughter."

When she said "our daughter," I became queasy and desperate to change the subject. I told her that once I was settled, I would send my address. However, I knew she would never visit the big city.

I had not expected London to be such a short train ride from Berkhamsted. There were few stops in between stations. I stared through the window and watched the countryside, and my past, fly by in a blur. My future lay on the tracks ahead. London. I was excited and nervous.

Expectations? I had many. A completely new life. Maybe I could even return to my Jewish roots again. Join a synagogue, meet other Jewish people, and perhaps even marry one day. Throughout my life with the Wickhams, I had kept my promise to Papa. I had never stopped remembering who I was, where I came from, and what I believed in. I was a Jew hiding in plain sight.

As the train rumbled into London, my thoughts about my tenure on the farm wavered from the good times to the bad. I would never forget her. I would try to forget him. She gave me a life, when others were not so lucky. He took away the opportunity of my giving birth to another life. She taught me how to sew, which I hoped would become my profession. She imbued in me the sense of goodness, strength and things only a woman can understand: appreciation and fortitude.

I had waited patiently for Max to come for me. He never did. My biggest fear was that he died in the war. That became the only logical conclusion. Papa and Aunt Gertie would not have survived. Of that, I was certain. I read about the atrocities that happened and that Nazi armies had stormed through Amsterdam shortly after I left. They left death in the wake of their march throughout Europe.

It wasn't until Japan awakened a sleeping giant—America—that the Nazis' strength began to wane. America could no longer ignore what was happening in Europe. It took Japan, a country on the other side of the world, to attack them before the colossus woke up. If they had awakened earlier and joined in the fight against Hitler, maybe my family would have lived. What had taken them so long? Many Europeans asked this same question. Where was the might of America?

The train arrived at a bustling Euston Station. I took my new suitcase and disembarked. With a paper holding my future address grasped firmly in my hand, I set off for my new life.

London had survived a terrible bombing, and slowly buildings were being rebuilt everywhere. It was exciting to walk the streets of this city. I was not used to so much pavement and cement. There were many big stores, not just small shops. Choices abounded in restaurants and pubs. People were everywhere, moving hurry-scurry with determination. I found myself walking faster to keep up. There was a lot to take in, and I was overwhelmed. My heart throbbed with excitement. I stopped a person to ask directions for the address on the paper, and they suggested I take a taxi, because it was too far to walk. I hesitated to spend any of the money Auntie had given me, except I did not know this city. I observed other people hailing taxis, and I waved my hand in the air. Almost immediately, a black taxi screeched to a halt. I handed the driver the address and was on my way.

RAINEE — 1997

Rainee greeted Red, signed the guest book and went to look for Jana. She was not sitting in her usual spot.

She returned to the reception desk and asked, "Red, do you know where Mrs. Bowman is?"

"Oh, sure. She disappeared into her room when she heard the doctor was here."

"Oh, right. Mr. Pritchard warned me about that. Where is the doctor's clinic?"

Red shook her head. "Dr. Wagner and his nurse see the residents in their own rooms since we don't have extra space. Keeps it private and all."

Rainee knocked gently on Jana's door, hoping not to interrupt her in case she was napping. There was no answer. "Mrs. Bowman, it's me, Rainee. May I come in and visit?"

She heard a very quiet assent from Jana. Rainee opened the door to find her in the wheelchair staring out the window.

"Good morning." Rainee approached. Jana did not turn around. "How are you today?"

Jana's hands were white-knuckled, gripping the arms of the wheelchair tightly. She turned slowly to face Rainee. At first, her eyes were distant. When Rainee smiled at her, her eyes briefly flickered to life. Then, almost immediately, they became vacant again.

"Is he here? Is he still here?" She looked out her window.

"Is who here?"

"*Der Doktor*. Is he still here?" Jana was trembling.

"I believe he's seeing patients, Mrs. Bowman. Other patients."

Jana noticed that Rainee had left the door ajar. Her eyes widened in fear. *"Shcnell! Shcnell! Schließen Sie die Tür."* She desperately pleaded for Rainee to shut the door.

Rainee shook her head and raised her palms. "I can't understand. I don't speak German."

Jana motioned at the door, "*Schließ!* Shut!"

"Of course. You want me to shut the door? Sure." Rainee was startled. She had not heard Jana using her native German before. She closed the door and returned to stand next to the frightened woman. "Are you okay, Mrs. Bowman? Is there something I can get you?"

"Nein! Nein!" Jana began rocking anxiously back and forth. She massaged her neck again, as if playing with something there. She quietly sang a song in Yiddish.

Rainee asked, "Would you mind translating those lyrics for me?"

She seemed unaware of Rainee, and continued to sing softly.

Jana's sudden departure from the present worried Rainee. "You seem agitated. Should I get the nurse? I'm sure they could give you something to calm your nerves. Tell me, what can I do for you?"

Jana remained silent. Rainee studied her and wondered what the doctor had done to cause such trepidation. Why was she so afraid of *Der Doktor*?

Slowly, Jana's body stopped trembling. She deflated into her chair in a relaxed state. Rainee heard a quiet, long sigh, like a punctured balloon.

"I brought you some chocolates. We know chocolate solves most of our troubles."

"Troubles? What do you mean?" Clear-eyed, Jana turned to look at Rainee again. Rainee realized that Jana was unaware of what had just transpired. *Could she have forgotten so soon? Where had her mind taken her during those moments?*

"You seem troubled. I just want to help."

Jana smiled and was no longer agitated. "Chocolates will help."

Rainee dug into her purse and produced her latest gift.

Jana looked over the box, took out several pieces, and put them in her bedside table. "For later. I am tired. I want to lie down and nap." Her smile vanished, and she looked exhausted.

That was unexpected. Rainee wondered, *Did fear overwhelm her and fatigue her so suddenly?* "Would you like me to help you to your bed?"

"That would be nice, dear."

Rainee helped move Jana from her chair into her bed. She covered her with a blanket and asked, "May I visit you later? I want to be sure you're okay."

"Okay? Oh, I'm fine. Yes, dear, I'd like you to come back. Make sure you close the door behind you." She closed her eyes, then took her blanket and completely covered her head.

Like a child in hiding, Rainee thought and went to seek out John to report what she had witnessed.

In his office working on his computer, he looked up and smiled. "Well, hello there."

She returned his smile. "Good morning. Thank you again for last night. I had a wonderful time."

"Would you consider it too forward if I asked you to the theatre this Saturday evening? I have tickets and would love your company."

"Thank you, I'd love to."

"You look perplexed." He offered her a chair.

"John, I just witnessed something. I'm hoping you can explain it. It appeared that Jana came in and out of reality. She was present and then distant. She reverted to German. She retired to her bed as if going into hiding from *Der Doktor*."

"Yes. That is curious. I wish I knew why. She was not afraid of the last visiting physician. You said that she started speaking German, eh? That I hadn't heard her do before."

Rainee said, "May I have your permission to speak to the doctor? I won't keep him long, I promise."

"Absolutely. I'm sure he'd be happy to speak with you. Come with me and I'll introduce you to him." He rose from his chair and led her down the hallway. They had searched several rooms before they found him.

John made the introductions, asked the doctor if he had a moment to speak with Rainee, and then left them to converse.

"Thank you for speaking with me, Dr. Wagner. I am concerned about a resident here who seems agitated by your presence."

"Ah, you must be referring to Mrs. Bowman. I'm aware of her apprehension. I understand they transport her for care. Please, walk with me."

They walked down the corridor. As they spoke, Rainee attempted to assess him. She guessed him to be in his mid-forties. He was not wearing a wedding ring. His posture was perfectly straight as an arrow. He had permanent frown lines on his brow; his hairline was slightly receding; and his nose was prominently bulbous. She found that his eyes unsettled her. They were deep, deep brown, almost black and very intense. When he looked at her, she felt he was looking through her. *I'd be a bit frightened of this man too, or maybe I'm reading too much into this?*

He continued. "Mr. Pritchard told me a little bit about her history. However, I never even got as far as reviewing her chart. She didn't want to have anything to do with me. I don't know if you're aware that Mrs. Bowman was a Holocaust survivor. To her good fortune, she managed to avoid the concentration camps. I have treated only a few survivors before, and I've seen some of the same behaviors in them. Mrs. Bowman is the one resident here who is a Jewish Holocaust survivor. There are some residents who fought in the war, but she is the only Jew."

"What do you mean? What type of behaviors, Doctor?"

"Well, for one, notice I am not wearing a white coat. That can be what we call a trigger, something that can elicit a reminder of the past. Certain triggers I've learned to avoid and I have trained the staff here as well. For instance, you never say to a Holocaust survivor that it's time to go to the showers, for obvious reasons. Also, needles are kept out of sight. A common behavior we have noticed is that some even hoard their food." Rainee thought of Jana and the chocolates.

"Doctor, do you find differences in the elderly you treat who are not Jewish or weren't soldiers?"

"Oh, certainly. Many differences. Soldiers who witnessed their pals blown to bits... well, they live with their own nightmares. No two people had the same experience, and their reactions to war manifest in different ways. To answer your question, not fighting but losing a loved one is equally devastating, especially if they weren't present at the time of death. Imagination takes over, and they create scenarios in the brain. It may not have happened the way they conceptualized the event, but it's very real for them. Simply put, war is anguish... for everyone." He glanced at his watch.

Rainee had an idea. "Dr. Wagner, I am presently writing a story about Holocaust survivors and Alzheimer's Disease. Would you mind if I interviewed you on the subject? You seem to have a wealth of knowledge. I could come to your office on any day that suited you."

The doctor hesitated. "I suppose that could be arranged. I'm certain you could find other doctors out there who have more knowledge on the subject than I."

"I'm hoping it will give me some insight into Mrs. Bowman's mind. I want to help her."

He reached into his wallet and produced his business card. "Call my receptionist and set up an appointment. In fact, my schedule has me in my office tomorrow. I usually take a lunch break, and that would be the best time to arrange it."

Rainee thanked him and returned to John's office. He was on the telephone, but he waved her in.

She listened as he spoke with patience and poise to whomever was on the phone. It sounded to Rainee that he was allaying someone's concerns. She thought, *Nice bedside manner.*

When his conversation ended, she told him what had transpired. He said, "What are you waiting for? Use my phone to call his office. I'll be right back."

She called and arranged a time. While she awaited John's return, her thoughts turned to the doctor's dark eyes. It caused her to shudder.

The next afternoon, the doctor's receptionist showed Rainee into his private office. "Doctor will be with you as soon as he's finished with this patient. May I get you some coffee or tea?"

"No, thank you." Rainee took a seat facing his massive desk.

She looked around his office. Neat and orderly. Even the papers on his desk were meticulously stacked. His lunch was awaiting him, not in a white Styrofoam take-out container, but spread out with good china, sparkling silverware, and a linen napkin.

Covering the dark-paneled walls were photos and certificates. She could not hear activity outside this room and guessed the walls required soundproofing for privacy. The only audible noise was that of the clock on the wall, with its steady tick, tick, tick. Rainee had been early and was in no rush.

She took out a pencil and pad to take notes, and then tried to get comfortable in the chair. It was wooden and unpadded, which made it difficult to find a comfortable position. Looking at the doctor's big leather chair behind the desk, she assumed that it was his intention that visitors do not get too comfortable.

Rainee couldn't put her finger on it, but something about the office made her uneasy. She thought again, *Perhaps I'm reading too much into this.*

The door opened and Dr. Wagner entered. He greeted Rainee with a curt handshake, then removed his lab coat and hung it neatly on a hanger behind his door.

"We are fortunate. The patient following my lunch break rescheduled, so we have extra time to talk, if you wish."

"Yes, that's lucky for me."

"My apologies. Shall I have my receptionist order you lunch?"

"Oh, no. I've already eaten. Thank you just the same."

"I hope you won't mind if I eat while we talk. I live on borrowed time, always guaranteed an interruption."

"Please, don't stand on ceremony. Enjoy your lunch."

Before he took the first bite of his salad, he asked, "Now, how can I be of service?"

Rainee told him that the story she was planning to write was still very loosely constructed, and she had many questions. She needed to know more about survivors and Alzheimer's and the triggers he had mentioned.

"For example, what percentage of your patients with dementia are Holocaust survivors? Have you noted any differences between those who were Jewish and those who were not? If so, what were those differences? In all patients with dementia, do they lose all touch with the present, or do they vacillate between present and past? Will they eventually live totally in the past?"

As the avalanche of questions flowed out in what seemed like one breath, she did not notice that the doctor, a bit overwhelmed, had stopped chewing his food. "Ms. Allen, I'm afraid I may not be the best source of information for you. I have so few patients who are Jewish and suffer from dementia. As you know, Mrs. Bowman will not see me."

"Yes, but do you know why, Doctor?"

"No, but I suspect it is because I am of German descent. She probably does not trust Germans." The doctor's tone was straightforward.

"However there are residents in the home that are German and her age. It is highly likely that the older men were soldiers, or Hitler Youth, who believed the propaganda that the Jews were a menace to society, yet she seems to tolerate their presence. She, herself, is German."

"Your point, Ms. Allen?"

Rainee readjusted herself in the chair. "I was with her when you were doing your rounds. The look in her eye was one of terror. She began to speak German. It appeared to me as if she had regressed to her younger self during the war. Even singing a lullaby—at least it sounded like a lullaby. She was terrified that you would come into her room."

"That doesn't surprise me. Nevertheless, what can I do to help her? She lived through a terrible time, *and* she has early-onset Alzheimer's. I can't change the past, I can't change what she may have witnessed, and I cannot, unfortunately, change her future."

Rainee stood up. Questions were racing in her mind, and sitting in the chair constricted her thoughts. The doctor continued to eat.

"I understand that, Doctor. You mentioned triggers. What happened during your first meeting with Mrs. Bowman? Did you notice the fear in her eyes? Did you say something that may have triggered her memories?"

The doctor took a sip of his coffee and pondered the question. "Let me think." He took another sip. "Nothing. I remember nothing out of the ordinary, at first. Well, I mean, other than she did not speak to me. She just stared. However, you must understand, many patients present like that. That's not a reaction that is uncommon. It wasn't until I reached for my stethoscope that she pulled her wheelchair back, out of my reach. I reached to roll her back, and it was then that she made it quite clear I was not to touch her."

Rainee stopped pacing. "How? What did she do?"

The doctor poured some more coffee into his cup. He dropped in two sugar cubes and took his time stirring. Rainee was impatient for answers and was about to jump out of her skin.

"She screamed. She screamed as if she had seen a ghost. Her face blanched, and she pointed a finger at me. 'You! You!' That's all she said."

"And what was your reaction, doctor?"

"My reaction? Well, honestly, I deal with the elderly, and I've been in many different situations with patients. No one has ever pointed what felt like an accusatory finger at me. Frankly, I believe I was a bit stunned at first. I regained my composure and asked her how I could help. She shook her head and started crying. I prescribed a sedative, and they took her to her room. It wasn't until I returned to my office that I found a memo from the home that she would be using a different doctor. I must admit I was baffled at first, but I soon forgot about it." He shrugged and started to cut up his fruit. He stopped for a moment with the spoon close to his mouth. "Hoek van Holland Strand—she did say Hoek van Holland Strand after she screamed. Yes, I remember that now. I think it's a city. Not sure where, though."

There was one quick rap at the door and his nurse requested to speak with him. The doctor excused himself, saying that he would be right back.

Rainee wrote that on her pad. *Hoek van Holland Strand... I'll look that up. I wonder what the association is.*

Rainee went to stand near the open window to breathe some fresh air. She wondered about the person behind the stethoscope.

On the wall were many pictures. There were informal family pictures, interspersed with pictures of the doctor greeting prominent figures. The most notable picture was of him sitting in an easy chair next to Prince Philip. They appeared to be chatting like old friends. He had a cigar in one hand and a snifter of brandy in the other.

In another picture, the doctor was shaking hands with Prime Minister John Major. From the background, it appeared to be a very formal event. There were white-gloved servers behind the Prime Minister, busy attending to tasks. In another, American Secretary of State Madeleine Albright was handing him what appeared to be a framed certificate and the doctor was wearing a tuxedo and a blue sash. Rainee looked around the walls to see whether she could recognize the certificate. She spotted it.

The doctor entered and excused himself for keeping her waiting.

Rainee said, "Not at all. It allowed me the opportunity to look at your very impressive collection of pictures. You move in high circles, Doctor."

The doctor smiled. "Recognition for research I collaborated on for *encephalomyelitis disseminata*."

"I'm sorry, you lost me there." Rainee said.

The doctor smiled warmly. "It's an inflammatory disease in which myelin sheaths around the axons of the brain and spinal cord are damaged. That leads to demyelization and scarring, which manifest with a spectrum of symptoms. You know it as multiple sclerosis."

Rainee nodded. "Please, goes on."

"It's an ongoing study. Fortunately, we are finding some real breakthroughs. Very exciting."

"I had no idea you were a researcher as well as an internist."

"Well, my interest started when my mother was diagnosed with MS. Naturally, I want to do whatever I can to help find a cure. If not for her, then hopefully for the next generation."

"Good luck to you. I don't know when you find the time."

The doctor walked over to his wall of pictures and pointed to a woman. His face softened. "This is my mother. Obviously, it's an older picture. Long before she needed a wheelchair."

Rainee peered closely at the woman. She was at the beach holding a beach ball and was about to toss it to a little boy. Her dark, flowing hair almost reached her waist. Rainee noticed her dark eyes and brownish complexion. "She's beautiful. Is that you in the picture?"

"Yes."

"You look like her. Even in this picture, you were what, nine years old?"

"Close. I was ten."

"There's a very good likeness. You mentioned she had MS. May I ask if she is still with us?"

The doctor's voice softened. "I am fortunate that both my parents are alive, doing relatively well and living here in London."

Rainee looked at the wall for a picture of his father but did not see one. Finding that odd, she asked, "You seem to have many pictures of family, which one is your father?"

The doctor straightened his posture and said in a brisk manner, "I don't have one here. Of course, there are some at home. He always claimed to be camera-shy. However, we have digressed. Shall we continue with your questions regarding Janet Bowman?"

At that moment, the nurse knocked and entered. "Doctor, the patient who canceled has shown up in great pain."

"Seat him in room two. I will be in shortly."

The nurse left.

Rainee said, "I still have many questions. Would I be able to return, Doctor?"

As the doctor put on his white clinic coat, he hesitated, and his countenance changed. "Ah, follow me. I think I have some information that may help."

He walked over to a door, which Rainee had assumed was a private lavatory. Instead, it was a tiny annexed room. Rainee thought it was probably a converted walk-in closet. It held many stacked papers, books, and more pictures lining the wall. He pulled a chain that illuminated the tiny, musty space. He mumbled, "I know it's here...."

Rainee stepped back as he started his search. To her left were more pictures, old and faded, from an era long past. What caught her attention immediately was a picture of a German soldier with his arm around two other soldiers. Cigarettes were hanging out of their mouths. One was aiming a luger at an imaginary target. However, it was the middle soldier that held her attention. He looked startlingly like the doctor. His hair was dark and receding. He had a bulbous nose. His eyebrows were almost touching. It was something about his eyes. They were black and unnerving. Even when he was smiling with his friends, his eyes were frightening and caused her to shiver.

"Ah, here it is," the doctor said as he reached for a medical textbook from his shelf. "I knew I could find it." As Rainee backed out, he pulled the light cord and the room went dark.

The doctor closed the door behind him and handed her a large medical volume. "Ms. Allen, you may find more answers in this textbook. It's a bit dry, but if you comb through, you'll find some information on Alzheimer's relative to different ethnic populations in general. There's not a lot of information out there yet. We are just now learning more and more about this dreadful disease. I'm afraid there's even less data about its relation to Jewish Holocaust survivors. But who knows? You may glean some things from it."

"Thank you, Doctor. I will be sure to return it to you."

What she had seen in the picture startled Rainee. *Could the doctor have forgotten the picture was there? Did he not notice that I followed him into the little room?*

"Ms. Allen, I must run. Like I said, borrowed time. Good luck with your research." He shook her hand and led her out to the reception hall.

Rainee managed a very weak goodbye.

JANA — LONDON 1947

I shared a flat with two other girls. It was a tiny basement walk-down on Flood Street in an area known as Chelsea. Even though below ground, it was regarded as the first of four floors. It had one bedroom, a living area, a tiny kitchen, and a loo that was so small only one person could fit at a time. We'd take turns cooking and had to learn to be creative with a one-burner stove. It was small and a huge change from the expanse of the farmhouse. I loved it.

The windows were usually open since all three of us took up smoking. It seemed so very fashionable then. On days when London became drenched with rain and the windows were closed, the air became dense with our smoke. On other days when the street sweepers came through, I believe they deliberately swept street dirt right into our open windows. We were always cleaning our flat.

We were happy and got along beautifully. The leader of our pack was Freda—Fearless Freda, we called her. She was a year older than I and very streetwise. She had grown up in London and knew it well. She knew the affordable restaurants, the best markets to shop, and the best bars to meet men. Fearless and a little fearsome, Freda had an attitude that I often wished I could borrow. When she made up her mind to do anything, she'd become unstoppable. Because of my naiveté, I looked up to her and often leaned on her. She had much to teach, and I was an anxious learner.

My other roommate was my age and straight off the farm too. She came from St. Ives, a seaside town and port in Cornwall, which was about as far west as you can go in the British Isles. Her name was Ivey; she was named after her home by the Celtic Sea. Ivey was a bit shy and needy. She came to London because both parents and three brothers were killed in the war, and she could no longer stand to live surrounded by the memories. Ivey was tall and awkward; she had bright red hair and a very fair complexion. Freda was of average height, with broad shoulders and a medium complexion, and she had bottle-blonde hair. I was somewhere in the middle with mousey brown hair, short, an olive-complexion, and in spite of my years on the farm, not very strong. We were quite the threesome.

We each managed to procure jobs. Freda waitressed in a restaurant that served a wealthy clientele and, although frowned upon by the management, a diner would occasionally slip her a tip. She kept the tip jar under her bed as "rainy-day" money, which confused me because almost every day was a rainy day in England.

Ivey worked at a hotel as a housekeeper. Some days she would come home with things left behind by guests. Often, it was half-used bars of soap or almost-empty liquor bottles, and sometimes, even food. On rare occasions, she even found money underneath the cushions, which may have fallen out of a man's slacks.

I worked as a seamstress at the London Palladium, a famous theatre in the West End. The manager, Val Parnell, interviewed me himself. He impressed upon me what an honor it was to work there. He reminded me that I was *just* a seamstress now, but that I might work my way up to being head seamstress someday.

The Palladium brought in shows and acts from all over the world. Famous people performed there and would usually bring along their own seamstresses. On those occasions, I worked doing housekeeping-type chores. Mr. Parnell always kept me working, because he knew how hard it was to save money.

Many times, I peeked out from behind the curtain and saw his Royal Majesty King George and other royals sitting in special boxes reserved for them. It was a magical place. Somehow, I felt a part of the lives of the privileged few who attended the shows. Then, of course, I'd return home to my tiny flat and my two roommates, and we would go over what was due the butcher, the proprietor, and others. We got by, though. And more importantly, we laughed a lot. Those were happy days.

It was early February and London was experiencing warmer-than-usual weather. Ivey and Freda told me to meet them at the Cock and Barrel. The neighborhood pub we frequented was just a short walk from our flat.

I was tired and preferred to go home and sleep. A new show was in rehearsal, and it had been a long, busy day at the theatre.

I entered the bar. A cloud of smoke and the smell of beer almost made me gag. The pub seemed crowded and lively for a Tuesday evening. Someone was playing the piano in the corner, and I stopped to peer through the smoke to find Ivey and Freda.

The piano player began the introduction to "For She's a Jolly Good Fellow." The entire bar turned to look at me, raised their glasses and joined in with the song. Ivey and Freda, who had been hiding behind the entrance door, jumped out to my surprise and conducted the rest of the song. Taken aback, I could not contain my tears. My roommates had arranged a birthday surprise. Now faces became familiar. My coworkers from the theatre must have taken a taxi to beat me here. They raised their glasses and sang along. Some neighbors from our building, Freda and Ivey's friends, and even the butcher had come to celebrate my twentieth birthday.

Never given a surprise party before, I wasn't sure what I should do. I kept smiling and saying thank you, thank you, thank you. Everyone clapped. Perhaps it was my work in the theatre, so like an actress taking her curtain calls, I took a deep, swooping bow. It was my moment in the spotlight.

Freda and Ivey hugged me and directed me to a corner where they had arranged tables and chairs. I thanked them and enjoyed a terrific evening. Of course, it went on much too late and into the next morning. I would never forget this particular birthday.

Throughout the party, Freda and Ivey introduced me to friends of theirs. The last of Freda's friends was a shy man named David Bowman. Now, I'm not sure how much Freda had pre-arranged or staged this, but since he was the last of my introductions, we had time to talk. He sat at my table and congratulated me on my birthday. We talked and talked and talked. Slowly the pub emptied. We were oblivious to the thinning of the crowd. I think Ivey and Freda were somewhere in a corner smiling with satisfaction at their conspiracy.

Before the dawn revealed itself through the fog of smoke, I had learned a great deal about this man. Before we parted, for he had to be at work in three hours, we had set up our first date. My first date.

David said, "I look forward to it with great anticipation." I did not admit this to him, but I did too.

Two days later, I was getting ready to go out on my first date. Ivey had to cover for a sick employee, leaving Freda to take control as she usually did anyway. She poked around her closet to look for the perfect dress for me to wear.

She pulled out four different dresses, holding them up against my body. "This one? No, not your color." She threw it on the bed. "Here, try this one on." I did as ordered. We looked into our one full-length mirror, and we both broke out laughing. Freda had a great laugh. At the end of each laugh was an involuntary snort, which always made me laugh even more. She accessorized the dress with pearls and bracelets. I fell on the bed laughing. "I really don't think so, Freda. It makes me look like a dowager. I'm only twenty."

The third dress showed more promise, but it was a little large on me. Freda got busy with pins and took it in in several places. Even though I'm the one who's the seamstress, she managed to make it fit my body with nary a pin showing. I applauded her deftness and told her she could get a job at the theatre. We both laughed until our knees went weak, and we collapsed giggling onto the floor. I suppose I could attribute my laughing to nervousness because David's arrival was nearing.

Freda sat me at her vanity, applied her makeup, and brushed my hair into a fashionable style.

We looked at her creation. I nodded with approval, and we settled back with cigarettes, awaiting the doorbell. Even though it was still February, my armpits started to perspire.

The waiter led us to a corner table and removed a sign marked RESERVED. I smiled, thinking how thoughtful David was to plan ahead. He held my chair as I sat down, then took his seat across from me.

"I hope you like this restaurant. It's one of my favorites. I'm sorry, Janet. Perhaps I should have asked what types of food you liked before taking you here."

"This is wonderful, David. I'm glad you chose this place. It looks lovely."

The restaurant was located in a hotel surrounded by buildings in the process of reconstruction from the Blitz. Its lighting was low and flattering; the linen was bright white without stains; and the silverware was sparkling and polished. The centerpiece was a small vase with a single red rose.

All around London, areas were still recovering from the Blitz. In September of 1940, seven years earlier, the German Luftwaffe had bombed London for fifty-seven consecutive nights. Nazis destroyed or damaged more than a million London buildings and killed more than forty thousand civilians.

Buildings either remained in ruin or were in various stages of rising from the ashes. Shops opened their doors; restaurants opened their menus; theatres opened their stages, and London was experiencing a revival. There was always cause for celebration whenever a new business opened its doors. Londoners guaranteed new restaurants were kept busy for the first couple of weeks. After a while, as people adjusted to their presence, it became business as usual.

David and I spoke of the Blitz. He said, "When the sirens sounded, my Mum, Dad and I ran to the nearest bomb shelter and waited it out. We were worried about my young brother, Samuel. I had no idea where he was. I held Mum's trembling hands while she kept murmuring Samuel's name. There were so many people crammed into this space. We were all relieved when the sirens stopped." He laughed. "I beg your pardon, the place was beginning to reek of human sweat, babies' diapers and... well, you can imagine."

I said, "I'm glad I didn't live in London then. A plane did drop a bomb into the center green of Berkhamsted. It destroyed most of the library, the town hall, and the church. Several people died. The entire community went into shock. We're a small farming community and couldn't imagine what the Germans gained in bombing us."

The waiter brought us menus. "Welcome to the Connaught. May we start you with a drink?"

"This place is famous for their martinis. Would you care for one?" David asked.

A martini? I drank beer. I'd never had a martini. They did look sophisticated in the magazines, with men in tuxedoes and women in gowns sipping them. "Sure," I said, sounding enthusiastic.

Pad in hand, the waiter asked, "Would you prefer gin or vodka?"

"Um," I had no idea. "David, why don't you decide for me."

He ordered me his favorite martini with vodka. A short time later, David started to fidget in his chair. He inspected the silverware, then he drummed his fingers on the table. It was nice to know he was more nervous than I was. Suddenly, he blurted out, "Did you know that the Connaught was built in 1897?"

"No, I didn't," I said. "Why don't you tell me more?"

"Happy to. It was originally named The Coburg Hotel, after Prince Albert of Saxe-Coburg, Queen Victoria's late husband. I think it was in... um... yes, it was in 1917 that the hotel was renamed the Connaught after Queen Victoria's third son, Prince Arthur, Duke of Connaught." He was talking fast, compensating for his nervousness, which helped put me at ease as well.

"Yes, I've heard about this hotel. Many famous celebrities who perform at the Palladium stay here. They rave about it. So this is the Mayfair section of the city. You know, I've never been here."

David's eyes creased with a smile. "Well, I shall have to show you around this lovely area."

As he studied the menu, I studied his face. He had a nice face, a kind face. Though we had talked into the wee hours of the morning when we first met, there was still so much to find out. I wondered what he did for a living and how he could afford this swanky restaurant. Auntie's voice whispered in my head: *A lady must not ask these things*.

I banished that tiny whisper. Who said I was a lady anyway? "What is it you do, David? I mean, what kind of work?"

"I'm a comptroller for an import/export company."

"A comptroller? Forgive my ignorance, but what is that?"

"Fancy name for bookkeeper. I received my degree in Business Accounting, and I hope to one day open my own business, doing accounting for other businesses. And, by the way, I don't consider that an ignorant question at all. Most people have never heard that term. I had never heard that term, even in college. Come to think of it, I think my boss made it up. Instead of raising my wages, he gave me a fancy title. Hey now, wait a minute!" And with that he took his linen napkin and slapped it on the table in feigned annoyance.

He joined me in laughter. He was funny. I liked him.

The waiter came to take our order. I am not sure what David ordered for us, and some dishes were unfamiliar to me. He had an undeniable charm, so I nodded approval with each item.

"And you, Miss Lutken, work at the Palladium. Quite a prestigious venue."

"You wouldn't think that if you saw my department. We are in the basement's basement's basement. No kidding. There are no windows, but the lighting is good. The management requests we not smoke, because not only is it stifling, but also the tobacco smell lingers on the costumes. There's no ventilation. Still we manage to sneak some smokes when we know the boss isn't in the building. I don't mean to sound as if I am complaining because I really do love it there."

We spoke of many things as we awaited our meal. Whenever I asked about him, he would turn it around to be about me. He was a gentleman in the truest sense of the word. His mother had taught him well.

A white-gloved waiter to my left placed our first course on the table. A silver dome covered the plate, and I looked up at David.

He smiled.

A waiter to my right lifted the dome covers simultaneously with David's two waiters. Impressive!

I must have looked delighted because David's face beamed. A wave flowed through my body, and I relaxed. My nervousness left. All apprehension about the first date, gone. Any trepidation about David, gone. One smile from him released those feelings from me. It was all so easy from there. It felt right.

After our dessert and coffee, we left the restaurant and decided to walk off our dinner. David took great delight in pointing out different buildings. The Mayfair section of the city was rebuilding quicker than my area. I mentioned that, and David said it was because many affluent people lived in this area.

"Where do you live, David?" There was Auntie's voice whispering again, and I waved it away. I was no longer a farm girl. I was now a city girl trying, at least, to appear sophisticated.

"I live with my parents. Same home I grew up in. I'm trying my best to save money to afford to open my own practice. It's in Marylebone. Just a few streets away from Regent's Park, on a street called Gloucester Place. If I were to walk straight through Hyde Park, I'd guess it to be maybe four miles or so to your place. Give or take."

We walked in silence for a few minutes. I knew it was important to introduce a topic that would or would not change the course of where I hoped this relationship was heading.

"Bowman," I said almost as a whisper.

"Yes?" He stopped walking.

"It sounds like a Jewish name. Am I too presumptive to ask if you're Jewish?" Auntie's voice was now screaming at me.

"Yes, I am Jewish, and I take no offense at your question. Is that a problem, Janet?"

Relieved, I said, "Oh my, no. Not at all. In fact, it's wonderful. I'm Jewish, too. I never dreamed I'd meet a man in London who was the same religion as me."

"There are quite a few of us in town," he laughed. "Oh sorry... I'm not laughing at you. Honestly, it was just so delightfully adorable the way you asked."

We both laughed. He took my hand in his and we continued our walk.

"Are you comfortable telling me your story, Janet? I know you are German, so I assume there's a story to be told."

I did feel complete ease with David. We found a bench and sat down, and I revealed my history to him. I started with a description of the village in which I grew up, my family, how growing anti-Semitism forced us to leave Germany, my stay at the orphanage, my exodus to the Wickham's farm and how I had ended up in

London. However, I did not tell him of that night of brutality. I had never revealed that to even my roommates. It was too painful, and what if I could never have children? I feared it would scare him off.

He listened without interruption. He held my hand, and his grip tightened when I told him some of the more poignant moments: saying goodbye to my father, the Nazis murdering the boys, how the Nazi commandant's black eyes became imprinted in my brain, and especially my wait for Max. There were times I had to look away from him as I revealed my story, but the gaze of his deep brown eyes never left my face.

I ended my story with the night I met him at my birthday celebration. When I looked up at him, there was a single tear falling down his cheek. I reached up and wiped it with my gloved hand. David took my hand and kissed it. He pulled me into an embrace and held me. He whispered, "I'm so sorry. I'm so sorry you had to endure all that."

I looked at him with a modest smile. "I suppose if I hadn't had to take those roads, I would never have met you."

It seemed as if our eyes locked for ten minutes, but it was only seconds. Then he pulled me to him and kissed me. My first kiss. Gentle, tender, and oh so splendid.

"Janet, there are organizations in London that help find people lost during the war. I will help you find your brother, if you'll allow me."

"It's Jana. My real name is Jana." I said my name and, not having used it in a long while, it sounded foreign to me.

"Jana. I like that. It's a good name. Jana, will you let me help you?"

Moved by his offer, I could not speak. Instead, I answered him with a kiss. There we sat, kissing until the dawn began to break and my heart began to heal.

RAINEE — 1997

On her way to visit Jana, Rainee stopped at the British Library to look up some information.

She read: *Hoek van Holland Strand: Hook of Holland (Dutch: Hoek van Holland, literally "Corner of Holland"), also known as the Hook (De Hoek), is a town in the western Netherlands and is situated on the North Sea coast.*

Rainee continued to read some uninteresting facts until she came to an eye-opener that started her heart racing: *During World War II, this was one of the most important places for the Germans to hold because of the harbor.*

She pulled out Jana's Holocaust ID card and read the passage aloud. "We were taken by train to the pier and put on *De Praag,* a boat." She tried to find information regarding a boat named *De Praag*. Unfortunately, she came up empty. Then she remembered Mr. Wickham mentioning the torpedoing of Max's boat. She dug further.

October 12, 1940 — Prinses Juliana (Netherlands): World War II: The cargo ship was bombed and sunk in the North Sea off Hoek van Holland, South Holland by Luftwaffe aircraft. The Royal Navy rescued survivors.

"Survivors?" Rainee's stunned voice echoed in the large room.

The people nearby immediately shushed her.

Could that have been the boat Max was on, and could he have been one of those who survived? The dates and place coincided. It was all credible, yet improbable. If so, why had he not looked for his sister? Mr. Wickham had gotten some information wrong. Luftwaffe aircraft bombed the ship, not a submarine torpedo. Nevertheless, it was common for information to get misconstrued. After all, how was information disseminated back then? It had to be through word of mouth, newspapers and radio. What access did a small farming community have to information from the outside world?

Until now, she had been searching for Jana's story of survival. Rainee decided to contact Ilana and see if she had any information regarding Max Lutken, but that would have to wait until she got back to the apartment.

Approaching the nursing home, she was alarmed to see an ambulance removing someone on a stretcher. John was accompanying the covered body, with one hand resting on it. She kept a respectful distance and hoped it was not Jana. Rainee watched as John took out a handkerchief and wiped away his tears.

He looked up as she approached him. "He was a resident here for nearly five years. Reminded me a little of my great uncle."

"I'm so sorry, John."

"I hate it. But unfortunately, it goes with the job. That's the downside of working here. You become very attached to the residents—even grow to love them—and then... well..." He wiped the tears from his cheeks.

Rainee wanted to take him into her arms to console him. Instead, she placed her hand on his shoulder.

He reached up and took her hand in his. "Thank you, Rainee. It's comforting having you here."

They walked inside, and he excused himself to tend to the final paperwork regarding that resident. He promised to look for her later.

Rainee found Jana in her room, staring out the window. Her view was of the entrance. She had seen the ambulance leave. "I knew Mr. Johnstone before he lived here," she said. "Before I lived here. He lived in our neighborhood and was a real talker, a real schmoozer. My husband David, and Shelley would take daily walks. Mr. Johnstone took his daily vigil and inevitably they would meet and talk. Well, Mr. Johnstone did most of the talking. David was more of a listener."

"I'm sorry for your loss. Shelley is my best friend's name, and she's here in London with me. Who was your Shelley?"

"Our dog. She was a sheltie. They're small collie-type dogs. Shelley, the sheltie. I know. Not very original. She made us smile a lot. We couldn't have children, so she became our baby."

"Your husband must have been a lovely man."

"Oh, yes. Would you like me to tell you about him?"

"I would love it!" Rainee sat down on the end of Jana's bed.

Jana turned her wheelchair to face Rainee. She smiled. "What can I tell you about the most wonderful man in the world? He was my... my life."

That was when Jana opened up her world to Rainee. She was articulate, in the present, and ready to reveal her entire life story. It was as if she had waited for this moment in time to erupt with information. She released everything from her heart. Everything emerged. She touched on her most personal information. Rainee wished she had brought her tape recorder.

Jana began with the story of her family's happy life in Frechen, Germany. She spoke lovingly of her family. She laughed with tears when she spoke of her brother, Max.

"I'll tell you a funny story about Max. I had come home from school one day very excited. Oh, I was so happy, because my essay had received the highest mark in the whole class. I earned five gold stars. They were stickers at the top of my paper. Mama was very proud of me. She said, 'Just wait until your Papa sees this!' I ran around the house waving the paper in the air. When Max came in, I shoved it in his face—he had never received such high marks." Jana laughed.

"I was putting on such a big show. With every chance, I would wave that paper with the gold stars around his head. He told me to stop. Over and over, he told me to stop pestering him. I was a stubborn girl and was getting even for all the times my brother had tormented me. He said, 'You are prancing around like a peacock. Like the peacock in Mama's song. You should not show off so much.' Still I did not stop, for it was my turn to torture my older brother for a change. Then he said, 'Ugh, stop parading around over a few gold stars. You act like you are some proud peacock!'"

"'Yes,' I told him. 'But a *golden* peacock.' We all laughed for that was the name of Mama's Yiddish song, 'The Golden Peacock.'" Jana paused to catch her breath. "For Hanukkah, Max carved me a peacock necklace and painted it gold. And from that day on, he called me his golden peacock."

She grew quiet for a moment, massaged her neck, wiped away a tear, then continued her story as Rainee sat and listened without interruption.

Jana revealed her family's expulsion to Amsterdam and her father's difficult decision to hand over his children to an orphanage.

She spoke of her friendship with a girl named Hannah. Her mood darkened as she revealed her emigration to England by way of a *kindertransport*. She spoke of standing on the docks, watching a Nazi's murderous rampage of young boys. Jana spoke of that particular Nazi, whose eyes she would never forget. "Black and empty. His eyes were searching right, and then left. He was looking to penalize someone, anyone. Then he murdered those boys and laughed. Oh, how he laughed! We girls watched in horror. I kept my eyes on Max, who was not one of the protesters. And I was thankful for that."

When Jana mentioned the Nazi with black eyes, Rainee's mind immediately flipped to the picture in the doctor's closet. Though full of questions, Rainee never interrupted. Jana was on a roll and Rainee did not want to cause her to deviate from her story. Jana was stirring up loads of memories, and Rainee was afraid it would act as a trigger. She was happily surprised that Jana remained in the present. It was most noticeable in her eyes. They were alive and bright.

Jana spoke about her life with the Wickhams. She spoke lovingly about Mrs. Wickham, although when it came to Mr. Wickham, she showed animus by practically spitting his name. She spoke matter-of-factly about an incident, which shocked Rainee. Through anger and clenched teeth, she spoke in a monotone of how he had raped her with a fireplace poker. Jana related in detail how afterward, while clutching her pained belly, she had to clean the house and prepared it to look like nothing had ever occurred. How Mr. Wickham awoke with no memories of the brutality he had force on her, and when her auntie returned, it became business as usual again on the farm. How much she wanted to leave, but she had to wait until after she graduated from school.

The story continued with her life in London with her roommates. Her voice raised an octave when she spoke of meeting David and their courtship. She said with all sincerity, "With the exception of not having children, my life with him was full."

With the mention of children, Rainee subconsciously massaged her own belly.

"My husband provided a comfortable life for us and we were happy." Jana's smile melted. "The doctors found his cancer, which had been in remission, returned and it was too late to help him. He passed away three weeks before our fortieth anniversary." Again, she took out her Kleenex and wiped away tears. Rainee borrowed some to wipe away her own.

That brought her to the present and living in this nursing home. Jana was aware of her memories fading and admitted, "My fear is losing all of them. What will life be like if I have no memories? What will it be like to have lived an entire life and not remember any of it? There's no one to remind me. My picture albums will be full of nameless people."

Rainee could find no words of consolation for Jana. How could she tell her that from her research into Alzheimer's disease, after a while Jana's brain would not signal her body that she was hungry, bringing on the eventuality of losing any appetite? Painfully, she would wither away, close her eyes and die.

Rainee said, "Perhaps I could help you label those pictures. We could start tomorrow."

"You would do that for me?"

"Of course I would." Rainee placed her hand atop Jana's and squeezed.

"Why? Why waste your time sitting with an old woman in a nursing home? You could be spending your time with that handsome Mr. Pritchard."

Rainee smiled. "Yes, he is handsome, isn't he? I enjoy spending time with you and getting to know you. Our time together is something I will always remember. I will never forget."

"Easy for you to say." They both laughed awkwardly. "Sorry, my dear. Bad pun."

Jana looked into Rainee's eyes. "Mrs. Wickham... Auntie... once told me that I was the daughter she'd never had. I like to think if I had a daughter, she would have been like you."

A tear trickled down Rainee's cheek. Overcome with emotion, they embraced.

A knock on the door had them scrambling for tissues and drying tears.

John entered and saw red eyes. "Oh my, how awkward. I've interrupted. I could come back later."

"No, it's all right," Jana said.

John's eyes widened as he looked at Rainee to be sure it was all right. She nodded.

"It's activity time, Mrs. Bowman. We have an ice cream social today. Make your own sundaes. Would you like to join the other residents in the great room?"

Jana looked from Rainee to John and her eyes clouded over. Rainee saw the transformation and became sad. It was as if a light dimmed and then went out. Reminded of her limited life here in the nursing home, Jana's world had just become smaller once again.

The words left Rainee's mouth as a whisper, "Oh no."

Rainee could not contain her excitement. "My God, John, it was amazing! If you could have been there to see her eyes light up. She was alive! I've never seen her like that before. She wasn't just *remembering* her past; she was *living* it."

John had some hot tea brought into his office, but Rainee was too excited to drink anything. She was pacing again, as she did when she felt energized. "John, the things she witnessed; the horrible brutalities done to her. Do you know why she never had children? I know her chart stated some gynecological problem, but do you know what caused it?" Rainee related Jana's brutal rape in detail.

John stopped drinking his tea, and his mouth fell open as he listen intently. "This certainly explains many things, Rainee. You're putting together pieces of the puzzle of her life. Sometimes, I've wondered whether patients with Alzheimer's have lost their memories or have chosen to have selective memory. Surely, a survivor of the Holocaust would choose to erase those horrible memories. It would be understandable."

Rainee lowered her voice and sat down to relate added information. "There's more, John. When I went to interview the doctor, his walls displayed certificates, honors, and the usual plaques you see hanging on walls. There were some family photographs of him with his mother. None with his father, and I questioned him on that. He was very vague with his answer, very enigmatic. Right before I had to leave, he took me into an annexed room where he stored lots of medical texts, pamphlets and other things. He seemed to forget I was right behind him. As I looked around, right there, hung on the wall, in a frame, was a picture of three Nazi soldiers. One of them looked exactly like him. Same coloring, same receding hairline, same shape of his face, and even that dark piercing look of his eyes. No question, they could be related. No question."

"Rainee, do you mean you believe that the Nazi was his father?"

"My gut says yes. It's just that I have no proof. He'd be the right age. Oh! Oh! And he said his parents were still alive and living right here in London!"

"You can't believe that was the Nazi that Mrs. Bowman was speaking of?"

"Yes. Well, no. I don't know, but stranger things have happened."

"That would explain her reaction to him. The doctor must be the trigger that brings back all those horrid memories." John rose and began pacing.

Rainee nodded. "Right. One more tidbit I should mention. Mr. Wickham told me there were rumors that a German submarine torpedoed the boat carrying Jana's brother, Max. I researched that. It turns out that he was close. The Luftwaffe sank the boat that Max was probably aboard. However, there were survivors. There's a chance that Max could be alive. A slim chance, perhaps, but still—"

"You didn't tell that to Mrs. Bowman, did you?"

"No, no, of course not. I couldn't. I have no way of knowing if he is alive. I wouldn't want to get her hopes up, but you can bet I'm going to do some detective work."

"All right, count me in. I want to help in any way possible," John said. "Where or how do we begin?"

"I think I'll contact Yad Vashem about Max. Nevertheless, I really want to meet the doctor's father."

"What? No! That could be dangerous."

"I thought of how to do it without raising suspicion. I'll return the textbook the doctor lent me. I'll just do it at his home. That way I can snoop around a little. See if there are any other pictures or Nazi paraphernalia hanging around. Honestly, can you imagine the nerve it takes to parade that stuff around?"

"Well, Rainee, you did say it was in an annex and not hanging on the wall in his office."

"Yes, but why was it even there?"

"I think you've missed your calling. You could have been an investigative journalist. Why don't we discuss this over dinner?"

"I'd love it... although, I can't guarantee I won't drive you nuts until I figure this out."

"Of that, I have no doubt."

The doctor's home address was easier to get than she had anticipated. Rainee called his office and spoke with the receptionist, reminded her who she was and told her she wanted to return a book to the doctor. As expected, the receptionist suggested that she drop it at the office. Rainee was ready and countered with a believable explanation of being across town. The woman readily told her the address. Rainee thought, *Easy... too easy. That could never happen in America.*

It turned out the doctor lived in a very tony neighborhood not far from Buckingham Palace. Lyall Street was a relatively quiet street in the section known as Belgravia. The doctor's white stucco house had topiary on either side of the entrance. Looking up, she saw window boxes with English Ivy overhanging. In fact, the entire street repeated the look. White stucco homes with window boxes only varying in choice of plants. Black iron balconies complimented the black-gated entrances. Regardless of the dreary rain, the whiteness of the neighborhood created a clean and very exclusive look.

Rainee knocked on the front door. No one answered. Disappointed, she was about to leave, when an elderly man opened the door.

"Yes, may I help you?" He held onto the door handle as if it held him up.

Rainee apologized, "I'm sorry for not calling first; I was hoping the doctor would be home. He loaned me this textbook, and I wanted to return it."

The old man said, "My son is not home yet. We don't expect him for another hour."

His son! A chill ran through her body. Her feet became lead, and she became immobilized. Rainee was standing face to face with a suspected Nazi. Then she noticed it—the similarities between them. Those black eyes and a bulbous nose. The old man's head was almost completely bald now, with a few silver hairs remaining. His bushy, overgrown eyebrows were gray.

She knew she had to assuage her own fears and get into that house.

Her heart was beating quickly, which caused her to sound out of breath. "Oh, that's a shame. I did so want to thank him in person. I even brought a thank you gift as well."

"Come in. You can wait for him. No sense standing in the rain." His voice was thick with a German accent. He swung the door wide for her to enter.

Rainee's heart was pounding. "Well, if it's not an imposition. Thank you."

She followed him to the living room. He walked slowly and was hunched over. As they walked the hall corridor, he said, "My wife and I are temporarily living with our son while she recuperates from a hospital stay."

Entering the main living room, she saw a frail woman seated in a wheelchair. She remembered the doctor had mentioned that his mother had multiple sclerosis. She went to shake her hand first and then his.

"Good day, Mr. and Mrs. Wagner."

"Hello." Mrs. Wagner's smile appeared genuine.

"My name is Rainee Allen, and it's a pleasure meeting both of you." She almost gagged on her own words.

"You know my boy, Martin?" Mrs. Wagner accent was not German. To Rainee's ear she sounded like Elsa, her college roommate, from Venezuela. However, she would not dare to presume.

"Only from the brief interview he allowed me. Dr. Wagner was kind enough to lend me this giant medical volume. I often wonder how these doctors get through these texts."

Mrs. Wagner grinned. "Please sit down. May we offer you something to drink?"

"Thank you, no. I just finished a very large cup of coffee. In fact, I would very much appreciate it if I could use your bathroom."

"Certainly. The loo is just down the hall, first door on your left."

As Rainee walked through the hallway, she made a mental note of the pictures that lined the walls. There were many family photos, excluding any with Nazi paraphernalia. She had hoped there would be a definite sign, proof of her suspicion.

She returned to the living room and stopped to admire some photos. "Ah, I can tell that this is Dr. Wagner as a boy. He does look like you, Mr. Wagner. And Mrs. Wagner, he has your smile."

"Yes, that is what they say." She seemed happy that someone noticed the resemblance.

"What are these beautiful mountains behind you?" Rainee asked pointing to a picture.

"Those are a very small portion of the Andes."

"I've read that the Andes are the longest mountain range in the world. That they cover seven countries."

"Yes, including Peru. That is where I grew up and where we lived. The picture was taken in our back yard." Mrs. Wagner became very animated, and Rainee could tell that she wanted to engage her in discussion.

"Peru? Really? You know, I've never been to South America, though I have always wanted to travel there. Is that where you two met?"

"Yes, Ralf had recently moved there when we, quite literally, bumped into each other in the market square. He says it was an accident, but I know better." She giggled like a young girl. "I had seen him eyeing me from a distance. You know men, Miss Allen. They make ridiculous excuses."

"I do know what you mean. Please call me Rainee." She looked over to Mr. Wagner and forced a smile. He was sitting quietly in the corner, absorbing the conversation. She now had a first name. Perhaps that would help her investigation.

"Yes, he was quite the looker back then. Strapping, confident and full of himself." She laughed. "Just one smile and I was smitten immediately."

"Paloma," Mr. Wagner said, "I think this conversation is not of interest to Miss Allen."

"Oh, on the contrary, Mr. Wagner, I enjoy hearing peoples' stories. I'm a writer and I learn a lot from other people. Personal histories fascinate me. As long as we have some time before the doctor comes home, I would love to get to know you, Mrs. Wagner. In fact, you remind me of my aunt... um, my favorite aunt." It was a little white lie. If she could ingratiate herself to this woman, she might be able to extrapolate some information.

"It is still fresh in my mind, like it was yesterday. He *pretended* to bump into me, and I dropped my basket of produce. He apologized profusely and picked it up for me. We spoke for a little while. He asked me when I would next come to market and if he could 'bump into me' again. I told him the day I would be there. Sure enough, he was there waiting for me, with flowers."

"Oh, how romantic."

"We sat at a sidewalk café and talked. He used what little Spanish he knew, and I knew no German. Instead, we spoke the international language of love. Does that sound too corny?" She glanced at her husband. "Am I embarrassing you, Ralf?" Then she looked back to Rainee. "He gets embarrassed when I tell the story of how we met. You know men."

Rainee looked over to Mr. Wagner, who looked uncomfortable, squirming in his chair. Did he feel his wife was giving too much information to a stranger? *I suppose when you lived a life that needs to remain hidden and buried, you keep any information close to the vest.* His wife had not revealed anything that could link him to the Nazi party, so she assumed that was why he had remained silent.

Rainee turned to him. "And you, Mr. Wagner? It seems you were understandably crazy about your wife immediately."

"Yes, I was. She stood out in the crowded market. Delicate and beautiful. She still is."

Mrs. Wagner blushed. Rainee wondered whether she knew of her husband's true past or whether she even cared. Perhaps she was just willfully naïve. *What would a young girl in Peru know of what was happening in the Pacific or Europe? There were parts of the world that were not involved with that war. Perhaps they lived in a remote area of Peru.* "Where in Peru were you born, Mrs. Wagner?"

The sound of keys opening the front door put an end to the conversation. The doctor walked in and was visibly surprised to see Rainee conversing with his parents. For only a moment, he stood like a deer in the headlights. "Ms. Allen, this is a surprise."

"Hello, Doctor. It's nice to see you again. I wanted to return your book and thank you for lending it to me. I did find some helpful information."

"Excuse me for sounding a little disconcerted, but how did you find out where I live? My office staff knows not to give out that kind of information." He put down his briefcase and took off his raincoat.

"Oh, I told your receptionist that I wanted to return it and had a gift of thanks." Rainee took a small package out of her purse and handed it to the doctor. "I've had the loveliest conversation with your parents."

"This gift was not necessary."

"I know. It's merely a token of my thanks. I noticed that you used a fountain pen, so this is another to add to your collection."

"Well, thank you. Hello, Mother. Father." He leaned over to kiss his mother. "Feeling better?"

"My spirits have been lifted talking with Rainee. She's a good listener. I told her about the first time your father and I met and how we fell in love. By the way Rainee, I didn't ask you if you were married." She glanced over to her son with a raised eyebrow.

Rainee laughed. "No, Mrs. Wagner. Guess I haven't found Mr. Right. I was not as lucky as you and Mr. Wagner."

"Well, don't give up dear. I'm sure he's out there. Perhaps you will *bump* into him sooner than you think."

Rainee said, "Well, I'd better go to the market more often then." Rainee liked the doctor's mother and winked at her.

Mrs. Wagner said, "I would enjoy it if you would visit again. We're moving back to our place as soon as I fully recuperate. We don't get many visitors, and I miss talking with a woman."

"I assure you that I'd enjoy the visit just as much. Thank you for the invitation."

Dr. Wagner offered his arm. "Allow me to walk you out."

Rainee recognized that was her cue to leave. She said her goodbyes to the Wagners.

There was no definite evidence to convince anyone that Mr. Wagner had been a Nazi. Nevertheless, Rainee could not deny her gut feeling, and now she had a first name. She could contact the Simon Wiesenthal Center, which she knew has a vast library of Holocaust information and was successful in hunting Nazis.

Even at an advanced age, if a Nazi was discovered, they faced deportation and prosecution. There was no statute of limitations on murder. In the 1960s, Israel's Mossad found Adolf Eichmann in Argentina, prosecuted him in Israel and then hung him. Nazis like Josef Mengele and many others had fled to South America. It was logical to assume that this German found his way to Peru, fell in love and married. *When did they return to London? How have they managed to keep their past life a secret for so many years? Was the doctor born in South America?* Rainee couldn't quite pinpoint his definite accent, a combination of Spanish and the Queen's English.

Arriving at the apartment after a long day of work, Shelley greeted her and suggested they go out to dinner. Rainee was relieved for the distraction and knew it was too early to make a call to the States. It could wait until after dinner.

JANA — 1948

David and I were married in a civil ceremony, along with twenty other couples. Ivey couldn't get the time off, so Freda stood up for me. David's younger brother, Samuel, stood up for him. I saved enough money to design and create my own dress. I copied a design in a movie magazine and borrowed beads from the costume shop at the Palladium with every intention of returning them after our wedding. However, I knew I would not be able to bring myself to dismantle my beautiful dress.

Feeling guilty, I did go to my boss, the head costumer and confessed. She laughed and told me, "Don't you dare be poppin' one bead out of that dress. We have hundreds, and darlin', they're not exactly real pearls. They're Lucite!" I was so relieved, since I had promised Ivey and Freda they could wear it when they married.

For our honeymoon we drove to Ellesmere Port near Cheshire. David had family there, and they owned an empty family cottage with a view of the River Mercey, which led to the Irish Sea. That meant I would see an ocean for the first time for the Irish Sea led out to the Atlantic. David would make sure it would all be very romantic.

Driving along the English countryside was an eye-opening experience for me. There were many farms along the route. I fought to keep my farming memories buried. I was determined that nothing would ruin this honeymoon.

We passed many enormous cathedrals. I marveled at how old they were, many built over five hundred years ago. How could they have withstood the destruction the war had brought? David was a wealth of information, describing how the masons built these cathedrals, and that many people had lost their lives falling from the scaffolding. I pondered how masons in those days could build a fortress, but not scaffolding that was safe.

We took our time driving toward Ellesmere Port, stopping for a picnic lunch and kisses.

When we arrived at the cottage, David's second cousins on his mother's side greeted us. They were very welcoming and kind. We were given a tour of our honeymoon cottage, which they proudly had garlanded with flowers. They went out of their way to make it special for us. On our first evening, they invited us to dine with them. Little did we know all his many relatives had been invited. Soon music filled the evening air. David and I loved it because we had not had a wedding party, and this festivity was a grand way to mark our nuptials.

One cousin, a burly man with thick black hair and arms as large as tree trunks, took a formal picture of us. I promised David that I would put the picture in the silver frame given to us as a wedding present by Freda.

We danced and drank and danced some more. At last, relatives began to disperse to their own homes and the party began to die down. Irmegarde, the eldest and wisest of his cousins, and to whom I will forever be grateful, suggested, "Everyone should be on their way and let the honeymooners begin their honeymoon."

David, who was quite drunk with a knowing grin on his face, nodded in accord.

He lifted me in his arms and those few who had remained cheered. He carried me to our honeymoon cottage, reeling a bit from drink. I was a little scared that we would fall, but he managed to open the door.

I had seen him tipsy on beer before, but never this drunk. Mr. Wickham's face popped into my head, and I became overcome with fright. I was frightened of the man I loved, a man whom I knew would never hurt me. I told him that I would change and meet him in the bedroom. I asked him to close the window in that room. He protested a little, saying that it would be too hot. I asked him again, saying that I was chilled. In truth, I wanted the room to get hot. I hoped it would induce sleep in him.

I went to the outside water closet to change and stayed there for almost half an hour. When I entered the cottage, David was in our honeymoon bed, fast asleep and snoring. I felt guilty but relieved. Very careful not to wake him, I slipped into the bed and allowed myself to fall asleep.

In the morning, I awoke to the sound of David vomiting outside the front door. Then he rinsed out his mouth. He came into the bedroom and back into bed. David was so apologetic about falling asleep that I felt bad for him and confessed my connivance. That's when it all came out. I told him about Mr. Harvey's rape, and that was why I had been so scared of his drunkenness the night before. He held me and cried. He promised he would never force me to make love with him. He promised he would never get so drunk that he would be out of control. I loved him for that.

I held back one crucial part of the story. I told him Wickham had raped me. I did not tell him about the fireplace poker. I had seen a doctor once and after his examination, he implied that scar tissue had formed over the opening of my cervix. He said it would make it impossible for sperm to get through in numbers large enough for me to get pregnant. The doctor had been very matter-of-fact about it. He didn't ask me questions, so I never asked him questions. I presumed the trauma of the rape caused my condition. I could not know for sure.

I knew I should have been forthright about not being able to have children, but I just couldn't, not then. Not on our honeymoon, when all possibilities of our life together were made of happy plans. I reasoned that perhaps in the future, when he would speak of children, I would nod and agree. Was I lying to my own husband or just omitting the facts? He would find out in the future; of that, I was sure. I wanted to enjoy our week together. After all, how many honeymoons does a person get?

The second night we made love for the first time. David was gentle and patient. However, the pain was excruciating. I wanted to yell; instead, I bit my lip. How could I do this to him, my sweet David? I endured the pain.

I was happy to hold my new husband in my arms as his body gave way into a giant shudder. His sperm entered me, searching for a target that was unattainable. He whispered how much he loved me. How happy he was. I could not say it back at that moment, even though I felt the same love. The guilt of withholding information from him stopped me. I just tightened my embrace. I was a lucky woman to find such a man.

We spent most of our honeymoon in our cottage near the canal. We would venture out to explore the land, and we always hurried to get back to the warmth of the cottage and the warmth of our bodies. I was relieved that the pain lessened each time we made love.

David suggested, "Let's make a pact to not allow any serious talk for the rest of our honeymoon. Life will surely bring that to us in the future. For now, we can be unaware and innocent of the real world. We can live in the magic of this remarkable week and hold that in our memories forever."

I agreed with unspoken appreciation.

RAINEE — 1997

At first, the receptionist at the Simon Wiesenthal Center was not very receptive. They received many calls from all over the world, and from many kooks. Rainee wondered, *Isn't that their job, to follow through on leads? There must be a way to circumvent the receptionist.* She realized her secret weapon had been there all along: Gary, her literary agent. He could make just one call, and she would be able to speak to anyone she wanted.

"I've been wondering when I would hear from you. Rainee, you know your deadline is looming." The voice that was once full of patience now sounded exasperated.

"I know, I know, Gary. I'm begging you to give me a bit more time. I have something here. Something that I think is big. It'll make a helluva story. And probably even a helluva movie."

"Okay, now you've got my attention."

Rainee related her whole state of affairs, everything that had happened to her since her arrival in England. Gary listened without interruption. Rainee could hear him take an occasional sip of what she assumed was one of his constant cups of espresso. She once had suggested he should have his caffeine delivered intravenously.

When she finished, he said, "So you never had a story for me? I mean, before you left for England?"

Rainee felt bad that he sounded aggravated. She owed him the truth. "To be honest, Gary, I was blocked and stalling. I'm sorry.

Really. Truly sorry. But when I came across Jana's ID card, I knew there was a story there. I'm just grateful she is still alive and that I was able to find her. She's an amazing woman. You must meet her."

"So this is a biography?"

"No, I don't want to do that. I'm not sure I could do her justice. You know I'm a fiction writer. She's become my muse, and I want to base this story on her. You know, change the names to protect the innocent, etc., etc."

"What about this Nazi? Should you be messing around with that?" The sound of concern in his voice reminded Rainee of the paternal presence he had displayed when her first novel came out.

"Well, here's the thing: I can't prove he is the Nazi that Jana believes him to be, or even a Nazi at all. This brings me to why I called. I need to ask another favor of you. Besides, your patience, I mean."

"What do you need?"

"I want to speak with someone at the Simon Wiesenthal Center. I can't get past the receptionist. They have a script with a list of questions, and I can't get them off that damned script. If you could speak with someone there as a representative of the publishing house, I have no doubt you'd be able to open the door for me. Ask about a Nazi named Ralf Wagner."

Reading from her notes, Rainee said, "Take down these facts: Disappeared to South America. Responsible for killing children awaiting a kindertransport from Holland to England. In collusion with the bombing of a cargo ship by Luftwaffe aircraft, October, 1940. The boat was the *Prinses Juliana* out of the Netherlands in the North Sea, off Hoek van Holland. Jana's brother, Max, was supposed to be on board that ship. Ask if Wagner is a person of interest to them." She could hear Gary writing down her instructions.

He asked her to spell out the foreign words.

She did, then said, "And get this, Gary: there were survivors who were rescued by the Royal Navy. Slim chance, but perhaps Max was one of them."

"Are you sure about all this, Rainee? Are you sure you want to keep investigating this? I mean, it sounds dangerous to me. And, if you're keeping it fiction, why even—"

"Because I want to see this man brought to justice. Not just for Jana, but also for all those families he obliterated. What right does he have to live and walk freely among those whose lives he affected? No, this has become personal."

"Rainee, I know you. You can be impulsive. Don't do anything stupid."

"Don't worry, Gary; they have no idea that I suspect anything. And even if I'm wrong, I'm still left with a great story. I'll fill in the blanks with my writer's prowess."

"Yes, but think this out. What if you're right? You could be in great danger. I understand there are underground movements that protect their own."

"That's why I need to find out about this guy. If the Center confirms him, get me a name of someone in charge there. I will contact them and get them pictures, anything they would need."

Gary sighed. "I hope you know what you're doing. I'll get back to you as soon as I know something. I'll email the information."

Rainee sat beside Jana as the older woman slept upright in her chair. She had arrived after lunch, and she did not want to awaken her. She took the opportunity to write some notes. The receptionist,

Red, had informed her that John was on a home visit and would not return for another hour.

As she scribbled her thoughts, she realized that she had not felt this passionate about anything since she had written her debut novel. The words came at high-speed and her pen seemed to have a life of its own as her thoughts spilled onto the paper. She'd left her laptop behind because it was heavy, and the weight hurt her shoulder. She would transcribe her notes later.

Was Gary right? And John? Was there danger here and was she being too impulsive? With all her suspicion, how could she stop now? Thoughts were beginning to cloud her writing. She had bitten down a fingernail to the cuticle and it was beginning to bleed. Wondering if she could find a Band-Aid in Jana's bathroom vanity, she entered the tiny bathroom and closed the door. Other than basic hygiene belongings, the vanity was empty. She knew she could go down the hall and ask Red. Instead, the thought occurred to her that an opportunity existed which had never cropped up before. Jana was deep in sleep; no one was around, and Rainee had the opportunity to go through Jana's bureau, bookshelf, and desk. She could dig about for some clues to her past life.

She had her hand on the top shelf when she stopped herself. *Wait one minute. You idiot. Don't be stupid. You have no right to invade Jana's privacy, rummaging through her private things. Who do you think you are? Stop this lunacy now. You would be crossing the line.*

Rainee looked at Jana. She had become fond of her and wanted to protect her in any way possible. If that meant searching for information, then so be it.

She very quietly opened the top drawer and reached in. Gently trying not to muss the contents of the drawers, she examined everything then put it all back as she had found it. She felt frustration mixed with happiness to find nothing unusual. She needed something... a clue to further her determination to help Jana.

In the last drawer was a jewelry box that held the wooden peacock necklace Max had carved. She gently removed and studied it. It had been crudely carved by a teenager, and she smiled recalling the look in Jana's eyes when she had related the story of how and why Max had made it for her. Was this the mysterious massaging of her neck... an unworn necklace?

In the bed, Jana stirred. Quickly and quietly, Rainee returned the necklace to its box and the box to its drawer.

Rainee sat back down, stricken with guilty thoughts. She had crossed the line. She entered into a virtual stranger's life and entangled herself in it. With no invitation, she had taken license to intrude. What license did she have? Literary license does not give you the right to invade another's life. She had to rethink this. She had to talk to someone about this. She knew that someone was John. She decided she would leave a note on his desk asking to get together. She left as Jana slept.

Gary sent an email with the name and direct number of someone to contact at the Wiesenthal Center. That person would be waiting for her call.

Rainee called the direct line to Lillian Frances. "Ms. Allen, I'm glad you called. Mr. Edwards told me to expect you. Please tell me everything you know. Don't leave out anything. I'll be taking notes, so I won't interrupt."

The entire story poured out while Ms. Frances listened attentively. Rainee heard her occasionally take a long drag of a cigarette, and then slowly expel the smoke.

At the finish of her exposition, Ms. Frances confirmed the existence of a known Nazi by the name of Ralf Wagner. "I have an entire file on him. He also went by the aliases of Wolfgang VonWagner and Rolf VanValkenburg. He escaped to Venezuela and disappeared somewhere in South America."

Rainee gasped. "It was Peru. No doubt he kept wandering until he ended up in a small village where anonymity became his companion. Probably, his young wife had no idea who she was to marry."

Ms. Frances continued with more information. "He is wanted for crimes unimaginable. Crimes against humanity. Though never implicated in the specific attack on the ship carrying Max Lutken, it is possible that he executed the orders to separate the children and later put the boys on the boat."

"He was the Nazi Jana saw?"

"Yes, it's possible he was responsible for the murder of those children whose bodies were left on the wharf. Apparently, the Nazis left expeditiously since the sounds of their Karabiner rifles echoed for miles."

"Running scared? Hard to believe they would be afraid of the townspeople. After all, they were the ones carrying the weapons."

"True." Ms. Frances shuffled some papers and continued to read. "When the townspeople arrived, the second boat had already left with the boys and there was no one found alive. The sight of blood and dead boys horrified them. Luckily, the citizens were courageous enough to photograph the remains of the scene, further proof of the massacre. The Center is in possession of those original pictures. I've seen them. Horrendous. The dead children's identification cards and suitcases were sent to the local authorities."

Ms. Frances continued her reading. "According to the dock master, the second boat arrived less than thirty minutes after the first departed and not the reported two-hour difference you had stated."

"Thirty minutes? The Luftwaffe could have easily caught up to the first boat."

Ms. Frances said, "Yes, it's surprising that the Luftwaffe didn't catch up with the first ship. However, there's reason to believe the captain of that ship may have been made aware of the impending attack and out-maneuvered them." She went on to report other well-documented atrocities that Ralf Wagner committed. "Eventually, he was ordered to work at the extermination camp, Sobibor. Right up his alley, no doubt. Other than one sighting of him in South America, we lost track of him. All documents were, of course, forged back then, and Nazis scattered throughout the world... even to America."

This was a lot for Rainee to take in. "Ms. Frances, what if what I suspect is true? What will happen to Mr. Wagner?"

"We would set the wheels in motion immediately. We'd send our people in London to collect him, interrogate him, his wife, son, and his friends. If we can prove unequivocally that this is the same Nazi, he will be deported and he will face trial. I would hope that he'd spend the remainder of his miserable life in prison. It's doubtful that they would execute him because of his advanced age, but that's always a possibility."

"What if I am wrong?"

"Well, either way the truth will come out."

"Isn't that like a judge telling the jury to disregard what they just heard? Who can really do that? I couldn't. To everyone he'd be guilty by inference. Wouldn't he? And what happens to his family?

His wife has multiple sclerosis and needs him. His son is a respectable doctor and has a thriving practice."

Ms. Frances' tone turned to granite. "It is not about them. It is about the father. Assuming he is guilty, then if they know about his past and can live with it, they should be living in shame themselves. There is the possibility that they know nothing of his past. After all, you said his wife met him in a remote village in Peru. His son was born there. There's no knowledge of when he moved to London. As I said, the truth will come out and then we'll be able to give you answers."

The dizzying image of a young Jana Lutken watching with horror as children were being slaughtered went through Rainee's head, and she said, "Okay, what do you need from me? What can I do to help?"

"First, we need an address."

"I don't have one. They were living with the son temporarily and may not be there anymore."

"Then just sit tight, Ms. Allen. We'll be in touch."

John and Rainee sat in a booth in a coffee shop not far from the nursing home. Rainee told him everything she had learned.

He became incensed. "The truth will come out? The truth will come out? Bullocks! That's easy for her to say! What about the danger you could be putting yourself in?" He paused. "Rainee, have you thought about the danger to Mrs. Bowman?"

The last sentence startled Rainee, and they both fell silent. Finally Rainee said, "My God, John, what have I started? What have I done?" Tears filled her eyes, and she reached for a napkin.

John moved from across the table to sit beside her. He put his arm around her as she wiped her tears. "Why the hell can't I cry like those Hollywood stars? I look terrible. My eyes get swollen; my nose fills up, and I can't breathe. Damn it! I'm a mess. Don't look at me." She hid her head in her hands.

John smiled. "You look beautiful to me." He pulled down her hands and lifted her face to his. Slowly, he drew her closer to kiss her.

"Wait," she said, then she blew her nose.

He smiled and waited patiently, then said, "Okay, where were we? Rainee, is this what they mean by a kissing booth?"

They both laughed.

The kiss was tentative at first, slow and gentle, their lips barely touching. Then he took hold of her waist, pulled her into him, and kissed her with deep longing. Rainee became lost in his kiss. Oblivious of her usual embarrassment with public affection, she returned his kiss passionately.

The waiter brought the check to the table, interrupting them. "You might want to get a room," he said.

Rainee whispered, "Good idea."

The short ride in the tiny elevator was filled with anticipation. They held hands as they walked to her apartment. She fumbled with the keys, dropping them. John picked them up and unlocked the front door. To be sure they were alone, Rainee called out Shelley's name and received no response. She pulled him into her bedroom, and their passion erupted.

He kissed her slowly; he kissed her deeply; he kissed her gently, and he kissed her hard. She followed his lead. He was on top of her and before long inside of her. He pulled out right before he brought her to climax. He was an experienced lover. Rainee was convinced he had five hands moving all at once. She was getting dizzy with his weight on her. He sensed that immediately, and with one swift movement, he flipped her so that she was on top.

He whispered in her ear, but she wasn't listening to his words, for her mind was on what was happening to her body. No lover had ever made her reach this level of ecstasy. She started to laugh right in the middle of making love. She laughed until she cried. John stopped and looked at her. He parted her hair, which had covered her face. "Are you okay? Am I hurting you?"

"Good God, no, John. It's just that I thought I was feeling... ecstasy." Rainee laughed "Ecstasy... it sounds like something out of a trite romance novel. No, please don't stop now. You are definitely *not* hurting me. I've never felt this good." They continued until fatigue defeated them, and they both fell into a contented sleep.

When he awakened, it was already late afternoon. Neither John nor Rainee had planned what occurred. He had missed two meetings, and he knew the nursing home would have been trying to call him. He moved Rainee's arm, which was draped across his chest, sat on the edge of the bed, and stealthily took his mobile phone out of his jacket pocket. Sure enough, there were four missed calls. He pulled on his slacks and went into the living room to check the messages. He called the office and spoke as quietly as possible into his phone.

Rainee awakened to the whispered sounds coming from the other room. She smiled, and her head swirled at what had happened. She remembered uttering the word "ecstasy" and started to giggle quietly.

John was leaning on the doorframe watching her giggle. "Something tickle your fancy?" He sat down on the edge of the bed and kissed her.

"You," she whispered. "You tickle my fancy."

"Rainee, I hate to leave you. I blew off two meetings and a host of other duties. And yes, I would do it again in a heartbeat. Meet me for dinner tonight. Please."

"Like you have to ask? I'll be here waiting." She walked him to the door, locked it behind him, and whispered, "Ecstasy."

To her astonishment, three of her eight weeks in London had passed, but she had come far in her research. Nevertheless, she had a relatively short time to solve the mysteries that surrounded Jana. She had uncovered enough information to make a nice fictional story, filling in all the blanks with literary license. However, this had become personal to her. Rainee was no longer associated with fictional characters. They were factual. They were real. They were human. She had feelings for two of them. She had suspicions about two others. Rainee had to see this through, even if it meant prolonging her stay.

Shelley was very busy with her training at work, and it was at sporadic dinners that the two friends would bring each other up to date. It would not be in Shelley's best interests to reveal all Rainee had learned. If there was any danger in her pursuits, she did not want to put Shelley in harm's way.

When the two friends went out to dinner, Rainee let Shelley ramble on about work and the people she had met. Rainee did disclose her growing feelings for John. When Shelley questioned the development of her research, she sidetracked the conversation back to John, knowing that Shelley was glad to engage in that subject.

Outside the restaurant, they hailed a taxi.

Both women were unaware of the black sedan with darkened windows that followed them to their apartment building.

They walked into the apartment and turned on the lights, inadvertently signaling the driver of the black sedan which apartment was Rainee's. He leaned out of his window, aimed his camera at the building, took some pictures, and drove away.

Inside the apartment, Rainee was pulling down the window shades. She frowned. She could have sworn a figure in a black sedan had pulled in what looked like a camera with a very long lens. However, it was all so fast. She waved the thought away, thinking she was just paranoid.

That night as she lay in bed, she began to contemplate the warnings of John, Gary, and Ms. Frances. There were dangers in hunting Nazis. What had begun as investigating a suspicion may have escalated to a new level. If she were right about Mr. Wagner, it would all be justified. But what if she was wrong? Alerting the Wiesenthal Center with mere suspicion had probably generated a signal to mobilize an army. They had told her to "sit tight." What did that mean? Were they taking control now? Rainee had given them the information that the Wagners had been staying at their son's home. Didn't they say they were going home as soon as she recuperated? What if they were still there? If she could obtain the doctor's address, the Center would have no problem getting it. She had the definite impression that the couple did not leave the house too often. The doctor had a housekeeper for shopping and chores. She could tell that the mother was desperate for female companionship. Perhaps she could get close to Paloma. It was hard to fall asleep with all of the questions buzzing in her head.

She needed information on how Nazi hunters worked. Perhaps her contact at Yad Vashem would know. She would call Ilana in the morning and then head to the library for more research. She had to figure out how to backtrack her steps in case she was wrong. Her suspicions, if erroneous, could ruin the lives of some innocent people. *On the other hand....*

Rainee looked at the clock. She was wide awake and it was three o'clock in the morning. She got out of bed and went to the living room window. Carefully, she moved the shade to look out. There did not appear to be anything out of the ordinary. At least, not to her untrained eye. Rainee dismissed the notion. "This is absurd, and I'm being paranoid. I have to get some sleep. I'm visiting Jana in a few hours."

The sun was trying its best to appear, but grey clouds were thwarting its attempts. Rainee opened her umbrella as the first drops of rain began to fall on her walk to the tube station.

Entering the nursing home, she inquired at the desk as to whether John was there. Red told her that he would be in meetings until noon. She went down the hall to Jana's room, hoping to find her in a lucid state of mind.

Dr. Wagner came out of a patient's room. Rainee smiled. "Hello, Doctor."

"Ah, Ms. Allen. A pleasure seeing you again."

"I hope you mean that, Doctor. I apologize if you felt my presence in your home was an intrusion. I assure you it wasn't meant to be."

"And my apologies for seeming rude. I was a bit startled to see you outside the office. Then again, you're not a patient, so there was no reason for concern on my part."

Rainee smiled. "Good. Friends again?" She thrust out her hand to shake.

He took it in his and held it for a moment. "Friends." His smile was boyishly charming, softening his dark eyes.

"Doctor, I—"

"If we are friends, please call me Martin."

She nodded. "Thank you. And... Rainee, please."

Rainee continued. "Martin, I'd like to offer to take your mother to tea. At the risk of sounding... no, *being* nosy, she appeared in need of some female company. She did ask me to return for a visit. She's a lovely woman, and I would enjoy it too." Rainee used her sweetest and flirtiest smile, hoping he would not say no.

"Well... um...." He looked down at his feet. "Because of her recent hospital stay, it would be nice to get her out of the house. Perhaps, and this is just a thought, my father could deliver her to you. They have a van, adapted for her wheelchair. He could drop her off with you and leave to get some much-needed respite. You know, I think that's a wonderful idea."

"I'm not familiar with London; would you recommend a nice place for tea? Or better yet, a place your Mom favored and has not visited in a while?"

"Brilliant. I'll find out from her. I'm sure she would love that."

"I hope she's well enough to go out?"

"Yes, they're back in their own place." Rainee experienced slight relief at hearing that.

They exchanged phone numbers, and he went on with his rounds.

Glad she had bumped into the doctor, Rainee hoped that with any luck, Paloma would reveal more information about her husband's past.

She knocked on Jana's door. When she entered, Jana's eyes brightened and her face lit up with a big smile.

Rainee smiled back and leaned over her wheelchair to hug her.

"Rainee, thanks for visiting."

"Ms. Bowman, you are the highlight of my day. How are you feeling?"

"I feel wonderful. I think I may have depressed you with my life story on your last visit. I'm so very sorry for that. Honestly, my dear, it felt like a purging. I feel lighter somehow. Thank you for letting me vent."

"Whenever you want to talk, I will listen."

"There's no one here I can talk to. Most of the residents are living with their own troubles. You might think that people who spend twenty-four hours a day together would get to know each other. Not so, Rainee. We live in our own small worlds. Look around my room. What is here? I have lived a long life, and this is all that is left of it. A few picture albums of people who are no longer alive. Some books, an oil painting that was already here when I arrived, some clothes that have other patient's names on the tags. Yes, the laundry confuses our clothes. That's not what matters."

"What does matter?"

"It is the memories of the past. My future surrounds me, and that won't change. This little room is sadly my future. So it is the past that matters. I live with memories that horrify me. I try to compensate with the good memories of my husband and our life together. It was a good life. Now I look forward to your visits,

Rainee. You bring sunshine when you come. I want to thank you for that." She reached out to take Rainee's hand.

"I feel the same. When I just entered and you smiled, it melted my heart. Do you remember when we met I told you we had a connection? Our birthday. Honestly, I feel there's more to our connection. I'm not sure what that thing is, but I feel it. Now that you have shared your past with me, I feel it even more. You've honored me." She squeezed Jana's hand.

"Well, now you know about me, but I don't know about you. Tell me about your life."

Rainee sat on the edge of Jana's bed and told her about her life. The two women laughed and spent a couple of hours exchanging stories. Rainee was happy to see that Jana was lucid the entire time. It had been the longest span of clarity since she had met her. She instructed Rainee to call her Jana.

"I have an idea, Jana. It has stopped raining and the skies have lightened up. Would you like to get out of here? Perhaps a stroll in your neighborhood? I can push your wheelchair, and you'll get fresh air. How about it?"

"You mean breathe London's smog? Sure, I would love that."

Rainee put a shawl over Jana's shoulders, grabbed an umbrella just in case, and signed her out.

They strolled the length of the street and took some turns to Regents Park.

All the while, they were unaware of the black sedan that was following.

Rainee remembered the little packet of Saltine crackers she had stuffed in her purse. She cracked them, and they fed the pigeons. She was pleased that Jana was having a day out, but she was very aware that the day would come too soon when she would say goodbye and return to Boston. Jana's world would shrivel again with no one to brighten it.

Despite the inevitable, she would enjoy this day and swore to herself that she would visit each day for the rest of her time in London.

Though it was only seven o'clock, she was drowsy when she returned to the apartment. She lay down on the sofa and fell into a deep sleep. She was unaccustomed to the amount of walking she was doing in London. Boston was also a walking city, but she either used her car or spent most of her days in her Copley Square neighborhood. Everything she needed was right there: shopping, the Boston Public Library, her favorite restaurants, and the best coffee shop in the city. She was feeling her age. *The forties are the new thirties. Do people really believe that crap?*

Her mobile phone woke her.

"Hello."

"Hi, Rainee. It's Martin."

She shook off the haze of sleep. *Martin? Oh, the doctor.* "Hi Martin."

"I wanted to let you know that my father's willing to drive my mother to meet you for tea. You said I should suggest a place. My mother used to enjoy meeting her friends at a hotel called the Rubens at the Palace. You'll enjoy it; it's across from Buckingham Palace. It's a bit pricey, so allow me to pay for this."

"Oh no, thanks for offering, but I wouldn't hear of that. This is a treat for me as well."

"Stubborn American, I see."

"You have no idea, Martin."

"Tomorrow at two o'clock? I'll call the hotel to reserve a table for you. I can have my father pick you up."

"Well, I appreciate that, but I'll be out and about, so it's best I meet them there. I've got a pen handy; the address is...?"

Martin told her the address and thanked her for giving his mother this opportunity to connect with another woman.

At two o'clock sharp, Rainee arrived at the hotel and followed the signs to the tearoom. The room overwhelmed her with its femininity. Vases were brimming with pink tea roses on tables covered with laced linen. Lit candles were centerpieces, and the aroma of fresh flowers and potpourri filled the air. Several elegant women with white gloves and hats were already seated. Rainee was decidedly underdressed. Official teatime began at two o'clock at this hotel, and these women were members of the old-school teetotalers. Their napkins placed daintily on their laps, they awaited the servers who knew each of them by name.

Rainee gave her name to the hostess and informed her she was waiting for Paloma Wagner to join her. Led to a corner table, she took her seat facing the entrance.

Soon she spotted Paloma being wheeled toward her. She smiled, stood and greeted both of them. Mr. Wagner maneuvered the chair into place. She noticed the white gloves and a hat. The flowered dress made her look years younger than when they had first met. Paloma chose to sit on the lace-backed chairs, so she rose from the wheelchair and transferred herself onto the chair. Mr. Wagner assisted his wife, kissed her on the cheek, told her he would be in the pub next door, and left.

"Thank you for inviting me to tea. It was lovely of you to ask." A broad smile crossed her face as she looked about the familiar surroundings.

"It's my pleasure. As a stranger in a strange city, I know I'll enjoy this. You'll have to walk me through this. I've never been to high tea before."

"Really? Well, you are in for an experience, my dear."

The server approached their table. "It's so nice to see you again, Mrs. Wagner. Welcome back. You have been missed." Paloma shook hands with her and introduced her to Rainee.

"Your return is special, indeed. We will roll out the red carpet just for you."

Rainee almost gagged from the server's solicitous manner.

"Margaret, be a dear and explain to my companion how tea works."

Rainee smiled as Margaret chirped on and on about high tea and its history and the Rubens Hotel. She was not listening. Her own agenda and the questions in her head drowned out the server's prattle.

Paloma drilled Rainee with questions about her life "across the pond." It was obvious to Rainee that Paloma had her own interests in mind—that of a wife for her son—so she answered the questions prudently.

The server returned and placed a three-tiered plate filled with finger sandwiches, scones and jams, petit fours and assorted desserts on the table. Tea was chosen and poured. Then Paloma talked and talked and talked. Her entire monologue was about her visits to this tearoom with her girlfriends. It was unmistakable that this outing gave her a huge feeling of liberation.

Rainee wondered, *If Paloma was a regular at this tearoom, what happened to her girlfriends? Did they dismiss her when her multiple sclerosis worsened?* It was a question that Rainee wanted to ask, but she refrained as it was not her place. "Tell me more about you and your life. Living in England must be radically different from South America. Was the move difficult for you?"

"No, not really. I knew we would end up here someday. Ever since my Martin was a young boy Ralf had said that we would live in England. In fact, he insisted we all learn English. Martin must have been about eight or so, when Ralf announced how important it was to learn English."

"Oh, why?" Rainee inquired.

"I can't remember his words exactly; of course, it was so many years ago. He was determined that Martin acquire a good education. He didn't think he would get that in Peru. There was an American piano teacher who was travelling, who wanted to learn Spanish. So we taught him Spanish, and he taught us American... I mean, English." She giggled at her faux pas.

"Did Martin go to school in England?"

"Not until medical school. He became a doctor here and then sent for us. He's a good son. He'll make a good husband someday." She smiled.

"Yes, he is a nice man. He was very helpful to me and generous with his time, allowing me that interview. My, he certainly looks like his father."

"Yes, I joke that we cloned Ralf. He does look like his father when his father was his age. I have no pictures of Ralf or his family, from before I met him, so it's hard to know what his ancestors looked like. For instance, I have hazel eyes, but Ralf has dark brown eyes, and Martin's are dark, dark brown... almost black."

"I think recessive genes factor in when it comes to eyes. You're right; it could be from an ancestor."

Tea was flowing and before long Rainee needed to use the powder room. As she was about to excuse herself, it occurred to her that Paloma might have the same need. "Mrs. Wagner, I need to use the powder room; I'd be happy to assist you, if you are in need."

"Oh, thank you dear. No, I've been drinking tea for many years now. I'm used to it. You go, and I will be right here when you get back. It's kind of you to ask." Rainee was certainly garnering points.

She found her way to the restroom. It was well-lit and filled with the scent of roses and potpourri. Rainee thought, *All this place needs is an estrogen pill dispenser*. On her way back to the tearoom, she noticed two men in dark suits sitting in the lounge. They appeared to be talking to each other; one glanced her way, then turned away abruptly when she looked at him. They both faked laughter, too loud and too disingenuous. A chill of fear went right up her spine to her neck. *Ah, that's where the word "spine-chilling" comes from,* she thought. *Who are these guys? Is this my imagination?*

Sitting down, Rainee noted that Paloma had ordered another pot of tea. "I selected a particular tea for you. I hope you don't mind, dear. This one was always my favorite."

"Not at all. Thank you." She paused. "Mrs. Wagner, may I ask you a question? As a writer, I love to hear the histories of people. You know, what makes them click and all. If I make you uncomfortable, just tell me it's none of my business. I'll understand."

Paloma smiled. "Please, I have no secrets. Ask away."

"Thank you. When you first met Mr. Wagner, you were a young girl living in a small village. Were the villagers aware there was a war going on in Europe?"

"Oh my dear, our village was so far from civilization, that we were hardly aware of what was going on in the next village. Seeing a foreigner come through became a major event. Mr. Wagner's appearance was fodder for talk. When I first heard of this visitor, I immediately left my chores and went to the market square. I pretended to be shopping for fruits and vegetables. I spotted him speaking with the café owner. He later told me he was looking for employment. Our eyes met, and at least for me, time stood still. You know, like in the movies. Everything stopped. He smiled, and I looked away. Nice girls did not flirt. I went home very flustered. A few days later, we saw each other again in the market area. He asked me to sit with him at the café. Oh yes, you knew that already." She stopped to sip her tea before it cooled.

Prodding her to continue, Rainee said, "Wow, this does sound like a movie. Or maybe a good book. Wasn't there a language barrier?"

Paloma put her hand to her chest as she laughed quite noisily. "Oh my, yes! His Spanish had a very different accent, so I assumed he was from a different part of South America. I had never met a German before. He had picked up a very small amount of Spanish, and we struggled to understand each other. He was so gentle and kind to me. I fell in love right then. Not so tall, just dark and handsome. And a foreigner! You could make this a romance novel." She started chuckling.

Laughing along and intrigued, Rainee persisted. "Did he explain what was happening in Europe?"

"Oh yes, of course. He told me he had received papers of conscription into the army, but he'd escaped before he had to show up at the post. He told me he had walked across Germany and most of Europe. He found work on a steamer that landed in South America. He kept walking, kept moving. He was afraid he would be found by the Germans in South America and be forced to return. He did not believe in fighting or killing. He was a peaceful man. So he kept on the move... well, until he saw me. He said he felt safe with me. He felt he was home at last."

Rainee had all she could do to keep from choking on her pastry. *A peaceful man who didn't believe in killing?* Her throat went dry, and she sipped her tea.

"So you married and started a family."

"Yes. We were so very happy. When our village finally heard about World War II, it was already over. I felt bad for Ralf because I knew he did not have a home to return to. He was very silent about his past life. Never talked about it. He forbade me to ask him. I guess it was too painful. You know he had to leave his mother and father."

Rainee's mind was spinning. *Painful? I'll bet it was painful. Getting caught would have caused him a lot of pain.* "Martin must have had questions growing up."

"No, not really. At least, he never asked me. He was forbidden to ask his father. Rainee, dear, are you all right? You look a little green."

"Guess I am not used to all these sweets. I'm fine, Mrs. Wagner. You picked a lovely place for my first tea. Are you doing all right?"

"Oh, you mean my MS? Yes, dear. I've had this heinous disease for almost twenty years. I've adapted. Now and then, I have a relapse and end up in the hospital. Martin allows me to recuperate at his home since he has a housekeeper to help Ralf watch over me. Men do fuss, don't they?"

"I suppose they do."

Placing more sweets on her own plate, Paloma asked Rainee, "Have you ever married, dear?"

"Almost, but it was a long time ago. I was young and hadn't yet experienced life."

"I think you should let Martin show you some of the sights of London. He's a good man... takes after his father."

"I'll be sure to ask him." Rainee thought perhaps that wouldn't be a bad idea. She could dig for more information. *After all, he has that picture in his storage room. He must know something.*

The timing was perfect as Mr. Wagner came toward them. He asked how they had enjoyed their tea and said that Paloma needed her rest.

The women hugged, and he wheeled her out to their van. Rainee eyed the two mysterious men as they watched the Wagners drive away. They put down their newspapers and left. She knew that was no coincidence. But who were they?

Ralf Wagner was very aware of the two men seated in the hotel lobby. They were there when he kissed his wife goodbye, and they were still there when he returned to collect her. His wife had spent two hours with Ms. Allen. He couldn't help be suspicious. Who were they?

He became jittery with paranoia and took a circuitous route to their home. He paced back and forth, from room to room. He kept looking out his front door window. He was well aware of a black sedan parked three houses down.

Why now? He wondered. *After all these years, why now? Does this coincide with the arrival of Ms. Allen? Is she really who she says she is?* He questioned his wife about what they spoke of during their tea.

Paloma was knitting and did not look up once. "Oh, womanly things. She talked about herself. Fascinating life, really. She's a writer, you know. Her book became a movie. We'll see about renting the tape. She asked about us and I told her about how we met. You know, I think she'd make a nice girlfriend for Martin."

Ralf's dark eyes darkened. "What did you tell her about us?"

Still knitting, unaware of her husband's growing anxiety, she said, "How I fell in love with you immediately. I told her that you had escaped Germany just in time. How you walked and walked until you walked into my life."

"Paloma!"

Startled at Ralf's tone, she finally looked up.

"I have told you to *never* talk about our life to anyone. It's no one's business." He fumbled for words. "What... what... what if the Germans became aware I am alive? I was AWOL. They could take me away from you."

"Oh, nonsense, Ralf. That was so long ago. Besides, Rainee was more interested in our love story, and I think she may be interested in Martin. Wouldn't that be nice, darling? I'd love to see Martin settle down. Wouldn't you?"

Ralf realized that his wife could not understand the seriousness of his concern. *Who were those men in suits?*

He left the room and went upstairs to make a phone call in the privacy of their bedroom. Ralf opened the safe in the wall, reached far into the back, and removed a piece of paper almost brittle with age. His hands trembled as he dialed the number.

"You can't begin to imagine the world of good you did for Mrs. Bowman." John held Rainee close in his king-sized bed. Her scent intoxicated him. "Getting outside of the nursing home and smelling fresh air was rejuvenating for her. I may have even caught her smiling."

"No! Smiling? Not really. Not our Jana Bowman." Rainee laughed. "I had fun too. We even laughed together. I think she's come to trust me. You know, John, in many ways she reminds me of my grandmother. Not her looks, but her.... What's the word I'm searching for? Grace. Yes, grace. She has a kind soul."

"Tell me about your grandmother."

"Well, she's an entire book, right there." She played with the hair on his chest, curling it around her fingers. "They share some of the same qualities. Really. I have become very fond of her."

"Yes, that's quite evident." He stroked her arm.

Rainee was unsure how to approach the next topic. She did not want to scare John, but she needed him to hear something. "Listen John, I need to tell you something. And please don't say anything until I get this out."

"Okay."

"I think I'm being followed."

John bolted straight up. "What?"

"See, I knew you'd react like that, not that I'm not a bit nervous myself. Look, I'm either paranoid or I'm being followed."

"What makes you think that?"

Rainee sat up and faced him. "Two men—London Fog raincoats, fedoras, sunglasses on those rare occasions when the sun comes out here, in a black sedan. Everything you'd read in a John le Carré novel. They seem to pop up wherever I go."

"Rainee, I warned you. You're tangling with the wrong sort. Perhaps now you should call in the police."

"I'm afraid I may have started something. As you know, I alerted the Wiesenthal Center. I thought maybe it's their people following me, hoping I'll lead them to the Wagners. When I had lunch with Mrs. Wagner, they were there. They sat through two hours of our tea. They only got up to leave when we did. I don't think they were aware that I noticed them. At least, I hope not."

"You say they followed you. Did they follow the Wagners when they left?"

Rainee frowned. "Y'know, I'm not sure." She wrapped the bed sheet around her body, got out of bed, and walked to his window. "Shit!"

John jumped out of bed. "What?"

"There's that black sedan. See?" She pointed. "Over there, three cars down." She pointed out a car with two men, one of whom looked like he was asleep. "Why follow me? I'm no Nazi."

"No, however you could lead them to the Nazi. I don't like this, not one bit." John started to get dressed.

"What are you doing?"

"I'm going to have a talk with those gentlemen."

"No, John! My God, now I've got you involved too. What have I done?"

John sat her down on the bed. "Listen Rainee, you did nothing wrong. You stumbled onto something that's too big for you or me to handle alone." He stopped, then said, "Okay, before I go out there and confront these men, let's talk this out. They're obviously not going anywhere."

They went into the kitchen, and John made a pot of coffee. He took out a pad and pen. "Let's start at the beginning."

"The beginning? All I wanted to do was to meet Jana. Who knew this would turn into international intrigue?"

"Summing this all up, you met Jana, and then you met the doctor. You had a suspicion and you interviewed him, and during that time, you saw a picture of Nazis, one of which looked like Dr. Wagner. You took it upon yourself to go to his house. You were met at the door by a man you believe to be the Nazi in the picture." He shook his head in disbelief. "Next you contacted the Wiesenthal Center with names. Am I getting this right?"

Rainee nodded.

"All right. You related your story to them, and that's when you started noticing these people."

Rainee sat in silence as she watched John organize her recent activities.

"You took it upon yourself to take Mrs. Wagner to tea to interrogate her, and then—"

"Interview. Not interrogate."

"Don't fool yourself, love. It seems you already had convinced yourself that her husband was *the* Nazi. You played judge and jury. My Lord, this does sound like a *le Carré* novel!"

Rainee got up to pour them coffees. "Milk and sugar?"

"No milk, four sugars."

"Seriously? Four sugars?"

He nodded and smiled. "My only vice."

"John, I have to admit that I enjoyed my tea with Paloma. She was lovely. It was during that tea that I started to have my doubts."

"Doubts?"

"Well, not about her husband being the Nazi—I was and am completely convinced that he is that person—I suppose misgivings would be a better word. You see, she needs him. She has multiple sclerosis and she depends on him for everything. What would happen to her if he were taken away?"

"She has her son."

"That's another thing. What will happen to his practice and his research if word gets out that his father was a Nazi? He would probably lose most of his patients."

"For Christ's sake, Rainee. His father was a *Nazi*! He was probably responsible for the murder of many people. There's a reason they still prosecute Nazis."

Rainee agreed. "Obviously, there is some correlation to Jana. I want to figure that out before Mr. Wagner is actually identified as a Nazi and taken away. Now, if you go outside and alert those men that we are onto them—without any proof I might add—they could deny it all. Then different people will appear. No, I don't think it's a good thing to alert them... not yet."

"Perhaps, you're right. It was my gut reaction, my need to protect you. Nazis be damned."

Rainee liked the sound of that.

"The question is, why are they following you? They could have followed the Wagners after tea."

Rainee nodded. "I didn't say they didn't. I said they got up at that point. Maybe there are more of them out there." She went to the window to look at the men. "Frankly, I can't say with certainty they are the same men. Now that I look at them... "

She sat back down and took John's hand in hers. "Dr. Wagner hinted at taking me out. I think it's a good idea."

"Bollocks! Absolutely not!" John was adamant.

She squeezed his hand. "I appreciate that you want to protect me. And you have nothing to worry about. Are you jealous?"

He was shaking his head. "Trust me, I am not jealous of that man. But it's too dangerous. You're getting in too deep. How will your Peeping Toms interpret this? They may think you are complicit with the Wagners. First a visit, then tea, then a date."

"I'll be careful. I promise."

John looked hard into Rainee's eyes. "I can't forbid you to do anything. It's just that I don't want anything to happen to you, Rainee."

Rainee smiled. "I don't either. C'mon, it's three o'clock, and you need to be up for your job. Let's go back to sleep."

She led him back to his bedroom.

"As if I could sleep now."

They snuggled into a spooning position, and Rainee fell asleep, comfortable in John's protective arms. He, however, couldn't close his eyes.

Leaving his apartment, or taking the tube, wherever Rainee went she was keenly aware of every car and every man who walked ahead or behind her. John had told her when the doctor was expected to do his rounds, and she arrived at the nursing home two hours before him.

She visited with Jana and found her in an upbeat mood. They played cards in the great room, and Jana invited another resident to join them. Before long, there was yet another resident at the card table. The four of them shared stories and laughter. Rainee stifled smiling when they often repeated the question, "Whose turn is it?" Ironically, it was Jana who kept them on track.

It was evident that Jana was coming out of her shell. She wasn't just staring at the television; instead, she was interacting with other residents. It was very different from when Rainee had first met her. John credited Rainee for the transformation.

The nurse who assisted the doctor entered the great room. "Dr. Wagner will not be available today. I will be doing his rounds. I'll find you when it's your turn." She left to start her assessments.

No one appeared disturbed with her announcement. However, Rainee was. John entered the room, smiled at Rainee, and spoke with the residents. One by one, they each disappeared into their rooms for the nurse's visit. Jana remained in great spirits, so Rainee spent another few hours with her.

She was trying to optimize the time she had left in London. The days were slipping away, and the idea of leaving Jana and John was clouding over her like a typical London day. She wanted to extend her stay and would call Gary and see whether his UK bureau had any apartments in London.

John left Rainee in his office to make her necessary calls.

Gary was intrigued. "Rainee, let's hope this turns out to be fiction and not non-fiction. Of course, you must realize the predicament you've created. A possibly innocent man may be suspect, and have to jump through hoops to prove his innocence. A possibly guilty man may go to jail for his sins—and hey, good for you—but his wife and son will suffer. Albeit, there will be retribution for his crimes fifty years later. And everyone gets to sleep better knowing an eighty year old Nazi is in prison."

"Why do I detect sarcasm in your voice, Gary? Don't you think if he is guilty, he belongs in prison? Is the fact that he helped killed thousands of Jews suddenly acceptable, because it's fifty years later? C'mon, there's no statute of limitations on murder."

"Rainee, is it possible that your creative mind is creating a scenario that may be beneficial to you?"

"What?" Rainee was incredulous.

"Okay, my real concern is you. You've entangled yourself into this family, befriending the mother, getting cozy with the son, and—"

"I am not getting cozy with the doctor. I am gathering information from him. After all, he was the trigger for Jana. I cannot believe that you have done a turn-about."

"Okay, maybe cozy was the wrong word, but I think you're too close to this thing, and you should distance yourself. If you're not paranoid, and there are people following you, then wake up! Can't you see the danger?"

"Listen Gary, I've committed to following this through. If I'm in danger, it's possible that Jana is too. I don't want anything to happen to her. Simple question: do you have an apartment here, or not?"

"No, we don't. However—and I know I'm going to be sorry I'm suggesting this—I have a friend who owns a narrowboat. He's here visiting New York. I'll check with him, though I have no doubt he'll allow you to use it. Just add his name in the acknowledgements."

"Narrowboat?"

"Yeah, I stayed on it once. The canals there are not very wide. Therefore, they came up with a resourceful idea called a narrowboat. His is about six feet wide and very long. It has all the comforts of home."

"I don't know how to steer a boat."

"You won't have to. It can stay moored where it is now. Plus, it's a short walk to the tube."

"Great. I'll stay with Shelley until she leaves. Please get back to me with the address and how to get the keys."

Gary voiced his concern. "Stay safe. Watch your back."

John walked in as she put down the receiver. She said, "Well, I am all set. Gary is on board." She stood to give him his chair, then explained the tentative plan to John.

John pulled her into his arms. "My family used to own a narrowboat. We used it for holiday vacations. But you could stay at my place. I want to protect you."

"I'm grateful for that, except if I am being followed, I don't want to bring any more of their attention on you. They already know we've spent nights together. This narrowboat sounds like a good plan. Since I'll take the tube to get to it, I could probably lose anyone following me in the labyrinth of your underground." She put her arms around his neck and kissed him. "I love that you're concerned."

"What word would a writer use? Desperately? Frantically? Crazily? Madly? Take your pick. I'm all of the above. Rainee, I am beyond concerned."

"It seems everyone around me is more concerned than I am. Maybe I *am* being naïve, but please understand that I have to play this out."

"Obstinate American."

"Overprotective Englishman."

The restaurant that Martin picked was a departure from what she expected. It was unconventional. Rainee would never have presumed the doctor would pick a restaurant that didn't match his stoic personality.

The tables and chairs were all artistically mismatched and very colorful. The paintings on the wall were original paintings with little price tags on them. The menu was eclectic; Italian, American, Indian, Chinese, Mexican, and some Rainee did not even recognize. Each dish was prepared with a twist to their traditional recipes. For instance, the special of that evening was Eggplant Parmigiana covered in a white sauce and served on a bed of Basmati rice. Somehow, curry snuck its way into each dish.

He seems relaxed in these Bohemian surroundings, she thought. *There's more to Martin Wagner than he allows the public to see.* Perusing the menu, Rainee said, "You know, Martin, this is tough to decide. Everything here sounds delicious and so... well, avant-garde, if you know what I mean."

Martin laughed. "That's exactly the reaction I wanted to get. This restaurant recently received a very favorable review. I figured since you were in the literary arts, you would enjoy an artsy meal."

"It's a very good choice. I like the atmosphere."

"Good. I'm glad." He smiled with satisfaction and looked back at his menu.

Their waiter took their drink order. When he left them, Martin whispered with sarcasm, "I sure hope he'll wear a hairnet over those dreadlocks."

"I doubt he's the chef, but I know what you mean."

She was nervous and hoped he could not detect her rapid heel-tapping under the table. She crossed her legs in order to stop the tapping. That didn't work, and a high heel shoe ended up dangling from her toe.

Martin said, "Tell me a little about yourself. To be honest, I did go out and buy your novel. I read your bio, so I know... well, not much, actually." His smile was genuine. "And, by the way, it was an enjoyable read. I can't tell you when I last read something that was not in any way clinical and mind-numbing."

She told him a little of her history, excluding her visit to the Holocaust Museum. She reminded herself that this was not about her. She wanted to find out more about his father. "By the way, you have a beautiful home. I love the neighborhood."

"To be truthful, I would never have been able to afford that neighborhood on an internist's salary."

"Really? Pray tell, how did you end up owning it?"

"I had a patient. He was the son of a sheik."

"No! You're pulling my leg! A real sheik?"

"Yes, a real sheik. I diagnosed his son in time for him to be treated back to health. The sheik was so grateful that he handed me the keys to his home. He told me he was going to sell it no matter what, and since I had saved the boy's life, he really wanted me to own it."

"My goodness! That only happens in Hollywood movies!"

"Naturally, I refused at first, but he was very persuasive. Quite honestly, I loved it the minute I saw it. I don't know, but there's something about it. The moment I stepped into it, I felt a sense of relaxation permeate my body. Hard to explain really. I just knew it would be a great place to come home to after a long day at the office."

"I imagine with all your research and maintaining a medical practice, it leaves you little time for relaxation."

"That's very true. That's why this is a nice break for me."

The waiter brought their drinks, along with a breadbasket. Martin raised his glass to her, "Here's to finding time to relax."

They clinked glasses, smiling.

A different time, different circumstances, who knows? Then she chided herself. *Don't even go there, Rainee.*

"You told me you had been researching multiple sclerosis. Any great breakthroughs?"

"Please understand that I'm just one of a team of researchers, and that's here in London. There's research going on around the world. My concentration was on interferons and their efficacy in reducing the rate of relapsing symptoms in patients with MS. Recently in America the FDA came out with acceptance of usage of interferon beta-1b for MS."

"That's wonderful. Great news for your mother, I'm sure."

"Well, not exactly. My mother's MS is more advanced, so that medication would be of no use to her. Of course, the good news is that many other patients will benefit by it."

"I have no doubt that she's very proud of you. That picture in your office—the one with Prince Philip—made me wonder about his interest."

"Oh, well, there is someone in the royal family with MS. No one in the direct line for the throne, just one of the many cousins. So naturally, he has reason to be curious about developing research."

"I enjoyed that wall. Very enlightening—all those pictures with prominent people and so many certificates. By far, my favorite picture was the one of you and your mother."

His eyes softened at the mention of his mother, and he smiled. "Yes, that was a lifetime ago."

Rainee wondered whether her initial opinion of his eyes, which had caused her to shudder, was an error in judgment. *He can be quite attractive when he smiles. Maybe I was wrong about him.* "Your mother said you were born in Peru. You must be fluent in Spanish."

"Sí, lo so. ¿Quieres beber otra?

"Huh?"

Laughing, Martin said, "I asked if you would like a refill."

"Si, por favor. That's the extent of my Spanish. Did I say that right?"

"You did, indeed." He snapped his fingers, caught the attention of the waiter, and pointed to their drinks.

The alcohol was helping her relax, and her foot stopped its rapid tapping.

After the waiter had set down their second drink, Rainee decided to add some ice to water it down a little because she was already feeling the effects of the alcohol. She turned to catch the waiter and was startled to see the two men who had been following her seated at a table in the corner.

She involuntarily gasped. Once again, that chill she had felt before returned. *So it is me they are following.*

"Did you need something?" Martin inquired.

"Uh, no... um, yes... uh, just some ice for my drink, please." She wondered whether Martin noticed that her resumed foot-tapping was now audible—at least to her.

He motioned to the waiter and placed her request.

Shit, now what do I do? I should have listened to John. Damn my leg, stop tapping. She pushed down on her thigh, but it didn't help.

"Are you all right? You look a little pale."

Rainee's mind was racing, and she missed his question. "Sorry?"

"I'm a doctor, Rainee, and you don't look well to me. Do you want to leave?"

"No, no. Absolutely not. It's just that... well, you see... I didn't eat lunch. Drinking on an empty stomach makes me a little woozy. I'm okay. I'll munch on this bread." She took a bread slice and buttered it. She hoped Martin didn't notice her hand quivering.

Bringing the conversation back to her date, Rainee said, "Now, where were we? Oh, right... you were telling me about your childhood. So let me see if I have this right. You were born in Peru, hence the Spanish-English accent. When did you and your family immigrate to England? And why here, of all places?"

"I certainly hope I won't end up the protagonist in one of your novels." Martin smiled.

Not the protagonist. More like antagonist. Rainee shrugged. "I'm the curious type. If I ask too personal a question, tell me to shut up. I promise, you won't hurt my feelings."

"I finished college knowing I wanted to be a doctor and applied to medical schools in different countries. I got into several. Still my father pressed me to accept King's College in London." Martin swallowed a piece of bread.

"Pressed you? Didn't you want to come here?"

"Maybe 'pressed' is too strong a word. You see, all my life, he said that someday he would move the family to England. As a young boy, I never questioned him. And since I was fluent in English, it was a better selection than the other countries."

"That makes sense." She hoped the perspiration starting to form on her brow was not conspicuous. When he looked away for a moment, she tried discreetly to wipe it with her napkin. *Who are those guys?*

"After medical school, I became an associate with an established physician, moved my parents here, and a few years later, opened my own practice. We've been happy here."

Rainee wanted to spin the conversation toward his parents. "When I met your parents, your mother was recuperating from an illness."

"Yes, she had just been released from the hospital. Her MS had flared up. It happens on occasion, and it's easier for both of them to move into my home... I mean, with a housekeeper and all. They moved back home two days ago."

"Yes, at tea your mother seemed in great spirits. You know, Martin, I enjoyed getting to know her. I would like to have the opportunity to spend more time with her."

"She expressed the same interest. Now I understand why." He looked in her eyes and smiled. "You have beautiful eyes."

She looked away, flustered and a little confused. Her thoughts shifted to John.

Fortunately, the waiter arrived with their meals.

Rainee could tell that Martin was embarrassed and felt foolish. He blushed as he stared down at his plate. "Well now, doesn't this look delicious?"

She agreed, and for a short while, they both ate in silence.

Martin looked up at her. "Look, Rainee, I... I'm sorry if I was a bit forward."

"It's okay. Really. American men are different, and I guess I'm accustomed to Boston's puritanical ways. Plus, I admit that I'm a little nervous," she added with a flirtatious smile.

"Nervous? I would never imagine Rainee Allen being the nervous type."

"Only with people I like." *Okay, so I lied... or maybe I didn't. God, this is confusing. Maybe I'd better stop drinking.*

Martin picked up his glass. "I'll drink to that. Cheers."

"Cheers."

Rainee missed most of their dinner conversation. While Martin spoke, her thoughts went in many different directions. She couldn't concentrate on what he was saying. The two men were in the restaurant, watching her— *Or are they watching him? After all, he's the son of Ralf Wagner.* Her thoughts changed to John and wished he would show up to whisk her away from this scene. *What am I doing here? I should have listened to John. He was right. There is some danger here. Those two men over there... could they not know I'm on to them? Who are they and where are they from?* Then an idea occurred. *What if I go over to them, introduce myself and ask them who they are? Are they following me, or Ralf, or Martin? If they say they're from the Wiesenthal Center, then I could be honest with them and tell them I placed the initial call.* She shook her head lightly and sighed. "Who am I kidding?"

"Excuse me? Who are you kidding about what?" Martin asked.

Startled, Rainee said, "Who am I kidding... I-I could never finish this steak. It's huge. Would you like to finish it, Martin?"

He declined.

Rainee put down her utensils. "Whew, I am full. But thank you; that was delicious."

Although he had not finished his meal, Martin followed her lead and put down his utensils.

"Oh please, don't stop eating because I'm full. A Peruvian with impeccable English manners. Very impressive, Doctor."

Martin hesitated, and then picked up his fork.

"Let's see now. We've covered you and your mother. Any siblings?"

"No. Just me."

"What about your dad? German man ends up falling in love with a South American beauty. Talk about a story for a novel." Rainee wanted to keep the subject light.

"Yes, how about that? My mother was a real beauty, too." Martin became serious. "I know I said it before, but I want you to know that having tea with you meant a great deal to her. When she was diagnosed with MS, she quickly ended up in a wheelchair, and her so-called friends began to disappear. When she needed her friends, they deserted her one by one. Sorry, it really angers me."

"I can understand why. I truly enjoyed talking with her. She's obviously proud of you and clearly still in love with your father. She talked all about his past."

"Really?" Martin had a look of incredulity. "That's odd. She doesn't know that much about his past. Before she met him, I mean. He never talked about it to us."

"How can I say this delicately? You never know what couples talk about behind closed doors, now do you?" Rainee watched him, trying to discern whether he knew anything at all.

"Well, he never told me. He's a very private man. For instance, of course he had parents... my grandparents... but he never told me anything about them. Not a thing. For all I know, they could still be alive and living in Germany. I wondered whether after we moved to Europe he would try to find out whether they survived the war. Well, if he did try, he never shared that information with me." Martin looked perplexed.

Rainee thought, *That's definitely the quintessential look of a doctor trying to diagnose a problem.*

"My father has taken charge of my mother's health issues. He makes all her appointments, confers with her doctors, and drives her everywhere she needs to be. She needs him." There was sadness in his eyes, and Rainee felt a little sorry for him.

Straightening his posture, Martin added, "It's probably a good thing because it gives him a project. He needs a project; otherwise, he roams the house like a lost puppy. So she is his project. And you are right. They do love each other."

He motioned to the waiter for the check. "Next time, we talk all about you, Ms. Allen."

"Sorry, I do have a bad habit of turning conversations around. I enjoy learning about other people's lives. It gives me fuel for my stories."

He smiled. "Well, when you write about me, please be kind."

Rainee was convinced Martin had no idea of who his father was and the savage acts he had committed. She was relieved that he was innocent of such knowledge. Still, she was confused as to why he kept that picture of his father in a Nazi uniform concealed in his office. Though she could not be one hundred percent sure Paloma was uninformed, she left the restaurant feeling less anxious than when she had entered.

Martin and Rainee decided to walk off their meal. There was a threat of rain in the darkened skies; otherwise, it was a nice night for a stroll.

Concerned the two men were following them, Rainee took out her compact to use the mirror surreptitiously. "Merely freshening up," she explained.

"Unnecessary, I assure you."

In the mirror, she saw one man following. He seemed to be walking step-in-step with them. Rainee was sure Martin was unaware.

She began to tremble from fear.

"Cold?" Martin asked with genuine concern. "Let's hail a taxi."

As they stepped into the back of the taxi, Rainee looked out the rear window. A black sedan pulled up to the stalker, and he got in.

The skies opened up, and it began to pour. The rain and the dark of night blurred vision and Rainee hoped they would lose the stalkers in the busy London streets.

Martin borrowed an umbrella from the cabbie when they pulled up to her apartment and walked her to the front door. Rainee noticed the light to their apartment was on, indicating that Shelley was home.

There was that awkward moment that comes with every first date. Rainee said, "I had a lovely time. Thank you, Martin. I would invite you up for a drink, but I see that Shelley's home."

"I hope we can do this again." He leaned toward her for a kiss. Though she was surprisingly tempted to kiss him, she thrust out her hand to shake his. "Puritan, remember?" She smiled.

He took her hand in his. "Right." He laughed, shrugged, and turned to get into the cab.

She watched him ride away. A tinge of guilt over using him crossed her mind. *Am I feeling guilty because of John and is it possible I'm attracted to Martin?*

She saw the black sedan pull up.

"Shit," she whispered. She fumbled in her purse for the keys to the front door. Her hands shaky, she dropped them as the men got out of the car and began to approach her. She tried the lock again—this time with success—and slammed the door behind her.

She ran up the stairs. Her heart was pounding in her chest as she reached her floor. She ran down the hall and stopped dead in her tracks. The door was ajar.

Not thinking of the immediate danger to herself, she shoved open the door and yelled, "Shelley? Shelley?" There was no answer. She stopped and surveyed the room. It had been searched. This was no professional job; they had been amateurs. Furniture was overturned; clothes strewn about, and drawers were open. Only her laptop was missing. The joke was on them because she hadn't entered any information yet. It was kept in her notebook, secure in her purse, which never left her side. All her emails were forwarded to a different address, which she could access on her home computer, and then delete from this laptop.

Rainee knew it was too coincidental to assume it had been kids looking to steal only a laptop. The television was still there. Jewelry was on their bedside tables. Whomever they were, they wanted her to know they had been there.

Where's Shelley? She should have been home by now. The panic of having brought this upon her best friend terrified her. As she picked up the telephone to call John, the sound of approaching steps in the hallway made her freeze. *Are those my stalkers? Are they coming for me now? Where can I hide?* She looked around for a safe place to conceal herself.

She breathed again when she heard the sound of drunken laughter. It was Shelley.

Shelley froze at the door. "What the fuck?" She gaped at the mess and then at Rainee. "What happened here, Rainee?"

Rainee ran to Shelley and hugged her firmly. "I'm so glad you're all right. I'm so relieved to see you."

"What's going on, Rainee? What the—"

"Pack your things. We're getting out of here. I'll explain as we move."

They hurriedly packed as Rainee told her about the mess she had gotten them into.

Shelley listened in disbelief, and she felt betrayed. "How could you not tell me? You put me, yourself, John, Jana, and whomever you came in contact with in danger. You should have at least warned me." She crumpled down on the couch and began to cry.

Rainee sat and put her arms around her. "I thought I was keeping you safe. I thought if you didn't know anything, you wouldn't be in any danger. When I came in, and you weren't here—" Rainee started to cry. "I was terrified that you'd been kidnapped. I'm so sorry, Shelley. I love you, you know that. I was trying to protect you. Really."

Shelley hugged her back, wiped the tears away, and took control. "Okay, the clock's ticking. Let's get out of here."

Rainee pulled the shades slightly back. Spying the black sedan, she said, "We can't go out the front. Let's go through the back yard and hope they aren't watching back there."

They left the lights on and made their way down the back stairs. Rainee stuck her head out the door. It appeared the coast was clear. A tall fence surrounded the back yard, obscuring their movement. The rusty-hinged gate squeaked as they opened it. The sound resonated in the night air. Startled, the two women looked at each other and then broke into a run through the back alleys of the neighborhood.

The sight of two women carrying four suitcases, bags, and purses, trying their best to run silently would have been amusing to the casual observer. However, a leather-jacketed man, with tattoos on his bald head, was watching from the rooftop of an apartment building, and he did not find it amusing. He lost sight of them as they followed the twists and turns in the alley. Speaking into his mobile phone, he sounded an alert.

However, the black sedan positioned in front of the building did not move.

Before leaving the apartment, Rainee had placed a call to John. He had instructed her to come to his apartment building and to use the back door. He would be waiting.

John was waiting by the back door when the two frazzled women arrived. He led them to his apartment, keeping the lights off. He pulled Rainee into his arms, and she fell apart. She kept repeating her apologies to him and to Shelley. "I am so sorry. What have I done? What have I started? What will we do?"

"Look, Rainee, we should contact the police. Let them handle it. After all, your apartment was ransacked."

"John, we don't really know by whom. Was it Nazi hunters or the Nazi protectors? Or, maybe it was neighborhood kids?"

Shelley had her hands on her hips. The glower on her face showed anger and disbelief that Rainee could be that naïve. "Come on, you don't really believe it could be neighborhood kids, do you? That is too coincidental."

John managed to calm them both. "You two will stay here. Shelley, have you noticed anyone following you this week?"

"No. Why would I have reason to suspect anyone would follow me?"

"Come to think of it, there's good reason to believe that they're covering this building, since Rainee has spent time here. Be careful leaving here. Use the back again." John pulled himself away from Rainee's embrace and went to look out the window. He saw nothing unusual on his street.

"Wait a minute," Rainee said. "I can call Gary right now. He'd still be at work. I'll get the information on the narrowboat and we can hole up there until you leave, Shelley."

"Narrowboat? I hate boats."

"You'll love this one. It's a floating hotel," Rainee said.

"Christ almighty, we're supposed to leave in two days, Rainee. Am I not supposed to show up for work? They were going to give me a going-away party."

Rainee turned to face her friend. "I'm staying."

Shelley's face twisted with confusion. "What? You're not coming home?" She looked at John. "Oh, I get it. Sure, I get it now."

Rainee walked up to Shelley and took her hands. "It's not just John, although he is a big part of it. I need to see this through. I feel responsible for opening this Pandora's Box. I feel responsible for Jana too. Try to understand, it's my job to undo this mess... somehow."

Reason returned to Shelley. "Yeah, I get it now. Scotland Yard would probably lead to Interpol. Once alerted, the Nazi would go underground again, and it would all have been for nothing." She shook her head. "I'm not sure whether you're crazy, foolish, or heroic my friend. Now that I'm involved, I'll defer to what you think is best. But I want to be clear—absolutely clear—about this one thing." She used her index finger to emphasize her point.

"What's that, Shel?"

"When this becomes a movie, I want a small part. Maybe a walk-on. That's all I ask."

For the first time that evening, they all managed to laugh.

Rainee had caught Gary as he was leaving his office and got the information about the narrowboat. Plans were revised. At the normal hour for John to be leaving for work, his car pulled out of the garage. If there were any onlookers, they would have seen nothing unusual—just him driving away alone. However, with suitcases in the trunk, and two women hiding in the back seat, he tried to act casual as he drove off. He looked into his rear view mirror to be sure no one was following him.

Driving a circuitous route to the narrowboat, he was convinced they had made a safe getaway.

The boat, moored in an area under the M4 Motorway, was surprisingly well isolated. It was also accessible by the Boston Manor Tube Station. John believed this was a good place to hide out, because the people who would be likely to see the boat were the occasional dog walkers, couples looking for a secluded area, or people using the canal as a route to walk to work.

John retrieved a key from the mooring office and was instructed that moorings were allowed for up to fourteen days.

John said, "I'll do a little research and find a place to moor elsewhere in a few days. I think it best we keep moving every few days." He looked at Shelley. "Shelley, my family owned a narrowboat, so I do know how to steer this thing. Now, let me drive you to work, and I'll pick you up when you call." They exchanged numbers.

Since she was late for work, Shelley left her suitcase behind. It would remain unpacked for the last two days of her trip.

When they left, Rainee did a thorough inspection of her new home away from home. She guessed the boat to be about forty feet long. It had lace curtains, an attractive, modern kitchen, and two bedrooms with a duvet covering each bed, and even a whirlpool corner bath with a shower. There was central heating, television, and something Rainee knew Shelley would like: a stocked bar. It resembled a floating country cottage, albeit a very narrow one.

Rainee stowed their suitcases in the bedrooms, took a soda from the bar, sat down, put her feet on the coffee table, inhaled deeply and let out a long, slow breath.

Though she wanted to visit Jana, Rainee knew it would not be a good idea to leave the boat. She spent most of the day napping, only to awaken to the sounds above and around her. The voices of occasional passersby, the creaking of the narrowboat, and when another boat motored past, a small wave lapping against the side. With the exception of some stale peanuts she found behind the bar, there was no food aboard. She was hungry, but John had called and said he would stop for provisions.

Shelley, John, and Rainee spent that evening going over every detail of the recent events. John had rented a van in the event that he was also being followed. He intended to change out rental cars every few days.

He lifted Rainee's spirits when he said, "Jana asked me if you would be visiting today. She looked disappointed when I told her you were unavailable. After I drop Shelley off at work tomorrow, I'll smuggle you in."

Shelley looked at Rainee and said quietly, "I'm not comfortable leaving you, Rainee."

John said, "I'll be staying on the boat with her. I'll provide as much protection as she allows me to give her. Hey, I took karate in seventh grade." John chopped the air with both hands.

"Oh, I feel so much safer now." Rainee laughed, leaning against him, then added in a more somber tone, "It's true, John. I do feel safer with you here. I can't believe it has all come to this. And I am so very glad that my best friend will be safely leaving tomorrow." Rainee went to sit beside Shelley and put a protective arm around her.

Shelley swallowed her last bit of take-out Chinese food. "Can't say it hasn't been fun... at least up until yesterday. My flight's tomorrow evening and John said he'd pick me up from work and zip me over to Heathrow." She started to tear up. "Rain, I don't want to say goodbye, especially under these circumstances."

"Me either. At least I'll know you'll be safe and secure in your own bed." Rainee squeezed Shelley's hand.

Shelley raised her glass and said, "Well, until we see each other in the good old U.S.A."

They clinked their glasses.

John drove the rented van up the driveway and into the attached garage of the nursing home. They waited for the door to close before Rainee surfaced from under a blanket.

"I'm too old for this." She massaged her lower back.

He led her through the back entrance and corridors. The nursing home was bustling with residents eating their morning breakfast. She immediately spied Jana sitting with three other people. She appeared to be holding court as the others listened intently while gobbling their meal.

When she saw Rainee, she smiled, and waved for her to join them.

John whispered, "Have fun. Stay away from the windows. As I drove in, I saw a black sedan out front."

"Shit. They followed us?"

"Doubtful. They've probably been there all night. And don't swear in front of the residents, please." He squeezed her shoulders, and left her to attend to his work.

She pulled up a chair and hugged Jana. "Good to see you. Sorry I was unable to visit yesterday."

"No worries, dear." She patted Rainee's hand. "I did miss seeing you."

"And I missed you too."

Rainee greeted the others seated at the table. "Was she regaling you with stories of her exciting work at the Palladium?"

No one responded. Their countenance unchanged, they continued eating. Many of their faces were nearly touching their bowls. Rainee thought, *It's as if raising their spoons to their mouths is too much of a burden.*

She recognized the signs of Alzheimer's disease, and realized that Rainee was talking to a vacant group.

"Shall we go for a walk today? Feed the pigeons?" Jana was almost like a child in her enthusiasm. "Tuppence a bag... tuppence, tuppence... tuppence a bag." She sang the words—a refrain from a song in the movie, *Mary Poppins*.

"It sounds lovely, but unfortunately, it's raining again. Perhaps tomorrow. In fact, I'll even get more crackers. That was such a nice day, wasn't it?"

"Oh, my dear, I cannot begin to tell you what that meant to me."

"I enjoyed it, too."

"It felt like a... a... oh, what is that word? A release. Do you know what I mean?"

"Tell me, Jana."

"This house has been my entire world: my room, the lounge, the dining room. Getting out, smelling the fresh air, feeding those pigeons, and most especially, being with you, was liberating. I feel like life has flowed back into these old bones. Look around—do you see my wheelchair?"

Rainee turned. There was nothing but a walker.

"I'm using a walker now. I had no reason to walk and so I lost strength in my legs. It was easier to be pushed about. I decided to give the walker a try. And look at me now!"

Delighted, Rainee clapped her hands, "Well, I'm surprised John didn't tell me."

"I don't think he knew. He hasn't been around these last few days. Been a bit preoccupied, I suppose." She winked at Rainee.

Rainee blushed.

"It's all right, dear. Young love is a wonderful thing. It's so uplifting for me to watch you young ones fall in love."

"I'm not sure it's love, Jana. Not yet. I do like him very, very much."

"I could tell by the way you blushed." She smiled at Rainee in approval. "He's a good man, a gentleman."

"Jana, you remind me of my grandmother. I sought her approval and yours means a lot to me too."

"Tell me about her."

They walked. Jana's legs gained strength with each step. Chairs lined the long corridors, where they could stop to rest. Rainee told Jana stories about her grandmother.

"Come with me to my room. I want to show you something."

Jana's small room was empty of life. Rainee decided she would bring flowers to brighten it.

Rummaging through her bottom drawer, Jana pulled out a small jewelry box and sat on her bed, with an involuntary, "Oy!" She patted the bed. "Come and sit beside me. There are some things I hold dear and want to share with you."

The first things she pulled out were her diamond engagement and marriage rings. She fingered the rings, and then handed them to Rainee to inspect. "Have I told you about my David?"

Sadly, she had forgotten the conversation she'd had with Rainee a week earlier. That was okay with Rainee as she had all day to spend with her.

"Tell me."

Jana repeated the story of her courtship, wedding and honeymoon. To Rainee's delight, she added more details of their marriage.

She pulled out her marriage certificate and David's death certificate, stapled together as one document. She spoke about his cancer and the difficulty she had experienced coping with it. Then she reached into the box and pulled out a handmade necklace. The dull gold chain was in need of polishing. The pendant on it was a peacock, whittled from wood and painted gold.

Feeling remorse for having rummaged through Jana's things earlier, Rainee reached to inspect it. A tear dropped onto it. She looked up to see Jana's eyes brimming.

"Can you tell me about this, Jana? Why does it make you cry?"

Jana was silent in her own reverie. Rainee was afraid she might have relapsed into her confused state. Finally, Jana spoke. "Max... Max made this... for me.... when we... were little."

"Max was your brother, right?" Rainee asked, hoping to stimulate more memories.

"*Ja, mein Bruder,* Max."

This was something Rainee had feared. She did not want to cause Jana to regress.

Jana looked up. "Oh, Rainee dear, I'm sorry. You don't speak German. Max was my brother."

Rainee exhaled with relief.

"He made me this peacock out of wood, and then strung it with my Mama's yarn. It was a Hanukkah gift. My mother liked to sing us a famous Yiddish song called 'The Golden Peacock.' Silly Max changed all the words to make them funny. It became our family song, and we'd laugh and laugh at his lyrics."

She stood to move to her window with the help of the walker. "I put it around my neck and never took it off. I loved his gift. One Hanukkah, my David replaced the yarn with a gold chain." She was staring at the rain, which had begun to fall steadily. "When we were separated, he promised to find me. *Mein Bruder, Max. Er versprach!* He promised! And he promised my Papa! I waited and watched. I watched for him every day." Tears were streaming down her cheeks.

Rainee brought her a box of tissues. She put her hand on Jana's shoulder and waited for her to continue.

"After the war was over, I moved to London. It was after I married David that I finally realized Max would not be coming, though in my heart, I still believed he was alive."

She sobbed as she gently placed the necklace around her neck. "I took this off the first time that doctor came to do his rounds. There was something about him... something that...." She fingered the necklace contemplating her next words. "I don't know. There was just something about him. I didn't understand why I felt the need to take off my necklace and put it away. I will not take it off again!"

She turned to face Rainee. "What is it about that doctor?" Her eyes filled with terror. "Why does he frighten me so?"

Rainee wrapped her arms around Jana and said, "I wish I knew, Jana. I wish I knew. I want to help you... if you'll let me."

The two women turned to look out the window as the rain beat a gentle rhythm on the panes of glass.

On the boat that night, John relayed to Rainee a cryptic message he had received at the office. The caller had warned him to "keep that bitch out of it" and then hung up before John had a chance to respond.

"That's your first warning, Rainee."

"Why would the Wiesenthal Center send me a warning? I'm supposed to be working with them. I'm supposed to be helping them. I don't get it. And calling me a bitch? That makes no sense whatsoever. None."

"Call them. Call them right now. It's afternoon there." He held out his mobile phone to her.

It didn't take long to connect to Lillian Frances. Rainee asked, "Why haven't I heard from you? I'm being followed. Are they your people? " Then she related the recent warning.

Ms. Frances said, "Yes, we have had people shadowing you... apparently, not that well. We did it for two reasons—two big reasons: the first one was that since you had not called us back with important information, we had hoped you would lead us to Ralf Wagner."

"What? What the hell are you talking about? You told me to—and I quote—*sit tight, we will be in touch*. Since then I haven't heard a word from you." Anger was building in Rainee, but she restrained herself. "And, furthermore, your shadows make terrible spies. They were always obvious, sitting there watching in that black sedan."

"That was their job, just to sit and wait patiently. Follow you to Wagner. However, according to them, you never went to his home. Now here's the second part, which makes sense to me now that you've received that warning."

"I'm waiting." Rainee was pacing the floor.

"Our guys became aware of someone—someone not related to our organization—also following you. Look, you have to understand—"

"What the hell does that mean? Another group? Who else hunts Nazis? Why would you people not know who they are? Why would you not tell me before now?"

"We tried. My operatives tried to approach you the other night. They said you ran into your apartment and then vanished. We have been trying to find you ever since. Where are you?"

"I'm not going to tell you that. Not now. Why should I trust you? Give me one good reason I should trust you now?" Rainee was practically shrieking.

"Ms. Allen, I want you to listen to me. You are in danger. The warning you received confirms my suspicions. My operatives' second order was to protect you. Let me explain."

"I'm waiting."

"Yes, we are Nazi hunters. We work with Israel's Mossad and, often when in the UK, they combine efforts with MI-5. Now listen carefully—there are people who are Nazi *protectors*. That's right; there are Nazi sympathizers. I suspect they have emerged. Their agenda will be to protect Wagner at all costs. He will probably choose to go underground again."

"He was never underground. He was living right here in London, in plain sight."

"Yes, he was living under an assumed name, an assumed identity. Once a Nazi's real identity is exposed, there are organizations that mobilize to protect them. There are two ways to accomplish that. One is to get him underground, and two is to eliminate the threat—that would be you."

Rainee became dizzy, and her knees weakened. She leaned into John, who had his ear close to the phone. He helped her to a chair.

He took the phone away from her, and spoke with quiet restraint, "I am going to guess that you know who I am. I want you to tell me exactly what I must do to protect this woman."

"I'll assume I am speaking with Mr. Pritchard. My best advice is to keep her away from the Wagner family and keep her hidden. Even from us. It's likely that since she was aware of our inept shadows, the other party is also aware. They may even be shadowing our guys."

"What do you plan to do about this?"

"The first thing will be to replace my guys. They will blend into the crowd and redirect the other party, confuse them—I'm hoping. I need you to persuade Ms. Allen that we are the good guys. She will need us for protection."

"Bollocks! She has me! I'll try to convince her, but I certainly can't promise anything now that you've botched it up. In fact, I am not all that bloody convinced. Perhaps, we need to call in Scotland Yard, Interpol, or maybe even James Bond."

"Look, Mr. Pritchard, these Nazi protectors are dangerous. They will stop at nothing—*nothing*—to protect their Fuehrer's protégés. Do you know what skinheads are? These groups are made up mostly of skinheads, modern-day Nazis. They worship

Hitler and the swastika, and *Mein Kampf* is their bible. Most are young, unemployed, angry, gun-wielding hotheads. If you can believe it, they are organized. They know every alley and sewer in London. They know how to elude the police. They have safe houses in every country on this globe."

Still angry, but exhausted, John said, "Ms. Frances, what do you think we should do?"

"Give me two hours. I need to confer with my superiors. I will call back. What is your number?"

John told her his phone number and collapsed onto the couch. He put his arm around Rainee, who was staring at nothing, still in disbelief.

He stood abruptly. "We are moving this boat. Now!"

John motored the boat with only the running lights. Narrowboats were slow moving through the canals. Because he was frustrated and angry, his heartbeat was racing, and he wished the boat could match that beat. He needed to provide Rainee a haven and find answers to this spy-versus-spy game, which was not something in which he wanted her involved.

Different scenarios played out in his head as he steered the boat. He could put her on a plane back to America, but why would she be any safer there? Both sides knew her face and could come after her there. Still, moving her through the canals of London was not the ultimate answer, but merely a temporary solution.

Or he could face Wagner with the truth—let him run. *What damage could an eighty year old man do now?* They would never convict him of his past crimes because he'd probably die while awaiting trial.

Helpless and frustrated, all he wanted to do was to look after Rainee and keep her safe.

He pulled the boat into a little cove to moor for the night and shut off the running lights.

He went below to find Rainee sitting on the sofa, wrapped in a blanket, hugging her knees to her chest.

The telephone's ring startled her. It was Ms. Frances calling as promised. "I'm sorry. We can't come to a collective agreement on this. Everyone has their own ideas for what is the next best step. We have a call in to Mr. Wiesenthal himself."

John was incredulous. "You don't know what to do? The great Nazi hunters themselves can't come up with a plan of action. Really?"

Not allowing his sarcasm to get to her, she said, "No, sir. We are not perfect. Otherwise, we would have found all the Nazis that have been in hiding since the war ended. Look, I understand your frustration, and I want to assure you that we are working on this and will come up with a plan."

"And meanwhile?"

"Meanwhile, we have assigned new people to shadow and protect you. They are some of our best agents. They don't look their age, so they can get away with wearing bandanas and running shoes. They'll blend in. There are three of them; one's a woman. Two of them will act like a couple, and the third will hang back. They will be armed."

Rainee whispered to John, "Ask her if we should know who they are? You know, in case we need to run to them for protection."

"I can hear her, Mr. Pritchard. Tell her it'd be best if you didn't know. Otherwise, you may give them away, looking over your shoulder and such."

"We'll be in my office tomorrow. I want to hear from you with a decision."

"I wouldn't advise you to bring Ms. Allen to your office. You know they're probably staking it out."

"Don't worry about that. I know how to get in without anyone detecting us. I assure you; I won't let anything happen to her. We'll speak tomorrow."

"We'll be in touch as soon as we can."

He disconnected the call.

Rainee smiled at him.

He put a protective arm around her and led her to their bed, where they lay in silence, staring at the ceiling. Finally he said, "We've got to come up with a plan."

Her trembling subsided as Rainee started to feel calm in John's arms. "I'm still dazed by this turn of events. It feels like everything is... I don't know... upside-down, I guess. No one is who they seem to be. The bad guys are really the good guys—now why the hell didn't they tell me that from the start?"

"Ms. Frances said they were there to protect you."

"I'd feel a lot more protected if I knew I was being protected."

"I want to know more about the Nazi protectors. They're the ones that worry me." John tightened his hold on Rainee.

She put her hand on his chest. "I know I've said it before... I am so sorry I got you involved and put you in danger. John, I—"

He put a finger to her lips. "Shhh. I want to protect you. What we need right now is sleep. We can talk in the morning."

They each closed their eyes but neither fell asleep.

They were both busy at dawn. One showered while the other scarfed down a quick breakfast. Despite the lurking dangers, Rainee had insisted on going with him to work.

Since they had left the van at the previous moorings, they decided it would be easier to take the Tube to work and pick up the van that evening. Getting to the Tube was a fifteen-minute walk, even at a brisk pace. In the Tube, they separated and took circuitous routes to the nursing home. John met up with her on the street behind the building. He led her through the alley to the neighboring house and rang the bell.

The owner, an older man with a kind face, allowed them to enter. John had requested the use of his back yard—no questions asked—for passage from building to building. They both had awnings that would obscure the vision of any onlookers. The man's father was a resident of the nursing home, and he felt indebted to John. He said, "This conversation never happened, my friend. Here's an extra key to my back door as well. I do hope there will come a day when you can clue me into what's happening."

Overcome, Rainee hugged him. "Thank you, thank you, thank you."

"Blimey, now she's a keeper." He winked at John.

John went right to his office and Rainee headed straight to Jana's room. Though it was still early, Jana was up and dressing herself.

"Hello, my dear. You're here early today."

"Yep, just wanted to see if I could join you in the dining hall."

Rainee noticed that Jana was not wearing her typical sweat suit. She had on an attractive dress and makeup. "You look lovely. Are you trying to impress anyone in particular?"

"No, I felt like dressing up. It makes you feel good to dress up, doesn't it?"

Rainee nodded. "I know what you mean."

They walked down the corridor slowly. Jana was using her walker and Rainee held Jana's purse. Rainee thought, *I wonder where she thinks she's going with this purse.*

Watching Jana eat her breakfast, Rainee sipped on instant coffee. She created small talk, attempting to keep Jana's mind busy. It was another rainy day, so Jana would have to be content playing games in the great room and watching the telly. Rainee was happy just to sit beside her.

That evening Rainee took a roundabout route to the boat. John had warned her that he needed to retrieve the van and would arrive a little later than she would.

While she was preparing dinner for the two of them, a sudden sound startled Rainee. Fear gripped her, and she began to tremble. She grabbed a steak knife and tried to control her breathing. Inching toward the window, she peered out into the dark. It was too dark to see anything. It had sounded like a thud and the boat had rocked. The noise was there again. Rainee looked at the doorknob as it began to turn. She raised the knife. Her heart was pounding as she backed away from the kitchen and crouched behind the bar.

The door flung open, and John stumbled in. He whispered for Rainee. She gasped. His raincoat had bloodstains. His eyes were swollen. He had cuts across his face, and he was holding his stomach, as he reeled into the room. He reached for the counter, missed and fell to the floor.

Rainee ran to him. "Oh my God, John. What happened?" Afraid to try to move him, she grabbed a pillow off the couch, lifted his head and placed it underneath it.

"I got mugged. I was fiddling with the keys to unlock the van. They surprised me from behind." He was groaning from the pain. "I think they broke a rib... or two."

"We've got to get you to the hospital."

"No. No. It looks worse than it probably is. Besides, they'll report this to the police, and they'll ask questions I can't answer."

"Yes you can answer them. You can tell them who did this." Rainee got up to wring a washcloth with warm water and cleansed his bleeding face.

"Rainee, I got jumped by two guys. I didn't see them; I was too busy protecting my face and keeling over. I did see a fist the size of a football coming at my face. Each finger had tattoos of swastikas. Before they left me on the ground, they saluted and yelled '*Sieg Heil!*'"

"So you do know who did this. We both do."

"Yes we do. Rainee, after I keeled over, one of them grabbed my hair and pulled my head back. He leaned in and whispered in my ear—"

"What?"

"Damn it. He said 'Tell that bitch girlfriend of yours to get on a plane and go back to America.' Then he did this—" John took his finger and mimed slitting a throat. Rainee gasped for air. "I'm sorry, Love. I thought about not telling you, but you need to know."

Rainee started pacing again. Half in panic and half in thinking mode, she was wearing a circle in the carpet.

She helped John get up and sit on the couch. The bleeding was slowing. "Where were you? Where did you go?"

He held her stare while reaching into his coat. He pulled out a gun. "I went to my father's house and took this. Good thing they didn't know I had it on me."

"You could have used it on them."

"No, it's not loaded." He reached into his other pocket and pulled out a box of bullets. "I was going to load it when I got here. Timing is everything, isn't it?" John attempted a laugh, then groaned with the pain it caused.

"Let me put some ice on your face. You're starting to look like a raccoon."

The ice made him wince. "Sorry, no raccoons in London. Badgers maybe, but—"

"Stop it. That's not funny."

"You know what hurts the most, my love?"

She liked the way he called her his love.

"My ego. I haven't been in a fistfight since I was twelve years old. I was protecting the honor of Mary Stubbles. I lost that one too."

"There were two of them. You didn't stand a chance."

"Sean Connery would have made mincemeat out of those two. "

"Oh, so now you're comparing yourself to James Bond?"

"Prichard... John Pritchard." He laughed, then whimpered again.

"Stop making light of this, John. You can't go to work tomorrow. You're in no shape."

"I'll call in sick, and you can stay here and nurse me."

"I promised Jana we would go to the park. The forecast is sunny for a change. I don't want to disappoint her."

"Like bloody hell you will. Who will be there to protect you? No! No way in hell."

"Speaking of protection, my protector, you look like bloody hell. Let's get you into a hot shower. It'll feel good."

She helped him stand, and he leaned on her. She undressed him, trying her best not to hurt him.

"If I'm in this much pain, how is it I am getting aroused by your touch?"

"Simple answer—you're a man."

While he took his shower, she finished preparing dinner, though her appetite had left her.

He came limping out in a towel; exposing a large bruised imprint of a fist on his ribs.

"What about the Wiesenthal Center? Did they call you at the office?"

"Yes, but all she said was that plans were in the works and she will call again. Oh, and apparently, Mr. Wiesenthal was not reachable. Must be hunting Nazis or something. Hello? We've got one right here!" He winced.

"Oh, John, shouldn't we at least see your family physician? What if your ribs are broken?"

"Nothing they can do about it. They wrap it. It's something that takes time to heal. I'll be okay. Honest."

In spite of her loss of appetite, he ate ravenously, though with each swallow came an involuntary wince.

Following dinner, she put him to bed with some aspirins and one of her sleeping pills.

He was out as soon as his head hit the pillow.

When Rainee was certain he was fast asleep, she packed a carrying bag with a change of clothes. Her plan was to awaken early, dress in John's raincoat and hat, borrow his keys to the back entrance and visit with Jana. She would leave a note. Even though she knew he would not be happy about this, Rainee needed to see Jana, whose spirits were elevated as of late. She hoped that maybe Jana was ready to tell her more about why she had reacted so strongly to the sight of Martin.

That night she stayed awake, cut, and hemmed John's pants to her height. They were too large, and she needed a belt to keep them from falling. Rainee wore four sweaters to fill out his raincoat. She put her hair up under his hat. She admired her handiwork in the mirror and slipped out of the boat.

Rainee took several different Tube routes, picking up some flowers from a street vendor as she exited the Tube station. She took long strides, attempting to walk like a man and was doing a decent job of it since no one was doing double takes at her.

She made her way to the neighbor's rear gate. Taking care to stay beneath the awning, Rainee unlocked the back door. Relocking it behind her, she leaned against it and let out a long sigh of relief.

There was a restroom to the right of the entrance hallway, and it was there she changed and stashed her clothes for her return.

Jana was walking to breakfast. Rainee sidled up beside her. "So what do you say we go for a walk in the park today?"

With a twinkle in her eyes, Jana smiled. "I'll bring the crackers."

MARTIN AND RALF — 1997

Martin and his father were taking a morning stroll through Kensington Gardens since the week of rain and drizzle had finally changed to London sunshine. There were many people outside enjoying the weather while it lasted: joggers sped past them; couples were holding hands; students were studying on the grass. Martin was talking animatedly about new advances in MS research.

Ralf was not able to listen to what his son was saying. His mind was on the two men in leather jackets following them. They were doing a lousy job of being inconspicuous. Or was he becoming paranoid and imagining it?

The conversation turned to his mother's tea with Rainee. "Did Mother enjoy herself? I know it has been quite a while since she had a lady's day."

"Yes."

"I'm glad. She needs to get out more."

"Yes." Ralf was weighing how to approach the subject he had avoided throughout Martin's entire life.

"Mother is after me to ask Ms. Allen on another date. I may do that. We did have a nice time."

"Don't!" Ralf turned to face his son. "Do not do that."

A bit taken aback with his father's brusqueness, Martin asked, "But... but why?

"Trust me. It's just... it would not be a good idea, Martin."

"What are you talking about? Why not?"

"It's enough that I ask. That's all."

"You seem so distracted and troubled. What's wrong, Father?"

Ralf knew that the time had come to have a talk with his son. The truth had to be told. He was an old man, and he needed his son now. He would need to be truthful with Martin and depend on him to prevent the truth from becoming public. Quite possibly, he would need Martin to protect Paloma and him.

They came to a park bench, and Ralf ordered Martin to sit.

"What is this about, Father?" Martin asked, sitting down.

"Shhh. Say nothing."

After a long moment of uncomfortable silence, the two men in leather jackets walked pass them, not even glancing their way.

Ralf waited until the men were a safe distance from them, then turned to his son. "Martin, you must understand... it was not my fault. I had no choice. It was kill or be killed."

Martin looked at Ralf, whose hands were balled into fists.

"I am haunted... so haunted by my past, Martin." He was agitated, and Martin became fearful.

"What are you talking about, Father?"

Rubbing his brow, contemplating his next words, Ralf Wagner looked weary and distressed.

"You must understand. It was the war. World War II. I was German. *Ja,* I was sixteen years old. No one else knew that. I looked older. I was a strong boy."

The fractured comments emerged illogically, creating a moment of panic for Martin. He wondered whether his father was losing his mind. "Father, you're not making sense. I know you're German. Take it easy. Slow down. What are you trying to tell me?"

"Listen carefully to what I am going to say to you. You must swear to me that you will never tell another living soul, not even your mother. Swear!"

Martin had never witnessed his father so disconcerted. "Yes, Father, I swear. What could be so awful that I can't tell Mother?"

"It happened a long time ago. I was just a young man. I had no choice."

Ralf stood up and began pacing. He was trying to gather his thoughts to be able to project them clearly to his son. He knew that what he was about to share with Martin would change his son's life. "I fear the past is about to catch up to me. Remember that what I am going to tell you, I tell you because I love you, son. You and your mother are my life." He looked directly into Martin's eyes. "I was born in Frechen, Germany. My real name is not Ralf." He took a lengthy pause to compose the strength to say his next few words. "My name is... is Max. Max Lutken… and I was born… a Jew."

Martin's mouth dropped open with surprise. "What? How is that possible?"

"Frechen was a nice town, and everybody was friendly. After World War I, Hitler promised all of us that he was going to bring prosperity back and make our country strong again. We all believed him. My father—your grandfather—did too. But Hitler's solution from poverty to riches was to eliminate anyone who was not pure Aryan. That meant the elimination of Jews. At first, the mistreatment of Jews was gradual. But then began to catch fire throughout Europe. When war broke out, if you were a Jew, your friends distanced themselves. Understand, son, that most people had no choice. Being a friend to a Jew meant you were an enemy of the State. Hitler's propaganda was growing everywhere throughout Germany.

"Father, I don't need a history lesson on Hitler. What did you mean when you said 'Kill or be killed'?"

"I will get to that. First I must explain what came before." He paused to gather his thoughts. "Our own townspeople ran us out of Germany. My father and my father's sister, Aunt Gertie, her two girls—and Jana—*Meine Schwester*."

"You have a sister?"

At hearing himself say Jana's name aloud, Ralf began to cry. He collapsed onto the bench. He put his head in his hands and wept. Martin put his arms around his father and allowed him the time he needed. This was a shocking revelation to Martin. He never knew he had an aunt or cousins.

Ralf wiped his tears on his coat. "Jana was three years younger than me. I promised my Papa I would take care of her. He made me promise. I loved my sister. Martin, you must believe me. I loved her."

"I do. Go on, Father."

"It was October, 1938. Our family was forced to leave Germany in the middle of the night. We went to live in Amsterdam. For a while my Papa worked, as did my Aunt Gertie. After a while, the Nazi party grew stronger. Nearly everyone was accepting Hitler's propaganda against Jews, and anyone who was not pure Aryan. It permeated Europe. Nazi troops were marching through cities and decimating them. The Luftwaffe was bombing countries in an effort to take over all of Europe. Even little villages with innocent civilians were bombed. Well, you know all this."

They both fell silent for a few moments so Ralf could collect and compose his thoughts. Martin was still in shock. He thought better than to interrupt.

"After a while, Papa lost his job because he was Jewish. Then Aunt Gertie lost hers. There was no money. Soon there was no food. My proud Papa had to beg for help." Ralf started to sob at the memory of his father begging on the streets of Amsterdam. Martin handed him his handkerchief.

"Papa and Aunt Gertie did the only thing they could. They put their children into an orphanage run by clergy. I was separated from Jana. They separated the boys from the girls. Now and then, I would catch a glimpse of my sweet sister. It nearly killed me that I could not take care of her, as I had promised Papa I would. I knew she was being taken care of. She was being fed, getting showers. We boys, on the other hand, had it tough. The clergymen claimed to be men of God, but what they did to us was not something God would have allowed."

Ralf balled his hands into angry fists. "It's hard to admit to you, and to myself, the horrors some of us went through. Every few evenings, a boy was taken in the middle of the night. It happened to me twice, Martin. Twice they came for me and took me into their rooms. It is difficult for me to explain what they did to me. I cannot even speak the words. Not to you, my son. Not even to myself. I did not know that this was something that could happen to a boy." Ralf's voice cracked. He trembled.

"Oh, Papa." Martin's eyes filled with tears and the two held each other and wept. "I'm sorry, Papa. I'm so sorry."

After blowing his nose, Ralf continued. "One night we were taken from the orphanage and the nuns marched us to the train depot. I was still separated from Jana. The train travelled several hours, stopping along the way to pick up more children. I later found out that this was called a *Kindertransport*. The people who organized these saved the lives of over ten thousand children. Jana and I were the fortunate ones. There was a change in the original plans, and we did not get to travel to England on the same boat. Some of the boys were angry with the Nazis that were standing guard around us. They started to protest. I was a coward and did not move from my spot on the ground. The soldiers shot all these young boys. Martin, I watched as these boys died. My brain did not believe what my eyes were seeing. My body felt paralyzed. How could the Nazis do this? Those same soldiers laughed about it. They took great joy in shooting little boys as target practice. My God, Martin, I sat and watched."

"What could you have done, Father? You would have been shot too."

Ralf said as a whisper, "I was overcome with fright. I was a coward."

"No, Father, no. You promised to take care of your sister. How could you have done that if you were dead?"

Trembling, Ralf said, "I didn't. I failed." He looked skyward. "Oh Jana, I failed you. Her last vision when we were together was watching those soldiers slaughter the boys. Imagine the horror in her young mind. I could not put my arms around her and comfort her. Her boat left for England, and the remaining boys were to wait for the next boat. It was the longest wait of my life. I didn't know if at any time, the Nazi would kill me, just for the joy it brought him. A couple of hours later a boat arrived and we boarded. Funny, I even remembered the name of the boat: the *Prinses Juliana.* There were many other children already on that boat. I don't know, maybe a hundred, maybe more. We were all terrified. We were told we were headed for England and that an English family would foster us. There was fear, but there was also hope. I vowed that I would look all over England for my Jana. I would never stop until I found her." Ralf paused to catch his breath.

Martin asked, "Do you need to take a moment, Father?"

"No, I must get this all out. It's important that you know all that happened." He continued. "We were on the boat for... I don't know how long, when there came a sound from the sky. An airplane started to descend. It strafed the boat, shooting and killing people on the deck. It was mayhem. Children everywhere were screaming and running in complete chaos, falling over each other. I watched as the plane rose in the sky and curved around for another pass. I knew I would die. I jumped overboard, swam as fast as I could away from the boat. The plane dropped a bomb, and the boat exploded. Debris flew everywhere, including parts of bodies. My God, Martin, I saw severed heads, arms, legs floating past me. The North Sea turned red with the blood of children. I grabbed onto a floating piece of the boat and pulled myself aboard. The explosion did not stop with the bombing. The plane had disappeared into the skies. Perhaps, it was the boat's fuel, I don't know. There were two more explosions, causing more debris to fly. Something heavy, maybe metal, hit me in the head, and I passed out. I drifted back to the shores of Holland and was unconscious. All I know is what I was later told. I awoke in an army tent set up by German medics."

"You awoke in a German army camp?" Martin was incredulous.

"Yes, and I had no memory of who I was. Amnesia, I had amnesia. The Germans nicknamed me *Vergessene Junge, Forgot Boy*. Since I spoke German and was German, they assumed I had been a foot soldier left for dead after fighting the Dutch army. I was conscripted back into the German army. Back? How ludicrous that sounds now. At any rate, the Germans nursed me to health and gave me a dead soldier's uniform and a gun. I became a foot soldier for the German Nazi Party. I didn't know who I was. I did not know my name. They gave me one: Wolfgang VanValkenburg."

Spellbound, Martin did not want to interrupt, but then something occurred to him. "If you were a Jew, weren't you circumcised? Didn't the Germans know immediately?"

Ralf placed a hand on his son's shoulder. "Yes, you are right. I was circumcised. When the aircraft first strafed the boat, there was fire everywhere. I was terrified. A young boy whose whole body was on fire ran right into me and knocked me down. He fell on top of me and, in seconds, my clothes caught fire. I instinctively threw myself into the sea to put out the flames, not just because the plane turn back towards us. When I awoke, the medics told me I had suffered second-degree burns from my waist down. Thank God, my manhood was not as damaged as my thighs. You've seen my thighs, but not my penis. It suffered a severe burn—painful beyond description—because of the scarring, you could never tell I had a circumcision. So, even I didn't know."

Martin winced imagining the pain, then said softly, "Go on."

"Being sixteen, I followed my superior's orders, as all soldiers must. I learned how to use my rifle, and I enjoyed this new knowledge. Martin, I felt a surge of power grow inside me. I could do anything I wanted. I was a soldier in the German Army, and no one would dare cross me. Hitler became *Mein Führer*. He was my leader, and I believed what he said about the Jews. I thought them a filthy, inferior breed we needed to exterminate for the good of Germany. Martin, I killed Jews. I killed my own people. I did not know." His cries turned into wails. "I... did... not... know."

Some concerned passersby stared, but when they saw that Martin was caring for him, they continued to pass.

Catching his breath, he composed himself in order to continue. "My troop was ordered to Sobibor, a concentration camp in Poland. It was an extermination camp. I did my job. I exterminated people by the thousands. I rose in the ranks and soon was commanding other soldiers. I became an important man, son. I was an *Unteroffizier*, a non-commissioned officer. I liked my power. I reveled in it. I took great joy feeling superior to the prisoners. To me they were less than human, anyway. I killed arbitrarily. I needed no reason. I had the power. I was young, stupid, and caught up in the momentum of our army's growing power. We felt entitled to kill."

Ralf's body had intensified with his commentary, then deflated slightly. "It was not until America entered the war that we began to lose it. I knew it, but was ordered not to convey that to my troops. I was to keep up morale. It was business as usual, and we continued to march prisoners into the ovens. We increased the numbers, and the ovens ran day and night. We awakened terrified prisoners in the middle of the night and marched them to their death. I could feel the frantic necessity as any soldier did. Then again, I also knew *why* we had increased the running of the ovens. It was just a matter of time before the enemy would arrive."

"Feeling the end was near, my soldiers started to disappear one by one. Orders were to shoot any deserters under my command. They were going AWOL for fear the Russians or the Americans would appear any day." Ralf paused. He knew what he was going to say next would be even more shocking to his son. He bowed his head and stared at his hands. "I did the same. In the middle of the night, I walked up to the guard and when he turned his back to me; I took him by the neck and snapped it. You see, my son, killing had become nothing to me."

Ralf averted his gaze from Martin. He did not want to see his son's disappointment or, even worse, his horror. "Then I left. I walked and walked and walked. I came to a farm, stole clothes and shed my uniform. I continued to walk until I came to a town. Starving, I begged for food. People were kind to me. Some gave me shelter, even though I spoke German and was obviously German. They must have understood I had escaped the army somehow and was seeking shelter. I would lie and tell them the Nazis forced me into the army by threatening my family. I did not have a choice. That was the lie I had to tell. These were the same Polish people that I would have given no thought to killing only weeks earlier. They were helping a stranger. I spent many nights crying over my guilt. But I kept walking. It took many months to make my way to a port. I found work aboard a ship headed to South America."

Martin recognized that Ralf was looking frail and pale. "Father, you look like you need a drink. I know I do." Martin helped his father stand. They walked to a nearby pub and found a table in a private corner. Martin went to the bar and ordered a couple of beers. The cigarette smoke hung low and dense like cloud cover. The pub was not crowded, and it was safe to talk.

"So is that when you met Mother?"

"No, not immediately. We landed in Venezuela. Over the next few months, I made my way down to Peru. I lived by working on ranches and doing menial work. Any work I could get, I took. I learned passable Spanish along the way."

A server delivered their beer and asked if they wanted to order food. Neither of them had an appetite and waved her away.

"I continued to walk, not caring where I headed. I walked; I worked; and I walked again. Sometimes, days would pass without seeing another human being. I first saw your mother in the small

Peruvian village where you grew up. One look and I knew I wanted to marry her. Well, you know that story. What you don't know, and she never will know, is that… I got my memory back."

"How? When?"

Ralf took a long sip of his beer. "We were married two years before your birth. We were very happy. The village was remote, and they knew little of the war. My German accent was as foreign as any other accent. No one knew my history... no one but me.

"My memory returned when you were about seven years old. We were in the town square where many other villagers had gathered for the Fiesta de la Virgen del Carmen, an annual festival. Maybe you remember because we attended each year. Everyone did."

Martin nodded.

"There were many foreign tourists that particular year. I don't remember why. However, I do remember that you were on my shoulders to watch the parade pass. I overheard a father singing a song to his child. They were standing behind me, and he was cradling his child, probably trying to comfort him. The song was in Yiddish. A famous Yiddish song called, 'The Golden Peacock.' I knew this song. My parents sang this song to Jana and me when we were small. I had changed the lyrics to make it comical. Also to torture my little sister, as siblings do."

Martin began to hum the song quietly, and then added the words as if lost in a reverie. "The golden peacock flies away. Where are you flying, silly Jana bird? I fly across the sea to the south. Please ask my love to kiss me on the mouth! I know you, and I shall bring a letter back to say, you better not kiss me now, or there'll be no wedding day!" He blinked away more tears. "Well, those were *my* changed words to the song. Our family song... the lyrics of a young boy who loved teasing his sister.

"That is when it hit me. I was standing in the town square when all my lost memories came flooding back to me. It was as clear as day. Papa, Mama, my Jana and my name: Max. I was Max Lutken from Frechen, Germany and, my God, I was a Jew! I felt sick. My legs buckled. I had to put you down. Paloma asked me if I was all right. I told her I had to go for a walk. I stumbled away like a drunkard, and I walked. I remembered it all. The guilt—oh Martin, the guilt of killing my own people overwhelmed me. Can you understand that?"

Martin nodded.

"I went into a depression that lasted for several months. Paloma was so confused, but I couldn't tell her. How could I explain?"

Martin was listening intently. This explained the photograph he had on his wall. "Father, I have a picture of you... in a German uniform, with other soldiers. I came across it years ago. I was looking to borrow a... a pen, I think it was, from your desk. I rustled through the drawers, and I saw this picture of you. I was confused and stole it. I was young. I should have asked. I was frightened that Mother would see it."

"You have it? I knew it disappeared. Frankly, I had hoped I had thrown it out by accident. It was the one thing I had from my past."

"When I got older, I became obsessed with it. I tried to find out whether it was you or someone who may have looked like a younger you. I tried to unlock the mystery. It always led to a dead end."

"Where is the picture now?"

"It's hanging in my office closet. I kept it there, as a reminder to keep trying to figure it out. The picture and my interest in it faded after a while."

"Destroy it! Immediately! I should have done that years ago."

"Don't worry, no one could see it. It's in my private closet." Suddenly Martin remembered that Rainee had entered the closet with him. "Oh, my Lord."

"What? What is it?"

"It's possible Rainee may have seen it."

"What? How?"

"I had to retrieve some medical information and she followed me into the closet. I wasn't even thinking. It had been hanging there for so long. It's probable that she didn't see it. Yes, it is likely that she never saw it. That part of the closet is not well lit. No, I'm certain it's safe to say she never even noticed it."

"But what if she did, Martin?" He was agitated. His hands were trembling.

"It's just a picture. If she did see it, there's no way she could put two and two together. No reason to believe that she— Father, you must try to calm down." Martin called over the server. "We'll both have a whiskey."

"Martin, after your mother had her tea with Ms. Allen, I became nervous that Paloma had revealed too much information to this lady. After all, we don't know her. We don't know who she is."

The server delivered two shot glasses. Martin took a swig of his and said, "I don't think you have anything to worry about with her. She's here to write about Holocaust survivors and Alzheimer's disease. She's a writer; that's all."

"Do you think it's a coincidence that just as she showed up my past became revealed? There is something else happening now. I can feel it. My instincts tell me there is more going on." He stopped and pointed to the front of the pub. "Look out that window, Martin. Do you see a black sedan and two men seated in it?"

Martin got up and walked to the window. He drew back the shade and saw exactly that. Sitting down he asked, "Who are they, Father?"

"I wish I knew. They have been following us. They were in the hotel lobby yesterday, when your mother was having tea. Then there were the two men who walked past us in the park before."

"I didn't notice any men."

"I did!"

"You think they are Nazi hunters?"

"I don't know. They could be following Ms. Allen for all I know. We don't know her. I keep telling you that she may not be who she seems to be. Maybe following us means they are gathering info on her. I have no idea." He finished his whiskey in one swallow. Martin motioned to the server for another round.

"Jesus, what do we do?"

Ralf drew in a heavy breath and let it our very slowly. "I made a call. I've kept a number in my wall safe for many years. I coded it and almost forgot the code; it had been that long."

"To whom?"

Ralf looked around and lowered his voice to a whisper, "They are called *Stille Hilfe;* it's German for 'Silent Help.' They're an underground organization. They've been around since after the war. They were set up as a clandestine society. At first, they helped Nazis escape to other countries. Gave them false I.D.s. Now they protect them. Mostly, I think they protect those Neo-Nazi skinhead assholes who still worship Hitler. They mobilize when a war criminal surfaces and get him underground again. That's who I am, Martin. I'm a war criminal."

"Jesus, Father. This is unbelievable."

"Believe it, Martin. Believe it. I have lived with this tremendous guilt all our lives and with the fear of this coming to light."

The men sat in silence. Martin was trying to take it all in and make some sense of this revelation. With two shots of whiskey in him, Ralf was becoming lost in memories of the past.

"Jana, my sweet sister. Martin, remember when I had us all learn English? You were such a young boy. Do you remember I said that someday we would live in England? It was because I knew that Jana's *Kindertransport* had made it to England. I made a promise to her that I would find her. That's why we moved here. Son, for years I looked for her." Ralf's tears fell into his shot glass. He sobbed inconsolably, and others began to look his way.

Martin put his arm around his father. Until today, it was a gesture neither man had been comfortable doing. "I wonder what became of your sister."

"I don't know. I just know that her boat made it safely. Many of the fostered children took the last names of the family that fostered them. I could never find out what the family's last name was. I lost the trail and after numerous years, I gave up. Though, I do still look at old women's faces as they pass me on the street, hoping that maybe, just maybe..." After a pause, he added, "She could be living anywhere, or worse yet, she could be dead."

"Don't talk like that. She could be alive. I'll try to locate her, Father. Let me try."

"Martin, they prosecute Nazis. They still prosecute them, and send them to prison. Your mother needs me. She needs me, Martin. No! They cannot find me."

"I know, Father. I know."

Father and son sat in silence as they finished their drinks. Martin reeled with this new knowledge while Ralf felt an odd relief from purging the secret burden he had carried most of his long life.

Martin said, "I need to process this. Let me drive you home. I still have to make my rounds. I will come by, and we will talk more tonight. I promise."

Ralf took a last swig of his drink. He kept repeating, "Jana. Jana. Jana."

A memory clicked in Martin's head. It was vague and one he could not grab onto it as it floated around in his brain.

"Jana. Your sister's name is Jana. Is that a common German name?"

Ralf was already standing and putting on his jacket. "Why do you ask?"

"It sounds so familiar. I mean recently familiar. Not sure I know why. When was her birthday?"

"Why does it matter?"

"It may help me to know, to find her for you."

"She was born on February 9, 1927. I will never forget my Papa placing her in my arms. She looked up into my eyes, this helpless baby girl."

"C'mon, Father. Let's see if we can lose that sedan in the London traffic and get you home."

As they walked through the door, Martin placed his arm around his father's shoulder.

JANA — LONDON 1997

It was a beautiful day for a walk in Regents Park. Jana decided it would be best to use the wheelchair in case her legs tired. "Ah, finally... sunshine." Jana's smile was heartwarming.

Rainee knew if she had given it too much thought, she would never have attempted this outing. In spite of the obvious uncertainties, she convinced herself that no one saw her coming and no one saw them leaving the back exit under the awning. Rainee pushed her fears of danger to the back of her mind, confident that they had left undetected and determined to give Jana a pleasant day.

Rainee knew that when John awoke he would be furious with her, but she had made a promise to Jana. Too many people in Jana's life had not kept their promises, and she did not want to be one of them.

Rainee spoke about her departed grandmother. "You know, Jana, I miss her a lot. There are times, like now when I'm with you, that I feel her presence. Maybe that sounds silly, but—"

"No, not at all. After all these years, I still feel my mother's presence, yet she died when I was very young."

"You look a little like my grandma too. Her family came from Greece when she was very young. She had an olive complexion and dark, dark hair. You both have the same sweet eyes. Yes, you do look alike."

"You know David and I never had children. I would have liked to." A shudder ran through her when she remembered the cause.

Though she did want to gather more information, Rainee was apprehensive that those particular memories would cause Jana to regress, so she changed the topic. "Do you have those crackers? How about feeding some pigeons?"

Jana took out her bag of crumbled crackers. Before long, birds were encircling them.

Arriving at the nursing home, Martin met his nurse and apologized for running late. She had already taken the vitals of some patients and reported her findings.

In the closet-sized office space designated for visiting doctors, he sat at the desk and tried to review the nurse's notes without much luck. He found it impossible to get his mind off what his father had revealed. The name Jana kept circling in his mind. Why did that name sound so familiar? Surely, he had met women named Jana sometime in his life.

He found he could not concentrate on his duties. Jana—Rainee—Ralf... no, Max. His father could be correct. Maybe Rainee's presence had put into action a series of events that were irreversible. Why? Rainee was here to meet Janet Bowman, a Holocaust survivor with Alzheimer's. What was it she called her? Her muse? And a woman who shared her birthday. Her birthday?

Martin went to the patient medical files. He fingered through the files and pulled out Bowman. Since Mrs. Bowman's initial reaction to seeing him had been so severe, he had no reason to read her chart at the time. Martin sat at the desk and opened the chart. The first three lines caused him to catch his breath.

He read *Janet L. Bowman. Date of birth: February 9, 1927. Place of birth: Frechen, Germany.* He thought, *L for Lutken?*

He tried to make sense of it all. He was stunned at the possibility that her middle initial could stand for Lutken. Why would she have had such a negative reaction to seeing him? He'd been told he resembled his father, but why a negative reaction? Why not joy? Could it be she could not recognize her own brother after so many years? There were too many questions crowding his brain. *Ah, but perhaps I do know someone who could answer that.*

He called a psychiatrist to whom he often referred patients. The receptionist told him he could come right over. He stuffed Janet Bowman's chart into his briefcase and left.

Martin found it challenging to tell the story to Dr. Lawrence. After all, he had to keep from exposing his father. They spoke of a "patient" and everything was hypothetical.

Dr. Lawrence had many years of experience dealing with elderly trauma victims, many of whom were Holocaust survivors.

Martin asked his main question. "Why would she react with such mental agitation to the presence of a young doctor?"

Dr. Lawrence tugged at his mustache, pushed his glasses to rest on top of his head, and took a few moments to consider the circumstances. "Ah, you say you think the patient may be the sister of the boy left at the pier? And she had just witnessed a mass killing before her boat left?"

"That's correct." Martin was trying to act uninvolved. His heart was beating fast, and he hoped his nervousness did not show.

"This is something I have come across once—maybe twice—before. It troubled me, so I sought out a colleague, another psychiatrist. She diagnosed it straight away, as if it happened all the time."

Martin was anxious for answers. "And what did she say it was?"

"The term she used was *transference*. Let me explain." Dr. Lawrence folded his hands and rested them on his ample belly. "It's an unconscious defense mechanism where feelings and attitudes like love or hate, which are associated with certain people in one's life, can be attributed to others in a specific situation. In other words, at that horrible moment, the last two faces that patient saw became indelibly etched in her mind as one: the German officer and her brother. Perhaps her brother's face faded with time or metamorphosed with the face of the officer. Yes, this makes sense. With confidentiality, I assume we are talking about an adverse reaction to you?"

Martin nodded.

Dr. Lawrence continued. "When she saw you in your white lab coat, she transferred the Nazi's face onto yours. She regressed back to that moment when her brother and the Nazi were in proximity to each other. And if—and I stress the word *if*—her memory of the Nazi's face was the last face she saw, it is probable that she sees him in you."

Martin realized how remarkably close Dr. Lawrence was. *After all, I do look like my father did when he was a younger man.* It was logical and a perfect explanation for Mrs. Bowman's regressions.

He thanked the doctor and left to explain to his father.

During his drive, it hit him how astonishing it all was. His aunt was in the nursing home he visited. Rainee's visit had brought this all together. He was thrilled about presenting it to his father and was elated with the thought of their reunion after so many years.

Ralf Wagner listened in stunned disbelief as his son disclosed his findings with enthusiasm. Martin told him that in the director's notes he had read, *Mrs. Bowman sits for hours by the window. She repeats the name Max.* There was no question; this was no coincidence. Janet L. Bowman had to be Jana Lutken.

That Jana was still alive filled Ralf with joy. He grabbed Martin and cried in his son's arms.

Martin could not help it. He shed tears for his father and himself. This opened a completely new chapter in his life as well. He had an aunt and a family ancestry.

Unexpectedly, Ralf pushed him away. "No! No! Oh my God, no!"

"What? What's wrong? I thought you'd be overjoyed with this news."

"We have to hurry. Oh my God, we have to hurry." Ralf was pushing Martin out the door.

"Where are we going? Why hurry?"

"I got the call. Oh no, no, no! Hurry!"

They were rushing to get into Martin's car. "What call? Where am I headed?"

"Regents Park! We must hurry!"

"Father, you are scaring me. What call?"

"*Stille Hilfe.* They called to say Rainee was in Regents Park with Mrs. Bowman. No, I mean Jana. *Meine Jana.* I told them to do whatever it took." He looked at his son, shaking his head.

"You mean you gave them the go-ahead to kill Rainee?"

"I was desperate that I was on the verge of being found out. They said they could 'get rid of her once and for all.' This way no one would ever find out. We would not have to go underground. My identity would remain a secret."

"You told them to kill her?" Martin was almost in shock.

"I told you this morning what would happen if this became public, Martin. I couldn't risk it. I did hesitate, but they were pushing me for an answer. They said there weren't many people at the park now, because of some construction going on. I don't know. I panicked. Hurry! Hurry! I must stop them."

"Can't you call them? Take my mobile." Martin reached into his pocket for his phone.

"No, it doesn't work that way. Not with these people."

"Can't we call the police?"

Ralf looked at his son, who was concentrating on maneuvering through London traffic. "You understand what this means now? Do you understand? It will all come out. I will be taken away from your mother. She will have no one to care for her. She's helpless without me. Your practice will suffer once people learn your father was a Nazi. No, we have to stop these people ourselves." He was frantically waving his arms.

Martin floored the gas pedal as they headed to Regents Park.

They arrived at the opposite end of the park. Construction was impeding traffic. Martin pulled into the first open spot.

"I see them across the park, I'm running for it. Father, you get there as fast as possible."

Martin jumped out of his car, leaving the door open, and Ralf got out of his side. Martin yelled across the park to Rainee, who was unable to hear him due to the noise of a bulldozer.

Rainee and Jana were laughing as the pigeons flocked when they threw crackers into the air.

Martin spotted two men in leather jackets walking toward the women. The men looked like roughnecks. They were concentrating on the women and appeared to be on a mission. One had his hand in his jacket pocket.

Martin kept yelling and waving his arms for Rainee. Ralf wheezed as he tried to run.

The person who noticed Martin was Jana. When she could make out the man who was approaching rapidly and wildly, she realized it was Dr. Wagner. Her eyes widened with horror. Here he was—*Der Generaloberst!* This murderer was coming for her. She began to panic and started babbling in German.

The transformation startled Rainee. "Jana! Jana, are you all right? Jana, talk to me!"

Jana pointed at the man running toward them, who was yelling something they both could not hear.

"No, Jana, it's okay. It's only Dr. Wagner. He won't hurt you, I promise. He's a good man."

Jana ignored Rainee's words. She was falling into a state of regression.

Jana screamed, *"Mörder! Mörder! Mörder!"* She was trembling so visibly that Rainee worried she would have a convulsion. Jana threw her shawl over her head as if hiding underneath would make her invisible. Her German was flowing, and she was inconsolable.

Martin was getting closer. So were the two henchmen. Rainee noticed them and became apprehensive about their rapid approach. They were skin-heads with tattoos marking their necks. They were wearing black leather jackets with German written on it. Rainee thought, *Are these the men who attacked John?*

The men did not see Martin approaching from behind them, nor could they hear Ralf ordering them in German, "Stop. *Ich befehle euch zu stoppen! Ich befehle euch zu stoppen!"*

One of the Neo-Nazis pulled a gun and aimed it at the women. Rainee instinctively covered Jana with her body. A shot rang out. There was sudden searing pain in Rainee's arm. Martin caught up to the man with the gun and jumped him from behind, knocking the gun out of his hand. They struggled, and the other Neo-Nazi went for the gun.

Martin shouted at both of them, begging, "Wait! Look! Look who's approaching!"

They turned to see Ralf.

The old man caught up with them, barely able to get a word out. He was wheezing and holding his chest.

Martin feared his father would have a heart attack. "Please stop and listen to him!"

They waited for the old man to catch his breath while Martin positioned himself between them. "Give him a chance. He's the man who called you. Give him a chance, please."

Finally, Ralf could talk. He spoke with the men with his back to Rainee and Jana. He explained who he was and ordered them to abort their mission. He took out a paper from his pants pocket with code numbers and read it to them. Once convinced, they retreated in a run before the police could arrive.

Martin ran to Rainee. Jana was in a state of panic. Through her shawl, she watched him approach. *"Nein! Nein! Geh Weg! Laß mir allein!"*

"Are you all right?"

"Christ, Martin, I've been shot! What the hell just happened? Who were those men?"

"They're gone now. We've got to get you to the hospital."

"No, I have to help Jana. She's almost catatonic with fear." She placed herself in front of Jana to block her view of Martin.

"You don't understand, Rainee."

"I understand more than you think I do. Your father was a Nazi and Jana saw him commit atrocities. You wonder why she's freaked out at the sight of you? You look just like him. Now, she's regressed back to that time. Martin, she watched him murder young boys. He's responsible for more than that. According to the Wiesenthal Center, he killed thousands of Jews in Sobibor."

"There's more to it. I'll explain everything. Please let me get you to the hospital and get Jana sedated."

Jana started rocking back and forth in her chair. She was speaking in German. She started praying in Hebrew. It looked as if she would fly out of her chair at any minute.

Ralf approached slowly. Rainee blocked his view of Jana. He was crying as he neared. With soothing calm, he began to sing *The Golden Peacock*, their family version.

Jana's movements started to slow as she recognized the song.

Rainee moved to stop him, but Martin said, "It's okay, Rainee. Watch."

As Ralf sang their song, Jana pulled her shawl down from her head. She held her peacock necklace tight. She started to sing with Ralf. Closing the distance, Ralf was crying. He continued singing. "The golden peacock flies away. Where are you flying, Jana bird?"

Jana's eyes became lucid again, and she continued to sing their family lyrics. "I fly across the sea to the south."

"Max? Max? You've come for me?"

"I promised I would find you, didn't I? *Meine Jana. Bitte verzeihen mir.*"

"Forgive you for what, Max? You came."

He knelt before her chair and they embraced.

Speechless, Rainee looked at Martin. "But... but how—"

"I just found out myself. I'll explain it all to you. Please, let me get you to a hospital."

She heard the whistles. She turned to see several Bobbies running toward them along with two men in raincoats. They were the original two men from the Wiesenthal Center.

"Please let me get you to the hospital!"

Rainee looked down at her arm, which was oozing blood. She hadn't felt the pain until she saw the wound. Suddenly, she was woozy. "Okay, you've convinced me." Then she fainted in Martin's arms.

Rainee opened her eyes to a blinding light. She blinked to clear her vision.

Someone was standing in front of that light, looking down at her and smiling. "Waking up... finally." It was Martin in scrubs.

"Where am I? What happened?" Rainee was still feeling fuzzy from the effects of the drugs.

"You were shot in the arm, very close to your brachial artery. You could have bled to death. They removed the bullet. I saved it for you. I thought you might like a souvenir from your trip to London."

"Where?"

"You're in the recovery room. They let me watch the operation."

"Jana?"

"She's fine. She and my father are in the waiting area, reminiscing. It's as if time stopped for them. They are so happy to be together. Mr. Pritchard is there, too." He placed a hand on her shoulder. "I was very worried about you."

Her mouth was dry. She whispered, "May I have some water, please."

He poured water into a paper cup, gave it to her and held her head as she sipped slowly.

"I think my head is clearing. Tell me what... what happened out there?"

"You like stories and this one's a real doozy. Are you sure you wouldn't like to rest some more first?"

She shook her head.

Martin pushed a button to raise the head of her bed. He sat down beside her on the bed and held her hand.

"This story begins in 1938. A Jewish family fled Germany for Amsterdam...."

EPILOGUE
LONDON 1999

Rainee was cradling the phone with her shoulder, leaving her two hands free to fold laundry. "Gary, it's finished! And it is better than my first one. I'll be sending a hard copy in the mail as soon as possible."

"I was following the trial from here. It was all over the news. Were you at the reading of the verdict?"

"Of course. I was sitting with Martin and Paloma. It was inevitable that he would go to prison. He knew that when he revealed himself in the park. Although it wasn't Max's fault that he lost his memory, he had no way of proving it happened the way he said it did. Even though the Nazis kept meticulous records, the prosecutors could find no record with his name. The defense was counting on that as proof. The fact is that he was indeed in the German army. Max never denied it. He had to pay for all the killing. The prosecutor's argument was very convincing."

"Still, it must have been hard on the family."

"Yes, Martin held his mother as she wept. I watched Max accept his punishment. He never flinched. It almost seemed like he was relieved and wanted the sentence. I think the judge was somewhat lenient, taking into account his age and history. And the fact is that he knowingly gave up his anonymity by protecting his sister."

"The news was full of protests from people upset that he wasn't condemned to death."

"I know. However, fifteen years is a long time. He'll be ninety-five when he gets out... if he's still alive. It probably would have been a tougher judgment had the trial taken place in Israel, instead of Germany. I guess we'll never know."

"How's his wife doing?"

"Honestly, before it all came out, I was suspicious of her knowing his past. But it was an awakening—a rude awakening—for her. All their years together and she was innocent of his past. Just shows you, you can never really know a person."

"Which reminds me; I've been meaning to ask whatever happened to that John fellow?"

"After I was shot, Martin spent a lot of time with me. As you know, I moved into his place to rehab. When the story came out, everything hit the fan. The media was parked on our stoop and we couldn't leave the house. John was kind enough to bring Jana to visit. He knew. He could tell I was falling in love with Martin. John and I grew apart as Martin and I grew closer."

"Yes, it was obvious even to me. I could hear it in your voice."

"Really? We invited him to the wedding, but he didn't come. I understood why."

"Well, Rainee, this was one helluva story and I suspect that it will be one helluva book. Congratulations."

"Thanks, but it's a bittersweet achievement for me." Rainee interrupted herself. "Excuse me a second, Gary."

She put down the phone and called into the other room, "Honey, would you mind checking on her? I can hear her moving around."

It had always been the highlight of his day, so he ran up the stairs two at a time. Rainee laughed at her husband's enthusiasm.

"Gary, you're welcome to come here for New Year's Eve. We're throwing a Millennium Party."

"Wish I could, Rainee. I'd love to see all of you. How is Jana doing?"

"Right now she's getting over a cold, but she gets all the attention she needs. I'll talk with you soon. 'Bye."

Over the intercom, she smiled and listened to her husband talking in a soothing manner. "You need your sleep. Get your rest. Doctor's orders."

The baby was not in the mood to take orders from her father. "Oh, being stubborn I see. Wonder who you get that from? Shhh, my little Jana, you'll wake your grandmother and your great aunt. They are resting, too. What? You want me to sing you a lullaby? Okay, rest your head on my shoulder, and I will sing you a song about a little golden peacock."

Martin sang in almost a whisper. "The golden peacock flies away. Where are you flying, Jana bird? I fly across the sea to the south. Please ask my love to kiss me on the mouth! I know you, and I shall bring a letter back to say, you'd better not kiss me now or there'll be no wedding day!"

As he rocked her, his baby's eyes gradually closed.

Downstairs, Rainee smiled contently at the sounds coming from the intercom. She put away the laundry basket and went into the kitchen. Soon Grandma Paloma and Aunt Jana would be awakening from their naps, and it would be time for high tea.

~End~

ACKNOWLEDGMENTS

Primarily, I wish to thank Bernie Jaroslow. Without his creative input I would still be floundering somewhere around Chapter Four. It was fun and I look forward to working together on a future project.

Thank you to my incredible and patient Beta Readers: Shera Cohen, Beverly Sbarge, Phil Jaroslow, Lynn and Jerry Greenberg, MD., Lillian and Larry Jaroslow, Ruth Garber, Beverly Sandock, Sondra Shapiro, Gary Jaroslow, The Writers' Table; especially Michaele Lockhart and Glenda Taylor, my friends across the pond Cathy and Adrian Evans, and Tanya Downs. Flemming Poulsen, thank you for correcting my German.

My never-ending gratitude goes to Yad Vashem, the Simon Wiesenthal Center and the U.S. Holocaust Museums.

Thank you to my editor Harvey Stanbrough for keeping my grammar in check. Thanks to my literary agent, Joyce Keating for believing in this story. The incredible artistry of Evan Jaroslow's cover illustration creates a haunting effect. Thank you, Evan.

My husband Michael, my rock and the rock for our family: I always feel your unwavering support and encouragement, and never take it for granted. I love you deeply and as we head into our thirtieth anniversary year, I can only ask you to continue to put up with me for another thirty years.

My children Rachel and Zachary: I love you both with my entire being. You make me proud to be your Mom.

BIOGRAPHY

Award-winning author Lauren B. Grossman found global success with her debut novel Once in Every Generation. With over 16,000 downloads, the e-version of the novel remained number one in an Amazon category for over a year, and reached number four overall for about a minute.

She earned her degree in theatre and has performed in, designed sets, directed and produced numerous productions.

Ms. Grossman co-founded, co-published, and co-edited a performing arts newspaper. Because of the success of that newspaper, she and her co-publisher created a weekly radio talk show. She has had articles published and has earned awards for her short stories.

Ms. Grossman resides in Southern Arizona with her husband, two children, two dogs and a desert tortoise.

CPSIA information can be obtained
at www.ICGtesting.com
Printed in the USA
FSHW04n2035070318
45451FS